Love needs only one chance to shine . . .

He followed in his family's footsteps and just graduated Marine boot camp. Now Mason Cutler's personal mission is to get plenty of sun, surf, and no-strings romance in his favorite laid-back Florida beach town before shipping out. But a chance encounter with reserved Kiran Shenoy becomes a golden day of conversation, connection—and an intense attraction Mason can't walk away from. They make an agreement—eight sensuous days together without regrets or promises. Yet soon Mason is longing to convince the spirited woman behind Kiran's sad beautiful eyes to take a chance on even more . . .

All Kiran dared hope for was a chance to heal after a tragic accident and a devastating loss. Mason's freewheeling energy and head-on courage warms her scarred body and soul—and ignites her heart. But with their lives going in different directions, the only commitment they can make is a pact to meet again. Can what they feel survive Mason's military duty, and Kiran's second chance to restart her life? And can a desire sparked one summer night be enough for forever?

I0630407

Books by MK Schiller

Unwanted Girl
Where the Lotus Flowers Grow
Eight Days in the Sun

Published by Kensington Publishing Corporation

Eight Days in the Sun

MK Schiller

LYRICAL PRESS
Kensington Publishing Corp.
www.kensingtonbooks.com

Lyrical Press books are published by
Kensington Publishing Corp. 119 West 40th Street New York, NY 10018

All Kensington titles, imprints, and distributed lines are available at special quantity discounts for bulk purchases for sales promotion, premiums, fund-raising, and educational or institutional use.

To the extent that the image or images on the cover of this book depict a person or persons, such person or persons are merely models, and are not intended to portray any character or characters featured in the book.

Special book excerpts or customized printings can also be created to fit specific needs. For details, write or phone the office of the Kensington Special Sales Manager:
Kensington Publishing Corp.
119 West 40th Street
New York, NY 10018
Attn. Special Sales Department. Phone: 1-800-221-2647.

Kensington and the K logo Reg. U.S. Pat. & TM Off.
LYRICAL PRESS Reg. U.S. Pat. & TM Off.
Lyrical Press and the L logo are trademarks of Kensington Publishing Corp.

First Electronic Edition: May 2017
eISBN-13: 978-1-5161-0068-2
eISBN-10: -1-5161-0068-9

First Print Edition: May 2017
ISBN-13: 978-1-5161-0070-5
ISBN-10: 1-5161-0070-0

Printed in the United States of America

To the bloggers and authors who have supported me, especially Sage Spelling and Aliza Mann, who spent eight hours helping me fine-tune this book! To my editor, Corinne, for making Kiran and Mason feel real. To the great team at Kensington. And, of course, the reader, who picked up this story. I hope Mason and Kiran leave a smile on your face.

Chapter 1

Kiran

It is a cardinal rule young girls do not vacation alone. It is simply not done. At least that was Papa's argument to dissuade me from taking the trip to the gulf coast town of Jasper, Florida. My stepmother, Linda, told him to hush, explaining I was returning to my childhood home to visit with old friends. That wasn't true. Having no other choice, I'd left Jasper to live with Papa and Linda when I was eighteen. I didn't keep in touch with anyone. I don't have any old friends to look up. Or even new friends to bring with me. Instead of correcting her, I clicked the big blue confirmation button on the computer screen to book my non-refundable ticket.

Even now, as the cab drives past all the beachfront hotels, I'm not sure why I wanted to come back. Maybe because I never had a chance to say a proper good-bye to the beachside city I loved. The air is ripe with the smell of saltwater and African violets. I inhale the scent. Maybe I am exactly where I need to be.

The cab pulls up to the Sandy Waves Resort. Not only is it the cheapest of all the beachside hotels, but I know a little secret. Sandy Waves has the best beachfront access and stellar views of the Gulf of Mexico. The cabbie pulls over. The sun shines so brightly I cover my eyes as I search through my purse for the right bill.

The driver takes my suitcase from the trunk. "Have a nice stay."

Handing him payment, I thank him.

A dusty plastic palm tree sits inside the corner wedge of the revolving doors. An unsettling feeling rises in my stomach. I'm not claustrophobic exactly, but once in a while a weird panic seizes me for no reason. I swallow down the fear, take a deep breath, and opt for the traditional door. I push it open and awkwardly pull my suitcase inside. Someone grabs the edge of the frame and holds it for me.

"Thank you," I say, not looking up.

"Welcome," comes the deep, masculine reply.

I doubt the lobby at Sandy Waves has experienced an update in decades. The décor is 1980s gaudy beach chic, complete with palm tree-patterned wallpaper and flowery couches. The floors are orange and white tiles. My flip-flops make an annoying clacking sound as I scramble to the front desk.

The guy who held the door open for me isn't far behind. His footsteps are sturdy and solid, almost clashing with the clatter of my flip-flops. I take my place in the line of tourists waiting to register.

There is a couple ahead of me. The girl has long brown hair, a few shades lighter than the guy. He's holding a surfboard with one hand and has the other wrapped around her. She's probably in her early twenties, close to my age. He looks a few years older. She glances down at the ring on her left finger while he keeps his gaze fixed on her. He smiles at her, a sweet, I-can't-believe-you're-in-my-life kind of smile. It's not for her, since she's not even looking at him. No, this smile bursts out of him like he can't contain it. I can almost feel his happiness as if it's a tangible, contagious thing. What is it like to look at someone that way? As if they are the best thing in the world, or at least, the best thing in *your* world.

When it's time for them to move up, his arm never wavers. The way he is looking at her, it's probably good they are getting a room. They need one.

"Mr. and Mrs. Robert Jorgenson," he announces to the woman behind the counter.

"Ah, yes," the clerk says enthusiastically. "You're in the Sweetheart's Suite." She starts rattling off a list of amenities. I almost laugh at the desperate look the dude is giving her. Apparently, there is fanfare involved when you sign up for the Sweetheart's Suite. The hotel clerk isn't about to let them leave until she gets through her well-rehearsed spiel. She hands them a small pink bag with tiny hearts all over it.

"This has sunscreen, bottles of water, and chocolates," the woman explains. "Just all part of the Sweetheart Suite experience."

"Thank you, ma'am."

I stifle a laugh as he takes the dainty, pink bag in his huge hands.

"Just one more moment," the clerk says loudly.

But wait, Robert, there's even more.

Another hotel employee places leis of fresh, colorful flowers on both of them while the bellhop loads their stuff onto a trolley. The bellhop's

Hawaiian shirt matches the wallpaper pattern. Now, Rob (I call him Rob) looks a little embarrassed, but his bride is soaking it all in as if this were a five-star experience.

"The Sweetheart's Suite must really be something," the guy behind me mutters.

His voice is deep and throaty with the slightest southern twang. Not Florida southern, but maybe Alabama? He's probably talking to me because who else is there? I don't respond. Instead, I pull the string of my hood tighter.

He moves closer to me. "I think it's your turn, miss."

The woman is now calling for me. How long had I been holding up the damn line? Shit.

I rush toward the desk. The girl who leid the Jorgensons moves behind the counter and gestures for Alabama to come up as well.

"Welcome to Sandy Waves. Name, please."

"Kiran Shenoy," I respond.

"Kiran," she says. "Kiran, it's good to see you."

I glance up to see Mrs. Waters, my tenth grade English teacher. Her eyes widen before she shifts her attention back toward her monitor. I swallow down the hurt. She's surprised. I get it. The scar that travels down the left side of my face isn't subtle. I don't look like the girl she used to know. Her reaction shouldn't upset me. But it does just the same. I bite on my fingernail hoping this goes fast.

"Do you remember me?" she asks when I don't respond.

Maybe she thinks my memory is screwed up as well. How could I forget the woman? Under other circumstances, I would be thrilled to see the teacher who introduced me to the Bronte sisters and Jane Austen. She wrote the same quote on the board the first day of every class. Thinking of it now, I can almost smell the tang of white chalk. *If you constantly depict yourself as the underdog in your story, it's highly unlikely you'll become the hero.* Those words stuck with me, even though I fully acknowledge I am guilty of doing just that. Acknowledging and changing are two different things.

"Yes, of course, I remember. Mrs. Waters, how are you?"

She once told me I was a great writer, even though she gave me a C on my Gatsby paper. No hard feelings there. The paper deserved a C. I had a love-hate relationship with Fitzgerald that translated to a long, rambling essay about narcissism and class distinction.

"I'm well, dear. How have you been? Are you in town visiting?"

"Fine." I decide not to answer the second question and counter with one of my own. "Are you still at the school?"

"Afraid not. The district had cutbacks. I took early retirement. I do love working here, though." That's too bad. She was a great teacher.

"That's great, Mrs. Waters."

"I heard you moved to New Jersey."

"I'm still there."

"Well, I'm sure you've missed the beach."

More than she can know. "Yes."

"Are you still writing?"

"No," I respond, although I'm pretty sure I just created a love story about the Jorgensons in my head.

"You're in college, though?" The way she asks, I'm sure she is readying a reprimand if I don't have the correct answer. I hand her my credit card for the incidentals, hoping it's enough of a hint I want to move on with this transaction.

I roll up the sleeves of my hoodie. "I'll have my business degree next year."

"That's wonderful, Kiran. I'm so glad to hear you're doing so well." She punches a few keys on the computer. "I see your staying with us for eight days."

"Yes."

"That's a nice long vacation. Is it just you? No one is joining you?"

Um…hello, awkward moment.

"Just me."

Mrs. Waters punches a few more keys. She still has the long acrylic nails. Today, they are bright purple. It seems at odds with the conservative bun, eyeglasses, and neutral clothes. "I'm going to upgrade you to a water view suite."

"That's not necessary."

"Nonsense, we have one that will just sit empty. It's not the Sweetheart's Suite, but it is on a high floor and has a balcony."

I thank her as she hands me a plastic keycard.

"I hope we can catch up later." She gives me a soft, heartfelt smile.

I nod. Swinging my suitcase, I speed walk toward the elevator bank. One of the cars is out of service. The other one is incredibly slow. By the time the doors finally open, I've silently sung the whole soundtrack of *Rent*, all five hundred twenty-five minutes and six hundred seconds of it.

"Hold it, please," says the guy behind me as the doors begin to close.

I press the open button, but the doors keep closing. I jab it. The metal doors don't stop.

"Sorry," I say. "Can't get it to open." I throw my hand in the gap between the doors. Nope. Still moving shut. Guess it doesn't have a safety. I pull my hand back before the doors slam.

He rushes toward me, a duffle bag slung across his shoulder. It's too late, dude. They close. Well almost close. I gasp as a very large sneaker wedges between the doors.

"Ouch," he says as the doors part.

"Are you all right?"

He smiles. "I'll live."

He presses the button for the tenth floor. The air in the elevator suddenly becomes heavier. It's the same guy who held the front door for me, the one with the smoky southern flare in his voice.

"I swear I was trying to hold it open."

"You were?" He looks straight into my eyes.

For some reason, I don't shift my head down like I normally do. I'm not sure if this makes it worse or better. He's a nice looking boy...man. Who the hell am I kidding? He's hot, like you-might-mistake-me-for-an-underwear-model hot. He's tall with defined, but not over-the-top, muscles. His jeans are ripped in all the right places and his faded gray T-shirt reads *free shrugs* in all caps. He's got a strong square jaw that's a day or two past a shave. His eyes are an intense light blue, my favorite color. The T-shirt might as well say *my superpower is being beautiful.*

The doors close, trapping us in a space that seems to get exponentially smaller now that he's sharing it with me. He runs his fingers through brownish hair. Umm...not exactly brown. I'd call the color milk chocolate spiced with threads of cinnamon and honey.

Get a grip. So what if he's good-looking? This is freaking Beach Town, Florida. Next to seashells and citrus, cute boys are the largest produced crop.

Wait. He asked me something, didn't he? Oh yeah, it was about the stupid elevator. "I pushed the open door button."

"It just closed anyway, huh?" He quirks an eyebrow, an amused expression on his face.

"It did. I swear. It isn't working," I say, pointing to the button with the picture of the triangles next to it.

"That's the button you pushed?"

"Yeah."

"You realize it's the close door button, right?"

I stare at it and the one next to it. The placement seems wrong, but the pictures don't lie. "I do now."

He offers a wry, teasing smile. "Don't worry about it. I'm just giving you shit. I swear, this elevator has gotta be older than Archimedes."

"Who is that?"

"The guy who invented elevators back in BC."

Now it's my turn to question him. "You made that up."

"Look it up, girl. It's true."

"How do you know that?"

"I think it was a Jeopardy question or something."

He watches Jeopardy? I'll take mind blown for five hundred, Alex. I thought I was the only person in my age group who enjoyed the show.

"I'm a spermologer too." I cringe, realizing how the word comes off versus what it really means. It sounds as if I own an assortment of sperm...gross.

He arches a brow. "Come again?"

"A spermologer, someone who collects trivia."

"I didn't know there was a word for us." Yeah, except a better title for me is Queen of Awkward Conversation.

"Yes, it's spermologer." God help me, can I please stop using obsolete words that have the antecedent sperm?

"Learn something new every day."

The elevator jolts before the car stops completely. I stumble back.

"You all right?" he asks.

"What happened?"

"Looks like we're stuck."

I press the button for my floor. Nothing happens. So I start pressing the other buttons. Still nothing. No... This can't be real. Getting stuck in an elevator with a super hot guy? This is the stuff of corny rom-coms.

"There's no need to panic."

"Not panicking," I say as I hit a few more buttons.

"Are you claustrophobic?"

"No." I sigh and lean back against the railing. I can still feel his gaze on me. "A little."

"Heard it helps to think about something else."

"Like what?" I curl my fingers around the steel railing at the back of the elevator.

He tilts his head, studying me. "Have we met?" he asks.

I replay the question in my head wondering if I heard correctly. When I laugh, the sound bounces off the walls and echoes inside the small elevator car. "Seriously?"

He does a face palm. "Crap, that sounds like a pick-up line. I swear it's not."

As if I'd think he was trying to pick me up. "I'm sure you'd remember if you knew me."

"That's true. How could I forget?"

For a second, I thought he might be making fun of me on some level. But there isn't anything malicious in his voice. Taking a deep breath, I force myself to relax.

"Kiran Shenoy, right?"

I lift my head, wondering if I did know him. I think back to all the boys I went to high school with, but his face doesn't register at all. It's the kind of face that would register in triplicate. "How do we know each other?"

"No idea. I overheard the lady behind the front desk say your name." He holds out his hand...his very large hand. "Mason Cutler."

I've been curling my fingers around the railing so tightly that I have to shake out my hand before taking his. His handshake is firm. I'm about to let go when he flips my wrist over. He presses his thumb against the ruby red mark there. Very few people notice it against my brown skin. His thumb slides back and forth in a short caress. The stain disappears against the pressure. It comes back slowly, deepening in color for a moment. My pulse spikes ten notches...maybe twenty. After an eternity, he finally lets go. It's really only been two seconds, but it feels much longer, or maybe not long enough.

"It's not a tattoo?"

"It's a birthmark. They call it a port wine stain."

"A fire stain."

"Right."

"I thought this was inked on since it's shaped like a heart."

The car starts up with a jolt. He gestures to the screen that signals we are moving. "See? No reason to panic."

The doors open, ending the weirdest elevator ride in the history of the world.

"This is me," I say, my fingers clutching the handle of my suitcase.

He holds one of the doors by leaning against it while I get out. I catch a hint of spicy, manly cologne and delicious boy. "Thank you."

"We made it unscathed."

"So we did." I nod, accepting what happened. He was just being nice and trying to distract me with an introduction.

"Maybe I'll see you around, Shenoy," he says.

"Maybe."

I turn just in time to see the doors close.

Chapter 2

Kiran

After calling Papa to tell him I made it, I unpack my things in record time and head straight for the beach. I purchase a Rum Runner from the thatched roofed bar. After I adjust my straw hat and secure my sunglasses, I make my way toward the sand.

I nab the first empty beach chair I come across. All the chairs are in groupings of two. Figures. I throw my stuff on the other one and toss off my flips-flops. My feet sink into the soft, warm sand. For the first time in a long time, I feel at home. Rum Runners, a good book, and a beautiful view. What the hell else could a girl want? I plop down and stretch out, letting the sun warm me like a blanket.

This beach holds so many memories for me. I'd ride these waves for hours until exhaustion set in. The good kind of tired that makes you feel more alive. When it got too dark to surf, my friends and I would circle around the bonfire, a stream of music playing in the background. We'd talk for hours about our futures. I realize now I'd spent so much time thinking about the future that I never enjoyed the present. I miss those moments of laughter and freedom. I even miss the angst that's part and parcel to being a teenage girl. Now, here I am again thinking about my future. This time, I decide to enjoy the present.

I glance at the waves. Elevator boy is here too. He's out in the water on one of those cheap blue surfboards the hotel rents. I squint to get a better look at Mason Let-me-feel-up-your-wrist Cutler. It was weird, right? I was sort of a shut-in since my accident three years ago so I'm out of practice when it comes to the art of conversation. Still, nothing normal about that moment.

I shake my head and hope the physical act will make the thoughts dissipate like I'm a human etch-a-sketch. I fish my e-reader from my knapsack and skim a couple paragraphs of the novel I'm reading. Then I reread them again because I'm not retaining anything. Having my mind hijacked by Mason Cutler has made it impossible to concentrate. So I peek over the screen and keep stealing glances at him.

One thing is for sure, he does not know a damn thing about surfing. He heads for waves right as they peak, wiping out every single time. But to his credit, he keeps getting back up and trying again. It's nice to know not everything comes easy to him. He emerges from the water, all golden tan skin and hard muscles. He wears bright orange board shorts slung low enough on his hips they reveal those indented V-lines that are almost impossible for most men to achieve. I notice it's not just me staring at him. He's captured the eyes of many girls and a couple of boys as he walks up the beach. A striped towel is draped over one shoulder and the long board is secured with his other arm. Water drips down his chest, which has a smattering of golden hair that naturally edges into a happy trail. There is a tattoo of a star on his right arm. The artist has made it appear as if the drawing is seared into his skin.

He smiles at a group of girls, who all turn radish red in an instant. Either the sun suddenly dipped a few inches or he's just got that effect on girls. There's a swagger in his step and cockiness in his smile. I want to borrow some of it. I have a feeling Mason Cutler has plenty to spare. God, he even walks in slow motion as he passes me.

Oh wait, he's not passing me. He's slowing down. Slowing down until he comes to a stop...right in front of me. He wicks away the water with his towel. "Hello, Kiran."

Are you there, God? It's me, Kiran. If you help me through this Judy Blume moment, I promise I'll do a special *pooja* tonight.

I struggle to come up with a great response. I settle for the all-encompassing, "Hi."

"This seat taken?" he asks, gesturing to the empty chair next to mine.

I grab my stuff and bring it to my chair. "It's all yours." I wonder if he's going to move the lounger somewhere. Perhaps by those giggly girls who were giving him the swoon-eye earlier. He doesn't. Instead, he slams the board into the sand and plunks down.

He glances over at me. "Aren't you hot?"

No, but I was pretty damn cute once.

He's talking about my choice of clothing of course. I divested myself of the hoodie, but I'm still wearing jeans and a long sleeve T-shirt. "I'm fine." Yes, because this is normal beachwear.

Sheltered by my sunglasses, I drink in his face and cut body at close range. His lips are full, always twitching at the corners as if he's fighting a smile, which is at odds with his strong, rigid jawline. Living close to the Gulf most of my life, I know all the different colors in a body of water. There are moments when the sun hits the water just right that causes it to shine with a slight gray reflection like hard glass over blue skies. That's the color of Mason Cutler's eyes—blue-gray beautiful.

My gaze shifts to his arm. There is writing inside of the inked star. He must realize I'm reading his tattoo because he holds his arm at an angle to make it easier.

"Did you know you mouth words when you read?"

Oh, that's how he knew. "I've heard that before."

In small, curling script it says *It always protects, always trusts, always hopes, always perseveres.*

"It's a bible passage, right?"

"Yeah, it's from Corinthians."

I have some working knowledge about the Bible. I try to remember what the "it" is referring to, but the answer doesn't come to me.

He moves to his side so he's facing me. "My dad quoted this particular passage to my sister and me before he tucked us into bed each night. The actual passage is much longer, but I don't have enough arm to cover the whole thing."

"That's really sweet. You captured the memory."

"It was a memory worth capturing." A flicker of sorrow flashes on his face before the smile returns. He juts his chin toward me. "Rum Runner any good?"

I'm sure that is a cue to change the subject. "I've never had one before, but it's really hitting the spot."

"You've never had a Rum Runner?"

"I've never had rum before."

He arches a brow. "Really?"

"This is actually my first legit drink."

"How old are you?"

"Almost twenty-two. You?" I can't guess his age because he's got that boyish smile, but everything else is carbon-dated man.

"I'm twenty-two." He brushes a hand through his disheveled hair. "So, you didn't get wasted on your birthday? That's a rite of passage where I come from."

"Is this really such a shocker?"

"Not a shocker, but definitely a surprise. Would you care for another or you planning to nurse that one?"

The glass is still half-full. If only my demeanor was. "I'm good."

"Yes, you are. You're incredibly good. You sure I can't get you anything?"

"Positive."

He stands and stretches. The hard, solid muscles on his waist shift for a second, confirming he is in fact not cast from marble. I force myself not to stare at his butt as he heads for the bar.

I change my mind, Mason. I do want something. Maybe a few more ice cubes in this drink. Or maybe just a cup of ice. Or a couple of polar ice caps.

There is no doubt I'm attracted to this wanna-be surfer boy, but I pretty much score an A+ in awkward, not to mention I'm a total loner. Yet there is something comfortable about him. Maybe because this is a vacation, and I won't have to worry about seeing him again.

He comes back with an amber bottle.

"I figured you for a beer guy."

He sets down the bottle on the small table between us. "Not just beer. This is Dos Equis."

"That fits." I laugh, thinking about the Most Interesting Man in the World ads.

His eyes are said to be lasers, so when they pierce a girl, not only do the panties she's wearing melt away, but all the panties she's ever owned in her life. He is the most interesting boy in the world. I'd end the commercial with a money shot of Mason taking a long drawn-out swig and then toasting the audience with the statement, "I don't always pick a random girl to chat up, but when I do, I make sure there is swooning involved."

Okay, so I'm definitely not cut out for advertising.

"Don't get me wrong, I am man enough to admit I enjoy the occasional fruity brew, but I think I'll wait to get my drink on. It's early still. I might go back in the water and try to catch a wave."

"I wouldn't."

"Why?"

"The sun will be setting. It's the worst time to surf." I watch him closely, thinking he might argue or do it anyway. In my head, I imagine him going under. "Just don't do it, okay?" The words come out with more conviction than I meant.

"Okay, you're right."

We're quiet for a minute, the sound of crashing waves and birdsong provide a soothing soundtrack. "What did you mean when you said I was very good?"

"Nothing."

"Tell me what you meant." I cringe, realizing my inflection added urgency to the statement. "I want to know."

"I just meant that you must be a very good girl to not consume liquor on your twenty-first birthday."

"You'd be surprised." A part of me wants to eat my words, while the rest is curious about his reaction.

He grins and cocks an eyebrow. There is a challenge in his expression. "Go on then. Surprise me."

"I was kidding."

"So you are fairly straight-laced then."

"I didn't say that."

"Then tell me something naughty about you."

An unwelcome heat uncoils in my belly like I've drank a whole pint of rum in one swallow. He wants naughty? I wish I could change directions here. I don't have much in the way of naughty. At least nothing recent. "When I was fourteen, I told my mom I was spending the night at a friend's house after school. I skipped that day and traveled for six hours and fifty-two minutes on a Greyhound."

"You remember the exact time?"

"You spend that long on a Greyhound in a scratchy, sparkly top and tight shoes, and you'd be counting the minutes too."

"I don't own any sparkly tops and all my shoes fit me so I wouldn't know. But I'll take your word for it. Were you running away from home?"

"No." I pause, not certain if I want to tell him the story. He waits patiently, the silence stretching but not awkward. "I went to a concert."

"All by yourself?"

"My friends and I made a pact to go together, but everyone bailed on me. I thought about forgetting it, but in the end, I decided I wasn't about to miss it. Who knows if I'd ever have the chance again."

"Well, now, you've got me curious. Who rocks it so hard for Kiran Shenoy that she'd take such a risk?" He holds up his hand. "Wait. Don't answer. I'm going to guess." He tilts his head, pressing his mouth closed as if he's giving it some thought. Bet he's counting back the years and matching it up to billboard charts. "Justin Timberlake?"

"Love Justin, but not enough to suffer slow death via Greyhound."

"Lady Gaga?"

"You're getting colder."

"Backstreet Boys?"

"One of my favorite bands, but no."

He gives me a wise-ass look. "Just when I thought you were cool."

"Have you ever listened to them, really listened? They have some great stuff."

"Eh, music is subjective."

"It is. But there's a difference between judgey and subjective."

"We'll have to agree to disagree. Boy bands are pretty much the bottom feeders of the musical ladder."

"Let me blow your mind for a second."

He narrows his eyes and nods at me in challenge. "Blow away."

"When you think about it The Beatles were the original boy band."

"Now that is a shocker."

"I know, right?"

"No, I mean it's a shocker you'd even make the comparison." He shifts his head toward the sky. "If you can hear me, please forgive this girl. She knows not how she sins."

"Are you asking God to forgive me?"

"No, sunshine. God will forgive you. I'm asking John Lennon to forgive you."

Did he just call me sunshine? "So there's no convincing you?"

"About the merits of boy bands? No ma'am. I'm an open-minded guy, but I will stand my ground on this subject. But now, I gotta know who you wanted to hear sing so bad you snuck out of your house and hopped on a bus for six hours all by yourself."

"Over six hours, thank you very much. It was Bon Jovi."

Mason nods in appreciation. "You do surprise me. You also won back a few cool points." He crosses his toned legs and stares at the waves. "The craziest thing I ever did was drink a mason jar of homemade liquor. I must have been about twelve at the time."

"Homemade liquor?"

"Nothing but moonshine. The stuff was strong enough to strip rust off steel." Mason winces as though the thought of it still makes him ill. He smacks his stomach. The sound is as solid as a steel drum. No bounce. No jiggle. "A friend of mine snuck a few jars from his daddy's liquor stash. I was sick for a week."

"That's really the most rebellious thing you've done?"

"Yeah, it is. I'm tame. Though I'll tell you if you can't hold your liquor back home, even at twelve, you get a lifetime of razzing."

I ask another question before I can analyze it too deeply. "Where is home?"

"South Carolina. I'm from a small town about forty-five minutes outside Charleston."

That sounds right with his accent. South Carolina must have a decent crop of beautiful boys too. Why did he come to Florida to hang out by the Gulf when he was so close to an entire Ocean? I want to ask him and find out more about this small town that produces boys with such delicious accents.

"Do you like living there?"

"Yeah, it's a nice place to call home. Tell me more about this concert."

"It was an amazing show."

"Did you get caught?"

"Oh yeah. The friend who was my alibi can't lie to save her life…or mine. I should have known better. You can't disappear for a whole day and night without getting caught. I was grounded for a month. God, my mom was so angry with me." I shudder, remembering the fury in her expression. But behind her anger were fear and disappointment and distrust. I'd put her through all that with my silly teenage rebellion.

"Was it worth it?"

I shrug. "No." It wasn't worth it to put my mom through that. But thinking of the show, I can't help but smile. Pinching my fingers together I say, "And maybe a tiny bit yes too. To hear Jon Bon Jovi sing 'It's My Life' was special. When I think about hearing that song in a crowded auditorium with a million other people and Jon's voice washing over all of us. Well, it's just one of those things that will always stay with me. Whenever I'm sad or I need a little push, I put on my ear buds and play that song. It helps." I laugh nervously. "I don't know why I'm telling you this. So silly."

"It's not. I get it." He places a hand over his heart. "I have a go-to song myself."

"What is it?"

"'Home' by Chris Daughtry. Know it?"

"Yeah, I do. It's kind of sad, though."

"Maybe. But there is something powerful about it. I listened to it all the time right after my dad died."

Maybe this is part of the connection I feel. We both lost a parent.

"I'm so sorry, Mason."

"Thank you." Holding the bottle by the neck, he takes another long drag of his drink. "Would I be a total douche if I ask you to take off your sunglasses? I can see my reflection in them. It feels like I'm having a conversation in the mirror."

I slip them off and lower my head. "Not at all. Sorry."

"You have pretty eyes."

I almost snap my sunglasses in two. Did he really say that to me? "Um…thanks."

"Why do I get the feeling you don't believe me?"

"No one has ever said that to me before."

"It's hard to appreciate them when you always have your head down." He taps on my e-reader. "What are you reading anyway?"

"*Ethan Frome.*"

"Edith Wharton? Not exactly an easy beach read."

"You've read it?"

"I tried once. I couldn't get through it. What else you got in there?" Mason asks the question as if he's inquiring what's in the fridge. "Anything less tragic? I'm looking for a rec."

So he's beautiful and he reads. I'm fairly certain this is some weird science shit and I've conjured him straight out of my fantasies. Now all I can do is picture him reading. For some reason, in this delicious daydream, he's wearing a skullcap and eyeglasses. It's too much. The brakes in my brain squeal when I divert them to funny cat compilations complete with piano background music. Thank you, YouTube.

I tap on the library icon and bring up my TBR. "Let's see."

"May I?" he asks, his large hand reaching out.

I surrender the e-reader to him. His fingers brush mine as he takes the device.

"Girl, I'm worried about how much you enjoy sad. Can you not read a book unless someone dies in it?"

"What are you talking about? I read all kinds of stuff."

"Hardy, Wharton, Conrad. Don't get me wrong, they are brilliant authors. But a tad heavy on melancholy, don't you think? What's the last book that made you smile or laugh out loud?"

This should be an easy question, but it's not. "Not sure." But I have read happy, funny stuff… I think.

His brow quirks as he scrolls down my library. My cheeks burn when I realize what's causing his smirk. Shit. He's browsing through The Fifty Shades section. "I see you do have some variety."

I snatch the e-reader back from him. Why the hell did I show him my library? I never realized how personal it was. Sure, I posted it to ten online book clubs I belong to, but this… This is on a whole different scale. "Don't tease."

He holds his hands up in mock surrender. "What? No teasing here. I think it's awesome. When you turn on your e-reader, it should return the favor."

I laugh so loud I startle myself. "You sure you're not making fun of me?"

He places his hand over his heart. "Scout's honor, I would never tease you about this."

I narrow my eyes. "Were you a scout?"

"Not a boy scout exactly, but I did make it to two cub scout meetings so that should count, right?"

"Not sure if it does."

"I earned a badge and everything."

"Well, as long as you have a badge."

"I do. Swear it."

"Sorry, I don't have a recommendation for you. It looks like we have different tastes."

"Have any idea where the nearest bookstore is?"

"That I can help with. If you turn left out of the hotel and go down eight miles and hang a right on Eighth Street, there's a store called Sam's Reads. It's a coffee shop slash book store. It's been ages since I've been there. I'm not sure if it's still there. You might want to check. But if it is, Sam will help you out with a rec. He's one of the most well-read people in the world. He has this amazing gift."

"What gift?"

"He's like a matchmaker of sorts. If you need a book recommendation, go to Sam. He can fit any person to the perfect book. I discovered some of my favorite authors because of him."

"I'll check it out."

"You might need to call a cab. It's a little far."

"I drove here. I have my car."

"Then you're all set. If you go, will you let me know how Sam is?"

"Why don't you come with?"

Him asking me to go to my favorite place in the world, a bookstore, is just a little too much icing on an already heavily frosted cake. Besides, I don't want to drop in on Sam like this. I have no idea how he'll react. "No thanks, but you should really go." I begin gathering up my things. He hands me my sunscreen and towel. I throw them into my beach bag with my sunglasses. "Bye, Mason."

"Why did you leave this place for New Jersey?"

"What?"

"Remember, I overheard you talking to the woman when you were checking in. Your teacher. You used to live here. Did your parents move?"

This question should not be offensive, but it freaks me out just the same. "Wow, you really were eavesdropping, weren't you?"

"Not exactly. Overhearing is different than eavesdropping."

I swing my legs to the ground. I pick up my bag and my almost empty cup. "I'm going to go now."

"Don't go," he says. "Look, I happen to have two ears, and they function whether I want them to or not. I only have one mouth, and luckily I can control that. I'll shut it now if you'll stay for the show."

"What show?"

"This show." He gestures to the horizon where the orange sun starts slipping behind the crashing waves. Sunset in Jasper is always spectacular and a sight I've sorely missed. "Okay."

He clinks his beer against my glass. "Here's to sappy songs and sunsets."

"Sappy songs and sunsets," I repeat.

We drink to the toast.

Chapter 3

Mason

This morning I went to the bookstore. She was right. Sam, the bookstore guy, is gifted. He shot question after question about my tastes, everything from my favorite authors to my career choices. He jotted it all down in sloppy shorthand, complete with numerical computations, a weird mathematical formula of his own devising. Then he opened a folder with meticulous lists in the same shorthand. But he knew exactly what he was looking for within the pages of slanted scrawls. I have a feeling he's high-functioning Asperger's. One of my buddies at home has Asperger's. He does the same thing. In a way, I suppose we all try to create logic from the chaos around us. For some folks, there is just way too much chaos to control.

I spent a solid two hours there, chugging strong coffee and hanging with Sam. He recommended several books, taking them off shelves stacked so heavy they were sagging. Just from reading the back covers, I could tell they were winners. I even asked him to recommend something for my sister, Dana. After I gave him a few pieces of data on her, he quickly located a book about a marine biologist who goes to a distant planet to study newly found organisms. As someone who loves sci-fi and sea creatures, it totally fits her wheelhouse.

When I was checking out, I spotted something for Kiran. The brightly-colored book sat upright on a shelf beneath a colorful row of stuffed animals.

"You're taking this too?" Sam asked, although there wasn't an inflection in the question.

"Yeah, it's a present." Not that I didn't have a copy at home.

When I asked Sam for a pen, his expression turned wary. "You're not going to write in the book, are you?" The question was so ripe with reprimand I almost dropped the pen.

"I'd never do that, man." Actually, I was going to do just that. But I grabbed one of the postcards by the register. "I'll take this." Before I changed my mind, I jotted a note to Kiran.

Hey Shenoy, thought you could use a happy book in your life. The kind that ends well and leaves you with a smile. This one always did the trick for me. I debated how to sign the damn thing. Love was way too much, but sincerely felt impersonal and cold. In the end, I just scrawled my name on the bottom. I stuck the postcard snugly between the cover and the front page.

When I got back to the hotel, I asked the clerk to deliver it to her room. I wasn't sure if the guy would tell me her room number, and I didn't want to knock on her door unannounced. I had a strong feeling this girl didn't just value her privacy, she protected it.

The book is not something Sam or anyone else would recommend for Kiran. Nothing she'd ever think to buy for herself. But maybe she needs it all the same. Or maybe she'd think I was a weird creep, but I'd risk it if it brings her smile out of hiding. I only caught a glimpse of it when we talked on the beach.

She has a sexy smile. Her mouth... Her mouth is nothing short of sensuous. Hell, it looks fucking delicious. She uses some kind of clear gloss on her lips, but they are naturally pink and plump. The bottom one juts out slightly. They have an indent, a little vertical line that runs down both lips. This girl can give Angelina Jolie a run for her money when it comes to sexy mouths. The way Kiran mouthed the words when she read to herself caused my dick to rear its ugly head. Wait a second. Scratch that.

I mean its beautiful head. Let me be clear. My penis has a lovely head.

Okay, enough about my dick.

Kiran also has a lovely head. Wait, now that sounds like I'm drawing a comparison between her head and that of my dick's. Fuck no.

Obviously, she's been on my mind, creating a little too much chaos for me to control.

Let me be honest, I can't talk about Kiran's physical appearance without mentioning the scar. The scar is definitely noticeable. It's apparent she lets it define her by the way she covers her face and diverts her eyes. I get it. It's a thick, angry welt across her left cheek that bends down to her chin. It's gotta be the first thing people notice. There's nothing pretty about it, but it doesn't make her less beautiful either. In a way, it speaks volumes about her strength.

To me, it's sort of like the heart-shaped birthmark on her wrist. It's unique, but it also diminishes against her other features. Although, I'd be lying if I said I wasn't curious. The question sits on the tip of my tongue. What the hell happened to you, Kiran? But I drown it in the back of my mind every time it surfaces.

Her deep, expressive almond-shaped eyes are such a dark brown they almost look black. They manage to show an entire range of emotion on the scale of sad. But when she laughs, there is lightness in them. Oh, and then there is that beautiful mouth of hers. Have I mentioned it? That damn mouth is killing me. Then again, I really enjoy the stuff that comes out of it too.

Between the huge-ass straw hat and oversized hoodie, I have no idea how long her hair is. Its pitch black, and I'm guessing the strands feel like spun silk. When she twirls a piece around her fingers, it stays in a curl for a few minutes before going straight again. She has a unique scent too. I got a nice whiff in the elevator. In the backyard of my house, there is a small tangerine tree right next to Gram's favorite shrub. Gram told me the name a million times. Hell, I had to weed around the damn thing often enough. I should know this. It's...jasmine. A jasmine shrub. Some seasons, depending on the weather, the tree and shrub would both blossom at the same time. As a kid, I used to stand between the two of them and suck in the air. That's the closest comparison I can make to Kiran Shenoy's scent. Jasmine, tangerines, and something else. A mystery ingredient I doubt I'll ever be able to single out, but it's probably the most important.

Judging from the way her breathing deepened and her cheeks flushed yesterday afternoon, I hypothesize this attraction isn't a dead end or one-way street. But the thing about troubled waters is that you either go with full diving gear or not at all. This is not a situation where you can just dip your toes. As curious as I am, I have no time for any deep dives outside of military exercises and drills.

Even as I make the decision, I realize I'm still searching for her. She wasn't on the beach today. She's not at the bar tonight. But there is a huge crowd gathered around the large tiki hut. It would be easy to miss her. A large bonfire crackles on the beach, and a wooden platform is set up to act as a stage. The band, five guys in matching Hawaiian shirts, goes through the entire gamut of beach music. The best of the Beach Boys, Billy Ocean, and Jimmy Buffet battle with the crashing waves.

The several beers I consumed created a decent buzz. Regardless, I'm definitely not drunk enough to mistake there are three girls flirting with me at the same time, and I'm not just seeing triple. We're hanging out and joking around. They hail from North Carolina, but I'm not going to hold it against them. Girl number one makes it very clear I am welcome back to their room where they have a huge stash of cheaper and better alcohol. All three of them seem as into each other as they are me. I gulp as two of them lock lips. Almost every guy at the bar nods or claps or shows some form of appreciation for the fine show we are witnessing. There are wet dreams, and then there are *wet dreams*. If this isn't every boy's wettest dream, I don't know what is.

"You ready to go, cowboy?" Alabama asks. Wait, is that her name? She's named after a state I think, but I was only half-paying attention. Outside of a Quentin Tarantino character, who names their kid Alabama? Especially if they are from North Carolina. Maybe I shouldn't feel so bad. She doesn't seem to know my name either. After all, she called me cowboy.

"Let me finish my beer."

"Hurry up and gulp it down, Mason," girl number two says, her fingernails digging into my shoulder. Well, guess one of them knows my name. Why the hell can't I remember their names? If anything, I am a gentleman, even in this scenario. But as hard as I try, their names elude me.

The offer is tempting. They are gorgeous after all, blond hair and creamy skin and bodies that could grace Penthouse. I am talking the October issue. Why the hell not? I'm not attached. I wouldn't mind a hook-up or five or three all at once. Hell, I marked it as one of the things to do on this vacation the way some people mark the sights they want to see. Tits, ass, and legs were on my to-do list. I plan to check all of them off tonight. This is easy. These waters are shallow enough that even my small toe would touch the bottom.

I am fully aware I sound like a sex-starved, horny teenager. But in my defense, I missed out on those crucial years. When all my friends were hooking up and satisfying their sexual appetites, I had to take Dana to Future Problem Solvers Club and coach field hockey practices or games. I've lived a life that a monk might be proud of…but not a straight-laced celibate one who sleeps on a hard bed or anything. More like the kind of monk that breaks a vow here and there. Still, I didn't date all that much, and I never brought a random girl home. My priorities never really matched my age. That is a choice I would never change, but now… Now I have a little freedom. So why am I not running full speed for their room?

Alabama is batting her thick, overly-done eyelashes at me. "We're going to have fun tonight, cowboy." For some fucked-up reason, I question the statement. One of the girls is groping my shirt. The third has her hand on my ass.

This is perfect, right? So can someone explain to me why the fuck I'm having second thoughts? Someone? Anyone?

I seriously need my head examined.

Taking a step back to extricate myself, I shake my head. "Thank you, ladies, but I'm going to stay for a while." To cement the decision, I order another beer.

"Oh sure," girl number three chirps, pressing her hand against my ass once again. "We can stay here for a bit."

We?

I disengage her palm from my backside.

"It's a little crowded here. I'm going for a walk." There, now I've gone and done it.

"Sounds fun," girl number two says, moving closer. Her name sounds like a musical instrument. She stands on her tiptoes and whispers in my ear about how she has never had sex on the beach. God, I hope she's referring to the drink.

"Actually, I'm really tired."

Girl number three slaps my chest. "Montana, can you believe this guy? He's tired, and we haven't even had our way with him yet." Montana. Her name is Montana. That makes sense. She has big boobs. Mountains. Montana. Her hand goes lower.

The bartender slides a shot to me. "This is for you."

I pick up the small glass filled with Baileys and topped with a huge mound of whipped cream. "Did you guys order this for me?"

The girls all have matching toothpaste commercial smiles. Viola, yes, Viola is her name. She speaks first. "Baby, if we wanted to give you a blow job, it would be the real thing."

"It's from her," the bartender says, pointing to the far end of the tiki bar. I do a double take. Kiran is sitting on the other side staring straight at me. She lifts up her glass in a toast, but her expression falls a few bars short of amused.

Staring at the shot and back at her, I'm curious as hell. I don't know what she means by this shot, but I sure as fuck aim to find out. "Excuse me, ladies," I say, already walking in her direction with my beer and my newly acquired Blow Job.

"Where are you going?" they ask, almost in unison. I wonder if they practice.

I turn back. "You girls have fun tonight. I am a cowboy, but this isn't my rodeo."

Three sets of heavily made-up eyes narrow simultaneously. I don't wait for a response.

Kiran has her hair down tonight, free of any cover. Turns out, it is long and straight. It hits the middle of her back. She's wearing a dark blue dress with long sleeves that manages to mask her from shoulder to ankle. Over that, she's got on a pink shawl. Honestly, I think Grams owned an outfit like that. Shit, Kiran, can't you give me something? A little leg or some clavicle at least?

"Thanks for the shot," I say.

"You're welcome, but you didn't have to come over here. I just wanted to thank you for the book."

"Did it make you smile?"

The corners of her mouth twitch. "A smile so big it hurt. No one's bought me a children's book since... Well, since I was a kid. I've never read that one, though."

I should have given it to her in person. It's a damn shame I missed that smile. "You're kidding. *Oh, The Thinks You Can Think!* is my favorite Dr. Seuss. It never goes out of style in my opinion."

"Definitely a classic. I read it cover to cover."

"Bet it took all of fifteen minutes."

"Ten times three."

"Three?"

"It took ten minutes, but I read it three times. Roughly, thirty minutes. Thank you. It was really thoughtful."

"Welcome."

"You didn't have to leave your little party over there." She waves a hand toward the three girls, who have their eyes fixed on me as if they are lining me up in their crosshairs. "Like I said, the shot was just my way of saying thanks." She doesn't look at me. She looks straight ahead like I'm not even there. There is an edge to her voice. Her mouth is tight. Is it jealousy from what she saw or annoyance because I'm in her space again? Kiran is one book I cannot read no matter how hard I try.

You're sending me mixed shots and mixed signals, Shenoy. I'm here and I'm gonna stay for a minute or ten. I wedge myself into the small gap between her and the person next to her. We're close...almost touching, but not touching at all. The narrow gap feels as wide as the Mexican Gulf. "I'm exactly where I want to be, Kiran."

Her straw stops in mid-twirl. She turns toward me. I desperately want to move a lock of hair so I can see her whole face. "Don't tell me you weren't having fun being mauled by three girls at once."

"Yeah, funny story. I thought it would be fun. Even figured it would make my very own personal greatest hits album. You know, something I can throw on the turntable in my head when I'm alone and in need of some good material. But in the end, it's just not for me. Besides, it's gotta be tricky to have an orgy." I lift up my hands like a sad surrender. "I mean the logistics alone...all those limbs and positions. When I have sex, I'd rather be an actor than a director."

She bursts out laughing. "You didn't look like you were too comfortable."

I wonder how long she's been sitting here.

She props her elbow on the bar top and leans her head against her open palm. "Before I came down, I was watching *Animal Planet* in my room and you had an uncanny resemblance to the baby gazelle."

"I look like a baby gazelle?"

"You do. Or at least you did right there." She tilts her chin in the direction of my previous location. "Right before a pack of hungry lions attacked it. Poor, poor baby gazelle."

I can't stop my smirk. "Baby gazelles are damn adorable, don't you think?"

"Adorable is a stretch. I'd say cute." She twirls a strand of hair. "Yeah, cute sounds right."

"I'll take it. But Shenoy, truth time, you sure you're not disappointed in me?"

"Because you were about to have mindless sex with three gorgeous girls?"

"Because I *didn't* have mindless sex with three gorgeous girls. When you put it in perspective, you just witnessed a man walk away from his dream. It kinda makes me weak on some level."

She shakes her head, but she does grace me with a smile that makes it clear she picks up on my sarcastic sense of humor. That is one beautiful mouth. "Maybe you're just not ready for it yet. I bet if you work real hard and it's meant to be, it'll happen for you one day."

"You think?"

"Yes. Dreams do come true." She puts her hand on my shoulder. "You learned a very important lesson about yourself today, Cutler." The statement comes out like the closing scene of a family sitcom.

"I did. Growing up is not easy."

"Never is." She looks down at the shot still sitting on the polished bar top. "You didn't drink it."

"Of all the thousands of shots in all the bars in all the world, why would you order this one for me?"

"What's wrong with it?" She asks it so innocently.

I hold it up. "Do you even know what this is?"

"No. I told the bartender to get you a specialty shot. Something you might like."

"Well, it's definitely special. It's a Blow Job."

She chokes on her own drink. "No wonder he started laughing. Shit. I suck at ordering drinks."

"Actually sucking is a very important part of a blow job."

She elbows me. "You have such a dirty mouth."

And an even dirtier mind.

I tip back my beer and swallow the last few dregs.

"Want another round?" I ask her, setting my empty beer next to her almost empty glass.

"No thanks. I should go. It's late."

I check my watch. "Shenoy, it's nine-thirty. Are you on grandma bedtime or something? Do you also have dinner at four PM?"

She laughs. "I want to get to bed early because I was planning to watch the sunrise tomorrow."

"Maybe you shouldn't go to bed at all?"

Her deep brown eyes widen. "What are you saying?"

God, what am I saying? "Why not just wait up for the sun to show?"

"Stay up all night?"

"Yeah. I'll stay up with you. It'll be easier to keep each other awake. Look here, you're on a beach vacation. Plans are for the real world."

"This isn't the real world?"

"No, Kiran, this... This is a reprieve from reality. This is a time to be spontaneous in a place where you don't have to set an alarm."

Either she's going to tell me off or dismiss the idea in a polite way. "What will we do all night?"

Don't ask me what I want to do with you all night, girl.

"You up for a walk?" I manage to spit out.

Chapter 4

Mason

We both decide our all-nighter should start with coffee. So we head north out of the hotel parking lot, away from the beach, staying on the sidewalk, in search of caffeine. We pass row after row of hotels lining the Gulf. She points out a few places of interest.

"The Hilton has a rooftop cigar lounge. The Sandmeridian has canopy beds on the beach and offers hula lessons. The Wilshire has a five-star rotating restaurant complete with a forties era dance floor."

"Ever been to any of these places?"

"Nope. Being a local means you know all about the tourist stuff, but you never do any of it. Although my prom was held at the Wilshire."

"How was it?"

"I didn't go."

"No date?"

"I had a date."

"Don't tell me the asshole stood you up."

She stops walking. We stand still for a moment. She tilts her head and stares up at the top of the Wilshire. There is something in her expression that spells regret in capital letters. "I stood him up."

"Why?"

"Just didn't want to go. He found another date anyway, so it's all good."

I doubt it was all good for Kiran. Although there is a story there, I can read the big red sign she's holding up: Proceed with Caution. I should heed it. I really should. "There is a lot of freedom between us."

"What do you mean?"

"When we leave here, you'll never see me again. You can say anything to me. Who am I except a stranger you met on vacation? I'll never hold it against you. I won't judge you. We don't have to play any games. I really suck at games, anyway."

She crosses her arms. "I'll keep that in mind. Can we talk about something else please?"

"Yeah." I say that, but I can't let go of the conversation. It feels unfinished. "I didn't go to my prom either."

She cocks her head. "You didn't have a date?"

"I had offers. As a matter of fact, Sheila McGovern asked me. That was a little too tempting to pass up so I agreed." Brilliant, Cutler. Inject another girl's name into the conversation. Nothing says I'm hot for you like talking about girlfriends past.

Kiran doesn't appear offended, though. "Oooh, Sheila McGovern." She arches an eyebrow. "And what makes her so special?"

"Besides the double cup size?"

Disappointment flickers on her face. "Misogyny doesn't suit you."

I jut my chin toward her. "What does?"

"Honesty. I think you're really honest. I like that about you. Besides, I have a feeling there was something really special about her because it's obvious you wanted to go."

She calls me out like a ref on home plate, and rightly so. I inhale a deep breath. "Sheila McGovern was very pretty and really sweet. I had a mad crush on her since freshman year."

"Then why didn't you take her?" She says it as if she feels sorry for Sheila... Or maybe she's sorry for me.

"Prom is lame. Anyway, I'm not a total dick. Sheila went with a buddy of mine when I bowed out. They got married last year, so you see it all worked out. In a way, I am somewhat responsible for bringing them together."

"Yes, you're a regular Cupid."

"Funny, smartass."

"You never answered my question."

"What question?"

"Why didn't you take her?"

"I told you, prom is lame."

"I would have believed you except you already committed to it. Maybe I'm reading you wrong, but you don't seem like the type of fellow to bail on a commitment."

I'm not sure how to answer or if I even want to answer.

She gestures between the two of us. "Or doesn't freedom work both ways?"

"Damn girl, if you gonna serve up some crow, at least sauté it in butter first."

She puts her hands on her hips. "The only way to serve crow is raw. Now spill it, Cutler. Why didn't you take pretty, sweet Sheila?"

"It wasn't about her as much as it was about me. I hate to tell you this, but you're wrong. I did bail on her. The whole thing was too overrated and expensive."

"Is that what you thought at the time, or what you think now?"

"At the time. Why do you ask?"

She wraps the shawl tighter, even though it is an exceptionally warm night. "No reason."

"You had a reason for asking. What is it?"

"It's an oddball thought for a high school senior. That's all."

"I have always leaned toward odd."

Her lips purse, her expression skeptical. "I doubt there is anything odd about you."

"It's time you knew."

"Knew what?"

"I'm the President of the Oddball Club, Shenoy."

She laughs and pats my chest. God, I want to hold her hand right there against my heart for a beat or two longer.

"That's my title, buddy."

"We'll have to share the title then. But prom? That was all about money. I've always been really careful with money. Not cheap, you understand, but responsible…maybe even frugal in a way."

"Money was a problem for you growing up?" She closes her eyes tight and clamps her mouth shut. "I'm sorry. That's crossing a line. It's none of my business."

"Don't be sorry. Cross lines all you want." I shrug it off, although a part of me wants to put up my own red sign with flashing lights to warn her to tread lightly. Why the hell I pried open this can of twisted worms, I have no idea. But I decide to share a part of me anyway because how can I ask it of her without reciprocating? "A year after my father died, my sister and I moved in with my grandma. It became apparent to both of us she was having some major memory problems and health issues."

"I'm sorry."

"It's okay. She was still herself in the end. Just confused sometimes. I know Alzheimer's isn't like that for everyone, so in that sense, we were lucky. The woman still beat my ass in *Jeopardy* every night. Funny, what the mind remembers. Anyway, I had to become head of the house. When I was sixteen, I got a job after school. I took over the bills and the groceries and the cooking."

"You cook?"

"Damn straight."

"Impressive."

"But doing that stuff makes you realize how little a dollar can stretch. Don't get me wrong. We weren't destitute or anything, but we didn't have a lot of surplus either. When it came to things like prom, I made another choice where to spend the money."

"What choice?"

"A few weeks after Sheila asked me, my sister had an opportunity to visit the Georgia Aquarium for a three-day trip. It's rated one of the best in the country. Only six students were chosen from the whole school district, and Dana was one of them. We couldn't swing both things. There was no way I would have stolen the experience from her so I could dress up in a rented tux worn by a hundred other guys before me. Sheila was upset, but she understood. She forgave me."

Kiran rubs her eyes and looks away from me.

"What's going on with you, girl? Don't tell me you're getting weepy on me?"

"No." Her voice cracks betraying her answer.

"Making you cry was definitely not in the plans."

She wipes a hand across her cheeks and sniffles. "I'm really not this sappy. It's just so…freaking sweet. I either had to cry it out or go into a diabetic coma. I chose tears."

I struggle to find a joke because the last thing I'm aiming to do is add to Kiran Shenoy's sad. She's has a huge surplus of sad. "It's not a big deal at all."

I wish I had a handkerchief for her. But since I'm a dude and this isn't the eighteenth century, I have nothing to offer her.

She's almost in control again except for the slight tremble of her lower lip. "I disagree. It is a very big deal." She wags her finger at me. "Do me a favor and don't make me cry again."

"Do me a favor and stop asking me probing questions, Barbara Walters."

Like a tornado changing course, she laughs. "Deal." As we pass the Wilshire, she takes another glance back.

"Hey, it's too late to go to prom, but we can still check out the revolving restaurant if you want." I twirl my finger.

She gives me a puzzled look. Yes, Kiran, I'm asking you on a date. Do I need to send you a formal invitation? Or maybe after all that money talk she thinks I can't afford it. I really hope it's the former and she's confused about my intentions. I rock back and forth on my feet, stuffing my hands in the pockets of my jeans.

"It's overrated and expensive." Well, that was a decline if I ever heard one.

Rejection stings like a swarm of pissed-off bees. "Are you trying to be funny? Because I wasn't joking."

"I'm not either."

"Do you think I can't afford it? Is that pity I'm sensing?"

She shakes her head rapidly. "That thought never crossed my mind."

For whatever reason, I believe her. What's more, I feel relief in her answer. "Then what?"

"How long are you here for, Cutler?"

"Eight days in total. Seven days in counting."

"Me too. You're the one who said plans are for the real world. We're both on vacation so let's not make any."

"Agreed," I say with a certainty I don't feel.

We resume our stroll, heading toward the downtown area. The stores are all closed save for a few restaurants and bars. We pass an ice cream shop with its lights still burning. A large neon sign in the window flashes Kirby's Ice cream. Kiran pauses and looks inside. They have it decorated like a fifties joint, or maybe they never redecorated. The floors are black and white checkers and the walls are a sky blue. There is a long, flecked Formica counter with red swivel stools.

"Want ice cream?" she asks. "This place is the best. They make it here themselves."

"Who would pass up ice cream?"

"People who suffer from lactose intolerance."

I chuckle. "No worries there."

I open the door for her. The bells chime above the door signaling our entry. A blast of cold air hits us both. The temperature's almost frigid compared to the Florida heat.

The girl behind the counter grimaces. "We're closing in ten minutes."

"Sorry," Kiran says. She turns back toward the door as if we've been caught trespassing. I reach for her arm. She stops instantly, her eyes scanning my hand. Not that I'm touching any skin. The shawl is thin and soft, but it's a barrier just the same.

"We'll take it to go," I say to the clerk.

I turn to Kiran so she can give her order first. She isn't like me. She checks out every carton inside the display case before making her decision.

She settles for some crazy chocolate concoction called Chocolate Overdrive. It's got chunks of fudge and threads of darker chocolate woven into the base. All my plans to kiss her go up in smoke. Fuck you, chocolate. I order a scoop of Blue Moon on a sugar cone. She opens the small purse she carries, but I hold my hand out.

"It's on me." I give her a look that says *do not argue*. She doesn't.

She grabs a few napkins for us. "Thank you, Mason."

"Welcome."

As soon as we're on the street again, I regret stopping for ice cream. Her fucking tongue is driving me crazy. I focus on my Blue Moon and try not to stare. Try being the keyword.

She holds her cone toward me. "Wanna taste?"

She must think I want some 'cause I keep staring, but it's not her scoop I'm interested in. "I can't."

"Oh, you're a germa-phobe." She turns back toward the store. "I can get a plastic spoon or something."

I reach for her wrist. The beat of her pulse rises in the few seconds before I let go. "No Kiran, it's not that. I'm allergic to chocolate."

Her eyes go wide. "Are you serious?"

"No lie."

"Is that a real thing?"

"For me it is. I've never officially been tested, but every time I have chocolate I end up with a migraine." If I wasn't staring at her so intently, I would have missed the slight tremble of her lower lip.

"You really are going to make me cry again, aren't you? That's got to be the saddest thing I've ever heard. You asked me if I pitied you earlier. I swear I didn't, but I sure do now." She takes a bite from her scoop. "You're missing out on so much."

"Yeah, it's…tragic."

"It is." She closes her eyes and licks her lips as if she's having a divine experience all by herself. The craving hits me in twenty places. I want a taste. And I'm not talking about the damn ice cream either. "Besides the fact you can't indulge in the awesomeness of chocolate, isn't this the best ice cream you've ever had?"

I'll admit the Blue Moon is pretty damn tasty. "Not bad, but not the best I ever had."

She tilts her head. "You've had better than this?"

"Affirmative. There's this little place called The Creamery back home. They not only make their own ice cream, the family actually owns the dairy farm that produces the milk. That milk gets turned into sweet cream that eventually becomes the best fucking ice cream in the whole world. This is a close second, but The Creamery wins all day long."

She narrows her eyes. "I think the hometown advantage is coloring your opinion."

"I am a proud, small town boy, but you haven't tried The Creamery, so until you do, you don't get a vote."

"Fair enough." The sidewalk narrows, forcing us to walk closer. Her arm bumps against mine a few times.

"Hey, I meant to tell you that you were right about Sam. He set me up."

"I knew he'd take care of you. How is Sam? Is he doing well?" She isn't asking it nonchalantly to make polite conversation. She asks it wistfully.

"He seemed fine. Nice guy. I told him you sent me. He remembers you."

She smiles. "Does he really?"

"Why are you surprised? You're not exactly…forgettable."

She leans against a wall. In the dim lights of the storefront, I can see her uncertainty. Maybe she thinks I'm toying with her. "He remembers me because of what I did, not who I am."

"What does that mean?"

"I wasn't a nice person when I was younger."

"Now that I have a hard time believing."

"I wish it wasn't true, but it is."

"Example, please."

"Did you seriously just ask for an example?"

"I did. I'll need some empirical evidence before rendering a verdict."

"Case in point, when I was in junior high, me and a few of the kids in my class threw eggs at his store. When you're a local, there isn't a ton of things to do even when you live inside a tourist attraction."

I shrug. "You were a teenager. Teenagers make stupid mistakes."

"Still feel like shit about it."

"So apologize to him. Make it right."

"I did already. I felt so guilty I came by his store the next day with a bucket and sponge. I scrubbed and scrubbed the front window and the door. But you can't un-fry an egg. Not even if you work at it for hours. Sam watched me the whole time. When dusk came, he came out of the store. He handed me a bottle of lemonade, thanked me, and told me to go home. I did."

"Is that the end of the story?"

"Nope. Feeling even worse, I went back the next day. I mean, the man thanked me as if I was doing a good deed. I let him. He didn't realize I was one of the egg-throwers. I needed to admit what I'd done. I expected Sam to call my mom or the police or at least yell at me, but he did something else entirely."

Even after all these years, she feels remorse for actions most people would have forgotten long ago. "What did he do, Kiran?"

She pauses to lick the drop of ice cream just before it lands on her hand. "He asked me what I like to read. At the time, the answer was nothing. I wasn't a huge reader. He gave me a book to take home free of charge. Isn't that what drug dealers do? Give you the first hit for free? But this was a positive obsession. He had me hooked. That story was the sort of book I really needed to read at that point in my life."

"What book?"

"*Fried Green Tomatoes at the Whistle Stop Café* by Fannie Flagg. It sort of spoke to me in a weird unexpected way. You think you don't fit in anywhere. Then you read a story about a girl who doesn't fit in, and you don't feel so alone. But she was better than me. She embraced the things that made her different. Whereas I tried to blend in and not make waves, even though I clashed with everything around me. I wanted to be brave like Idgie."

I remember my grandma watching that movie. Grams was a huge Kathy Bates fan. I get what she's saying. We both speak the same oddball language. There are books that have stayed with me, too. Ones I even give credit for shaping my life. "You'll never convince me you're not a nice person. And you're brave, too, Kiran."

Her laugh isn't bitter, but it holds little humor. She kicks a small rock. "Brave? Hardly. Why do you say that?"

"I have my reasons."

We're close. My palm is against the rough brick of the building. We're staring at each other. Her breath hitches. Fuck the headache. I want to kiss her. I want her soft, sexy mouth against mine. I want to run my hands through her long hair and down her body. I want to make her moan. I think she wants it too. I swallow it all back and drop my hand instead. Because even more than the kiss, I don't want her to stop talking. I want more Kiran Shenoy.

She walks away from me, faster with clipped steps, heading farther north as if we're late for a destination. Content not to push too hard, I keep step with her. The silence circles us. The light breeze from the Gulf plays with her hair. I get a sweet whiff of citrus and jasmine and that other flavor…the mystery one I have no name for, but it's driving me crazy just the same. We ditch the paper wrappers from our cones in a receptacle. A group of rowdy drunk guys past us. Keeping a wary eye on them, I move closer to her.

Once they pass, I shove my hands in my pockets again, a physical reminder of the boundaries I've set for myself. "Does Sam know? Did you ever tell him how much you enjoyed the book?"

"Sure, he does. You read a story that changes you, the first thing you do is tell someone. At least I did. I came back the next day and begged him for another book. After that, I spent a lot of time there. Sam's bookstore became a second home. My friends thought it was creepy. But I ignored them. What would Idgie do? I asked myself. Then I would do that thing. Sam and I became friends. He even let me arrange the shelves. That's not as easy as it sounds. Sam has a really specific method. If you screw up, he gets royally mad." She smiles, but not at me. She's smiling at a memory of her past. "Who knew *Jane Eyre* and *Wuthering Heights* could not be on the same shelf?"

"Why not?"

She lowers her voice to a whisper, the way girls do when their sharing juicy gossip. "Apparently, the Bronte sisters don't get along with each other."

"You don't say."

"I do say."

"You should go see Sam. He remembers you not as the egg-thrower but the girl who loves books as much as he does."

She shakes her head. "Our friendship didn't end well, Mason."

"What happened?"

"My mom found out where I was really going when I was supposed to be at the library. She thought it was inappropriate for a young girl to have a friendship with an adult male. She thought his intentions were...evil. Sam doesn't have a sinister bone in his body. To me, he was just another friend. But no matter how much I tried to convince her, she refused to believe me. Sam asked all the time if my mom knew where I was. I lied to him and said she did. So you can imagine what happened."

"I can imagine it, but I'd rather hear it from you."

She swallows, her hands clutching the shawl. "She caught me there after I promised I wouldn't go. She threatened to shut Sam down. She even called the police. They came and messed up Sam's books. It sent him over the edge. They almost arrested him. He gets upset when it comes to someone mistreating one of his books. It was a big, ugly scene. People talked and rumors spread. Customers who had been going to him for years boycotted the store. I kept waiting for the For Sale sign to go on the door or, worse, the Out of Business one. That would have been my fault. But I should have known better. Sam has weathered bigger storms."

I have a feeling Kiran Shenoy weathered her fair share of storms too. Maybe even a few hurricanes.

We pass signs for a Farmers Market. Apparently, they have the best lemons in all of Florida. "You never saw him again after?"

"I never went back, but I did see him from time to time. Jasper isn't that huge. He'd wave sometimes. I'd ignore him. He probably thought I was mad at him, but I wasn't. I was trying to protect him in a way. So stupid, really."

I gently shoulder bump her. "Or brave," I counter.

"No, it was stupid."

"I get where your mama was coming from, Shenoy. It sucks, but it's natural to worry about those things, especially in today's world."

"I get it too. I don't blame her. I just wish it hadn't turned out the way it did. I wish I wouldn't have gone back." She bites her lower lip so hard she might draw blood. "I can't believe I'm telling you all this."

We walk past a garage with a bright yellow door. I stop walking. I want her full attention. She follows suit. We both stare at each other.

"I'm happy you are." I place a finger under her chin and lift it until we are eye to eye again. "Go see him now, Kiran. I'll go with you if you'd like. He's not angry with you."

"Maybe."

We reach the outskirts of town where there are no more stores and the streetlights are farther apart.

"Should we head back?" I ask.

"Probably a good idea."

But we don't. We just keep walking north. We pass an old-fashioned kind of movie theater. There is a sign advertising some Hitchcock film. Not one I've seen.

"Why are you here, Mason?" she asks.

I wanted to go on a moonlight stroll with a pretty girl. Except it sounds too much like a cheesy line. Instead, I say, "We decided to go for a walk."

"I mean, why are you here in Jasper, Florida on vacation?"

"To surf."

She gives me a look that has wrong answer written all over it. "There's a lot of water to be had in South Carolina and a ton of beaches between the two cities. The waves are gnarly here, but the Atlantic is cranking too."

"Did you say gnarly?"

"I've lived here since I was four and moved away when I was eighteen. You don't think I've surfed?"

"I wondered," I admit. "Someone who wears winter clothes on the beach doesn't strike me as the surfing type."

She crosses her arms, her back straightens. "Well, I do." She sighs in frustration, causing a wisp of hair to blow off her forehead. "Or at least I did. I could give you some tips. I'm seriously worried you might drown out there."

"I can handle my own."

She laughs, shaking her head. "Oh Barney, what am I going to do with you?"

I don't know what Barney means, but I doubt it's a compliment.

"Don't you realize how dangerous it can be out there?" The last bit comes out a concerned warning.

I raise my hands in defeat. The truth is I know I've wiped out one too many times to claim any level of expertise. "Give me some tips, and I'll do my best to listen."

"We'll save that for another day, Cutler." She jabs me with her finger. "But that day has to come before you get on a surfboard again, okay?"

"Fine by me."

"So answer me now. The whole truth this time. Why are you here? Why by yourself?"

"Is that so weird? You're here by yourself, aren't you?"

"I have my reasons. I asked you first."

"It's a long story," I say.

"It's a long night," she counters.

"I just graduated."

"College?"

"Boot camp."

A shudder goes through her. A wind I do not feel.

"You're in the military?"

"The Marines to be exact."

"Wow. I asked you all these personal things, but I never asked what you did for a living."

"If you'd asked a few months ago, I'd tell you I was a mechanic. At least that's what I've done since I was sixteen. When I graduated high school, I did it full-time."

"But now you're a soldier."

"A Marine," I correct.

"Don't people enlist at eighteen?"

"Usually, but it's not a law." This story is so fucking long and raveling, I'm not sure where to start.

Her gaze is quiet and assessing and patient. "So why the wait?"

"I wanted to enlist then, but it wasn't the right time. Gram passed away and Dana was only fifteen."

"You took care of her?"

"We took care of each other. But yeah, I was of age so I petitioned for guardianship. I did my best. I'd say I did a pretty damn good job."

"I don't doubt it, but you were so young."

I shrug. "Thankfully, the state didn't agree with you."

"There was no other family to help you?"

"None I would trust." There was sharpness in my voice I didn't mean to project, but it came out anyway.

She sits on a large flat boulder in the parking lot of a convenience store. I'd give a million pennies for her thoughts. She pats the vacant area next to her and scoots over for me. "Sit with me." It's a tight space and not all that comfortable. I feel bad for taking up most of it. But not so bad that I don't enjoy how our thighs touch. "Are you all right, Kiran?"

She plays with a strand of her hair, twisting it tightly. "You said I was brave, but this… What you are doing is the epitome of brave. I'm in awe of you right now."

"I don't see it that way."

"Don't be humble."

"Honestly, it's always been my duty, but not one I ever resented. It's my honor to serve. That's the only way I can explain it."

"You always knew you wanted to enlist?"

"My dad was a Marine and my grandpa and even his dad and etcetera."

"Etcetera?"

"The line goes back forever. Matter of fact, when you look at my ancestral tree, almost every branch begins or ends with a war. I always had my sights set on joining the family business."

"I see."

"You asked why I'm here earlier. I had plans for my leave. I was going to find a realtor this week to get Gram's house ready to rent out for the next few years. Neither Dana or I need the house, but we're too attached to let it go. It turns out Dana took care of all of it while I was at camp and found renters before she left for Pasadena."

"She's in Pasadena?"

I can't help the pride in my voice. "Yeah, she got into the Marine Biology program at the California Institute of Technology. Got a scholarship too."

"That's amazing."

"Anyway, when I dropped her off at the airport, she made me promise I'd use my leave to do something just for me. So here I am."

"Why here, though?"

"My family used to vacation in Jasper. I thought of inviting a few buddies, but it's kind of special to me, and I didn't want to share it."

"I feel the same way."

I stand and hold my hand out for her. "Let's head back."

We're silent the whole way as we retrace our footsteps, the path now familiar and comfortable. She yawns. We never did get coffee.

"Are you conking out on me already?" I ask.

"Not a chance. This sunrise is mine."

"It's probably crap, but I saw a coffee vending machine in the lobby."

"I'll take crappy coffee over no coffee."

We make it back to the hotel and head straight for the vending area. Between my pockets and her purse, we find enough change for two cups. I don't even know if you can call this stuff coffee.

"Where to now?" I ask. "The beach?"

"What about the roof? I bet it's a good view."

"Think it's open?"

"Yeah, I checked it out earlier."

The elevator is as slow as ever. I don't mind being alone with Kiran in a small space, but I sure as hell can do without all the damn creaks and grunts that occur when we pass a floor. If there's going to be grunting, it should be coming from one of the occupants.

"Mind if we stop at my room?" I ask.

A look of panic flashes across her face.

"I want to grab a blanket."

Her shoulders relax. "Sure." Did she think I wanted something else? I do, of course. But not tonight. Not now. Maybe not ever. That's fine too. Disappointing, but fine.

Neither of us feels too great about getting back in the elevator of potential doom so we head for the stairwell. The door to the roof is open. You can see almost the whole shoreline from here. It's not set up for people, but there are a few plastic chairs stacked in a corner. I place two by the ledge. We each take a seat, lean back, prop up our feet. I drape the blanket over us.

The moon is ripe, almost full but not quite. It provides just enough light to see the peaks of the waves as they crash upon the shore. She closes her eyes but then snaps them open again.

"You can sleep, Kiran. I will wake you."

She rubs her face. "No. I'll stay up." Kiran fishes her phone from her purse. I expect she's going to text someone, which would be a real turn-off for me. Instead, she pulls out ear buds.

"Want to listen to music?" she asks, offering me one end.

"Depends. Is it going to be boy bands?"

"Maybe." When she laughs, it's almost wicked, her version of a villain's laugh. "Don't worry, I have a variety."

I hold out my hand. "Let me see."

"You've already peeked at my library and now you want at my playlist too? This is definitely getting personal."

"It might be your playlist, but it's my ears. I'd rather they not bleed."

She mocks an offended look before handing over the phone. I scroll down the long list. Yeah, this girl likes her fair share of boy bands and top forty pop, but then I get to the Pearl Jam and Led Zeppelin. Nice. I go further, curious what else is on here. I'm happy I do.

"Kiran Shenoy, you never stop surprising me."

"What?"

"You're a fan of country. The new country is cool enough, but the old country is kind of shocking me right now. Hank Williams, Jr.? Johnny Cash? And a little Reba too. You realize I'm ten guitar licks away from proposing."

She laughs, her cheeks turning the darkest shade of crimson. "Told you I like variety. You didn't believe me, did you?"

"Not this much variety. How did this happen? You just decided to try out some Bocephus one day?"

"Something along those lines. I get your surprise. It doesn't fit me."

"It doesn't fit most people our age."

"It's actually my stepmother's influence. Linda's from Tennessee, and her parents owned a bar where some of the greats performed. When I moved back to New Jersey with my papa, Linda would play these records all the time. I hated them at first. I made fun of them. I threatened to break them a few times. But it wasn't long until I was singing along to Patsy Cline and Charley Pride. The lyrics spoke to me. And all my complaints were really just me hating Linda because I always thought of her as the enemy."

"How could you hate anyone who loves Charley Pride?"

"I wonder that myself sometimes. Papa had an affair with her when he was still married to my mom. He told my mom he was in love with another woman, but they could keep up the marriage if she wanted, although it would be a sham. She asked for a few days to think about it."

"You're kidding. What's there to think on? When someone tells you they are in love with someone else, it's time to say so long."

"You don't understand, Mason. Their marriage was arranged in India. The word divorce isn't even a part of their vernacular. Plus, they had me to think about. Anyway, my mom came here to Jasper. To this very hotel actually. She wanted to be by the water. It reminded her of the Arabian Sea back in India."

"So she left your dad?"

"Not only did she go through with the divorce, she moved us here permanently. She was a software developer so she could work anywhere. She never liked New Jersey anyway. Thinking about what she did, I realize now how gutsy it was. Their divorce was a huge scandal in our conservative extended family. I blamed Linda for everything my mom went through. Every year I'd spend my summers with Papa and Linda. They would take me on these crazy vacations to Disney World and buy me all kinds of stuff. Papa tried to make up for the whole year in those few months. Later, when I was older, we'd go to Paris or Rome or London. Twice we went to India for a visit. The whole time, I was so nasty to Linda."

"Not anymore, though?"

"Not after living with her the past few years. She's a good person. Papa is too. Maybe they did a bad thing, but they aren't bad people."

I reach out and tuck a strand of hair behind her ear. I've never wanted to kiss anyone so damn bad in my whole life. But this is her move to make. I wait for her to lean in. To pucker up her lovely mouth. To give me an indication she wants it too.

But we've shared enough sad stories to fill up a whole fucking country album. Hell, we may have even crossed the line and hit a few chords toward the Blues. That's some pretty tragic shit. Country can make you feel. But the blues, well, they can tear a person's soul to shreds. I think that's the space we're in now. Torn, fragile, and so exposed we're already naked. She doesn't make a move. It's probably for the best. After all, if I start kissing her, I won't want to stop.

I hide my frustration and shift in the uncomfortable plastic chair. "Damn, Shenoy, your whole life is a Disney movie in the making. You even have the moral of the story figured out. I can't decide if I'm on a beach vacation or at Sunday sermon."

Thank God, she laughs and doesn't freak. It really could have gone either way. She nods in agreement. "Oh my God, I do read a little like a fable."

"A little?"

"Shut up, Cutler." She playfully punches my arm. "Ouch." She shakes her hand out.

"I will say this, you're a whole lot cuter than my pastor, even if you didn't offer me any wine or crackers."

"Hey, you're no better, Mr. Take-a-girl-for-a-walk-and-make-her-cry."

"That was not my intention."

"I guess there's just one thing left for us to do."

"What's that?" I'm grinning way too wide for my own good.

She claps her hands. "On with the music, Mr. DJ."

Again, not my goal.

She slips on her ear bud. I take the other. I scroll down her list, passing up any songs that are too heavy, too numbing, too boy band. I finally find something that fits the mood. Or at least my mood.

"Sister Havana" by Urge Overkill.

We listen to music until the night fades into day. The sky turns a deep rose color. She's asleep, her head on my shoulder.

"Get up, Kiran. You're going to miss it."

She mumbles something incoherent. Whatever it is, it sounds sexy as hell. A language I'd enjoy decoding. Her hair falls against my arm. It is soft as silk. I almost don't want to wake her. "Kiran, it's time."

She lifts her head just in time to see the golden light come over the water.

She rubs her eyes and straightens. "It's beautiful."

"It is," I say, except I'm not looking at anything but her.

Chapter 5

Kiran

I sleep until late afternoon. I think I dream about him. Or maybe last night was the dream, and none of it happened. Maybe he went to bed with three bouncing blondes, and I went back to my room to hide under the covers.

Except, this smile I have? It's plastered onto my face as if someone pinned it in place. Yeah, I walked around with Mason Cutler last night. We shared some crazy intimate stories. He's as beautiful inside as out. I told him some things I buried so deep I thought they had suffocated and died years ago. But there are no regrets.

Of course, I'd be fibbing if I said I didn't want him to grab me at any given moment and sweep me off my flip-flops. Even though it didn't happen, it was perfect nonetheless. Then we watched the sunrise. I'm so giddy about it I might just play myself a little air guitar for no reason at all. I'm killer at air guitar.

But I don't do any of those things. I think of a much better use for my fingers. With my eyes still shut, I trail them down my body, dipping them inside my panties. I imagine he didn't just walk me to my door this morning and made sure I got in. No, he came inside with me. He threw me on the bed. He ripped off my clothes. In this fantasy, I don't have any scars. Or maybe he just can't see them. Either way, it's not awkward. His blue eyes bore into me until I'm squirming from the intensity. What's better than honey? That tiny second before you taste the honey, AKA, anticipation. Last night, I indulged in gallons of anticipation. It's all pent up inside me, aching for release. I cry out as my fingers penetrate.

I imagine fisting my hands through his chocolate-cinnamon-honey hair. The sides are shaved but the top is long enough for a satisfying tug. His hands are massive. What would they feel like on my body? They would touch me everywhere, commanding and teasing every inch of me until my flesh screamed for him. I press my thighs together and rock faster.

It's so real I can almost hear him calling my name. "Kiran." It's soft, a notch above a whisper. "Kiran." His voice isn't louder, but it is more forceful, keeping in tune with his thrusts. He pushes himself deeper still. No wait, he's pounding into me. There's nothing gentle. It's raw and lusty and needy for both of us.

"Kiran?" His voice is so clear...so real.

Wait, what?

Shit! I stumble out of the bed, almost falling.

"Are you okay?" comes the deep masculine voice of my fantasies, except it's not in my head. It's on the other side of my door.

"Fine. I'm fine." What I am is a hot mess.

I wait until my breathing gets under control. Checking to make sure my T-shirt is long enough so it's not indecent, I open the door a crack.

"What were you doing?" he asks, looking at me as if he already knows.

"Sleeping."

"You weren't dreaming?" He's wearing a smirk. Do I have it written on my face?

"What's up?" I ask, trying for nonchalance and hoping for a change of subject.

"I didn't mean to wake you." He holds out his surf board. "I promised I wouldn't go into the water until you gave me surfing lessons. I'm upholding my end of the bargain, but I've been up for a few hours, waiting on you, Sleeping Beauty. I'd really like that lesson now."

I'm not sure whether to slam the door in his gorgeous face or grab a fistful of his T-shirt and pull him out of my fantasies and straight into my bed. His T-shirt does little to hide the muscular frame beneath it. He's wearing navy blue board shorts today. His hair is messy and damp and oh so tugable.

"Why are you so sweaty?" I ask.

"I went for a run to pass the time." He leans closer. Even his sweat smells good. "Why are *you* so sweaty?"

"I'm not."

He runs his index finger down my neck. My very slick neck. "No?"

I take a deep breath. "First lesson, you need a new surf board."

"What's wrong with this one?"

"Never rent a surf board from a hotel." I reach out and feel the side of his board. "You pick a board based on your experience level, but it should also be a reflection of your height and weight. You're too big and thick for this board."

His grin is pure mischief. A heat creeps up my spine as I replay my words. It's like everything is filtered through a sex-scope.

"So you think I'm big and thick?"

"For this board."

"Uh-huh."

I'll take stupid sexual innuendos for a thousand, Alex.

"I'm being serious." I try my hardest not to encourage him, but I laugh anyway. "This board is more suited for someone my size."

"What else?"

I try to bend the board, but it won't yield. "The board has to be softer."

"Softer?" He arches an eyebrow. "You lost me now, and we were doing so well."

"A softer board will be more flexible, which means it will be easier for you to control. If you have the right board and start your strokes earlier and faster, you might catch a wave or two."

"No one has ever accused me of not stroking myself fast enough."

I choke back a laugh. "Are you always this cocky first thing in the morning?"

"It's late afternoon, sunshine. And no, not always this cocky, but you're the one who's all sweaty, talking about stroking and thickness to me." He gestures between the two of us. "Call me kettle, cause guess what? You're the pot."

"Well, listen up, Kettle. There's a place about a block north of here that rents boards." I remember seeing it yesterday when we went for our walk.

"What's it called?"

My mouth tightens as the name comes to me. "A Thousand and One Bodacious Boards."

"Seriously?"

"No lie. It's a cheesy name, but they know what they're doing. They'll hook you up with the right board."

"What will you be doing while I'm getting...hooked up?"

"I have to take a shower and eat something." And maybe finish something too.

He checks his watch. He wears a real wristwatch in the age of smart phones. Just add that to the growing list of items labeled reasons why Mason Cutler turns me on, twists me in every direction, and flips me inside out.

"I'll meet you on the beach in an hour then."

"An hour and a half," I say, closing the door before he can respond. I lean against it, all perma-smile and drenched panties. A part of me thought last night was a fluke. I even cringed thinking of the awkward moments when we'd run into each other during the rest of the stay. Yet, here we are.

After a grueling session of self-love followed by a rousing rendition of air guitar, I take a long hot shower singing "Sister Havana" at the top of my lungs.

By the time I find Mason, he's waxing a surfboard much more suited to his build. He's shirtless, the lean muscles of his chest and abs flexing as he runs the bar of wax from nose to tip, the muscles in his arm flexing with each glide. It's wildly erotic. Of course, he is doing it all wrong.

"Bitchin' board, dude," I say, throwing down my hemp beach bag next to him.

"Yeah?" his eyes narrow, the naughty grin surfacing. "You think its thick enough?"

"It'll do."

I take the bar of wax from him. It almost slips from my fingers. I don't even have to look at the label to know it's sex wax, the dry hump variety for higher temperatures. "You wax to create grip and traction."

"Friction."

I tuck a strand of hair behind my ear. As much to get control over the runaway train of Mason Cutler as anything else. "Right. It's more of a sanding motion, though." I demonstrate for him. I trace the line that marks the rails. "But not on this area."

"Got it. No coloring outside the lines."

"Right."

I hand the bar back to him. He follows my lead, his fingers gripping the bar tightly, rubbing wax onto the board until the surface is covered.

"You never told me why you came here, Shenoy."

"I didn't?"

"No."

"For the same reason my mom did. I have a decision to make. I thought being here might help."

His mouth tightens into a thin line. "Trying to decide if you should leave your cheating husband? Probably something you should have told me."

"What? No, not that kind of decision."

"So no cheating husband?"

"No husband at all. Geez, I'm only twenty-one."

"Yeah, just making sure." He looks down at the board again. His head snaps up suddenly. "Or boyfriend?"

"No one."

He nods and returns his attention to the board again. "So what's the big decision you're debating?"

I've actually been itching to discuss it with someone. I rifle through my bag and bring out the book he'd given me. It seemed appropriate to put the letter in here. I take out the envelope with the official school seal and hold it out to him.

"Iowa?"

"The University of Iowa to be exact. I decided to apply again as a fluke. I was accepted into the Creative Writing program. It's one of the best in the country."

"And this is what you want to do? Be a writer?"

I nod. "It's always been my passion."

"What's the problem then?"

I pull my legs up against my chest and wrap my arms around them. "I've been taking online business courses for the past few years. I'm only a few semesters from my degree in finance. Hardly any of my credits will transfer. I'll be starting over and in a new place where I don't know anyone. I'll be a twenty-one-year-old freshman." I'm ashamed to tell Mason about my fear, especially since he's going off to God knows where, and here I am freaking out about college. But there isn't any judgment in his expression.

"The other day I read something about a lady graduating college at eighty."

"At the rate I'm going I might be eighty by the time I get a degree. Papa thinks it's a waste of time. I'll have to get loans and pay my own way. He's basically told me he's not in the business of funding dreams. But I have some money my mom left me, and I even got a partial scholarship. Still, it'll be a challenge."

"Sounds like you have the money part figured out. That's good."

"I do. But my dad really disapproves. We had a big fight about it before I left. He called me a quitter. Said I should finish what I started."

Mason narrows his eyes, a few hard lines form around his mouth. "It's not quitting. It's starting something new, something better."

"He's not trying to be a jerk. He's disappointed. I'll be letting him down if I go."

"How so?"

"He owns a financial advising firm, the biggest privately owned firm in New Jersey. He wants me to take over one day. That's always been the plan."

"His plan or yours?"

"I'm not sure anymore. What I am sure of is that dreams always sound better in the abstract. Do I really want to invest four more years going to school?"

He flaps the letter in the air. "You think you'll hate it there?"

"No." Even thinking about it, I can't help smiling. "Reading literature? Talking about literature? Working on my own writing? That's this side of Nirvana. It just…isn't very logical." I take the letter from him, carefully fold it, and place it back in the book. I slip it all into my bag.

"Your argument isn't logical. You don't want to go to a school you know you're going to love because you might have to do it longer?"

I never thought of it so simply. "Maybe I'll have to move that reason from con to pro."

"I think you should."

"Move the argument?"

"Go to Iowa."

"We'll see. I have a few days before I have to give them my answer."

He looks out at the Gulf. I wonder if he's thinking about the waves. "Know what a barnacle is, Shenoy?"

That's a weird question. "Yes."

"So then you know how the average barnacle survives?"

"I'm not really up on my barnacle knowledge."

"Dana explained it to me once. I always thought it was interesting. Typically, the barnacle attaches itself to something such as a whale or a boat or even a rock. Once they find a place to stick to, they hang on for their whole life."

"Crappy life."

"Or an easy one. Think about it, the barnacle doesn't have to make any decisions. They follow a course they don't navigate themselves. They literally spend their lives going with the flow."

"What's your point?"

He leans forward. "Sometimes you're the barnacle and sometimes you're the boat. Which one do you want to be, Kiran?"

"Are you seriously comparing me to a barnacle? This is the analogy you're making?"

He shrugs. "If the ship fits. Look girl, you want something deep and profound, crack open a fortune cookie. You want some straight-up country boy philosophy, you come to me."

"I'll keep that in mind." I shift so I'm on my knees. "Let's wax."

"Never had a girl ask to wax before."

Never had a boy compare me to a barnacle. "Focus, Grasshopper, I don't want you slipping off this board. It's been a long time since I've used my first aid training."

"You did first aid on someone?"

"Once."

"When?"

"I was maybe fourteen. Luckily, I'd just taken the course at school. This wanna-be surfer got caught in an undercurrent."

"He should have taken a lesson from you."

"Yeah, right."

"So what happened?"

"Nothing really." I wave my hand in the air. "I dragged him back to the shore and lost my favorite surfboard in the process. He took on a lot of water. I had to give him mouth to mouth, but he was fine after a few compressions."

"Kiran Shenoy, are you telling me you saved someone's life? And you said I was humble."

"I'm not being humble. It's just an old memory." It's difficult to reconcile the person I am now from the girl who used to take risks and be courageous. Maybe I have become a barnacle. I break the bar of wax in half. "We need to switch it up now." I start making diagonal hatch marks. He follows my lead, crossing each of my marks to make a perfect X. Our hands pass by each other. We both lean forward to gain better access. Everything inside me tenses once more. I always hated waxing my board, considered it tedious work, even though it doesn't take a long time. Now, I find myself wishing it took longer.

"Enough," I say. "It's waxed enough. Let's work on your stance."

He laughs. "What position do you want me in?"

There's a loaded question.

We set the board flat. I toss off my beach shoes. I show him a few stances. It's nice to be on a surfboard again, even if it is on the sand. Then Mason stands on it, his feet apart. I adjust his arm. Actually touching the sleek muscles I've been admiring is enough to make a girl wipe out on dry land. Mason is all business now. He listens to all my advice. He asks questions too.

I notice the blue board he rented from the hotel lies near us. "You never returned it?"

"You said it was more suited for your body." He jerks his head toward the water. "Come out with me?"

Why not? I want to. But when I turn my head and scan the horizon, all I see is dark water. Every reasonable thought vanishes. Fear grips me, and the response gets stuck in my throat. The irony of what I'm doing, of who I have become, hits me like a tsunami. I am a complete fraud. I'm teaching him to do something I can no longer do myself. I beg my legs to stop shaking as the panic swells in my gut. I close my mouth tight before he can hear my rapid breaths.

"It's okay, Kiran. I understand," he says, although I never answered him. His voice is low and soothing. How could he understand? I don't even understand. He places a hand on my shoulder and rubs slowly. "Thank you for the lesson. I don't need to surf today. We can do something else."

"Yes, you do. The waves are good." I can't even meet his eyes. Can't look at the water. Can't do a fucking thing. I just want him to go so I can deal with this. I place my palm flat against his chest. I push. He doesn't move. Not even an inch.

"Kiran, are you all right?"

"Fine. Go…please." The words come out so meek, almost a whisper. He does. Thank God.

Now that I don't have to contemplate going into the water, I can breathe again. I can watch him. I even do a silent cheer when he barrels through the tube of a wave. He's out there for a good two hours. When the sun starts dipping, he heads back with all the other surfers. His shadow covers me.

"You did well, Grasshopper," I say, forcing a huge smile.

"I had a good teacher." He takes the seat next to me. His feet are covered with sand. "What happened, Kiran?"

"When?"

"You know when."

"I told you I don't surf anymore."

"Why not?"

"There are lots of things I don't do anymore."

"That's not an answer."

I clasp my hands together. "It's the only one I have."

"You realize you had a panic attack, right?"

My laugh is so freaking high-pitched it's almost a shriek. "What? No, I didn't."

"Dana used to have them, and I recognize the signs. Bottom line, you had one. When I tried to comfort you, you begged me to go away. I feel like a total asshole for listening to you."

"You shouldn't."

"Why don't you surf anymore?"

"There are lots of things I don't do now." I pick up my bag. I stuff my sunscreen and e-reader and all the other crap back inside. "I'm going to go. I'm tired."

"Talk to me." He takes my wrist and rubs his thumb across my birthmark. "Can you at least look at me?"

I tilt my head to stare into the brilliant steely blueness of his eyes. I want to towel off that look of concern etched on his face. Want to wipe it clean away. I manage a weak smile. "I'll see you around."

Chapter 6

Kiran

Choosing to read, I avoid Mason for the rest of the day. I almost convince myself that's what I want to do. But being cooped up in my room is driving me nuts. So when the sun goes down, I come out of my hibernation and go for a walk along the beach. Every hotel is hosting some type of beach party. The swarms of people laughing and drinking are overwhelming so I walk until the hotels scatter farther apart.

A DJ plays Chris Isaak's "Wicked Games." Really? Chris Isaak and his hypnotic sexilicious voice singing about desire and falling for someone is the last thing I need right now. I keep moving until the music is washed out by ocean waves.

I come to the fenced area that separates the private hotel beaches from the vacant Lancaster property. The chain-link fence is still there and so is the sign that reads Private Property. As a teenager, my friends and I used to hop this fence and hang out on the other side. I have no idea what makes me place my fingers in one of the chain-link openings and then a foot in another. I just want to be that girl again, the one who was carefree and a little careless too. The fence stands at least eight feet high. I struggle with each push upward. I tell myself the fence has changed. It's higher and the footholds smaller. Except it's not. This is the same fence that's stood here for ten years. It's me who has changed. What was once easy has become monumentally difficult. My fingers tense, the metal cutting into them as I grip harder. The scar that runs across my stomach smarts with each stretch as if warning me to stop this foolishness.

Fuck you, scar.

"Need a hand?"

I stumble for a second before I catch my grip again.

"Take it easy, Shenoy. I wasn't trying to startle you."

With a sigh, I resign and climb back down to where he is. The sand is soft, but a sharp pain shoots up my legs anyway. He catches my wince. He looks at me with a mixture of concern and curiosity. And maybe a little sympathy too. Take it back, Mason. All of it.

He's taken a shower. He's wearing a white T-shirt and dark jeans. His spicy cologne mingles with the salt air. I struggle not to stand on my tiptoes, nose up to his neck, and take a long whiff. Yeah, because I'm not weird enough.

I cross my arms and lean against the chain-link fence. It's cool on my back. "Were you following me?"

"I was."

I didn't expect him to answer honestly. I'm not sure how to respond. I want to be angry, but I can't funnel the emotion, no matter how hard I try.

He places his palm on the fence right next to my head. It sways for a second. "I saw you leaving the lobby."

"Kind of stalker of you."

"Or we could just call it friendly reconnaissance. Why were you hopping the fence?"

"To get to the other side."

"Funny."

"It's a private beach. No one uses it, though. I used to sneak in all the time when I was younger. Guess I'm feeling sentimental."

"You want help getting over the fence?"

"No."

"I'll see you on the other side then."

Wait. What?

He walks a few steps back before running, jumping, and practically leaping over it. The fence wobbles against his weight, but only for a second. My mouth drops as I watch him hop over the fence in one fluid movement, as if it were nothing more than a small bump in the road. "Are you Captain America?"

He gives me a sly smile. "Shhh, I'm incognito." He puts his fingers into the chain link in the hole next to mine. "Are you coming?"

I take a deep breath and start my climb. It's not as graceful as that crazy catapult thing he did. When I get to the top, I make the mistake of looking down before I swing my leg over.

"I'll catch you if you fall. Do you trust me?"

The answer comes quickly without any thought or hesitation. "Yes, Mason, I trust you."

I take the last step, sighing with relief when my foot touches the sand.

"Nice job, Shenoy. You did it," he says.

"Don't patronize me." It comes out like a sharp snap. This time it's Mason who winces. I replay his words in my head, hunting for the note of sarcasm, but I can't find it.

"I wasn't. I would never do that. I know that's physically hard for you. If you think for one second I'd belittle you for that, then you don't know me."

"I'm sorry. I just..." I can't find the right way to express myself. So I just look up at his face. "Please forgive me. I'm a jerk."

"You're forgiven." He shoves his hands in the pockets of his jeans and looks around. "Who owns this?"

The area is desolate and peaceful. I would go so far as to say it's pristine. In a beach chock-full of huge hotels standing next to each other like linebackers, this spot has always been my favorite. Although it all comes from the same stock, there is something serene and pure about the sand here. The moon is full and low, giving off a translucent light. It highlights the chiseled planes of his face.

"The Lancaster Corp. They had plans to build a hotel here a while back. But they never got their act together to get the proper permits. They still own it, though, as far as I know. So it just sits here vacant."

"Except for the pesky kids who occasionally come here to make out?" He arches a brow, the question ripe with amusement.

"Mostly we smoked pot."

"Kiran Shenoy, you naughty rebel."

"In my defense, we always cleaned up after ourselves, and we never did anything too wild or crazy."

"You were probably too paranoid."

"Yeah, we were pretty freaked out the whole time." I turn my gaze toward the ocean. "I did have my first kiss here, though."

"Tell me about that."

"Are you kidding?"

"No joke. Tell me the deets. Where were you? Who was the dude? Was it a hit or miss?"

I take his arm and walk him backward a few steps until we're behind the only palm tree in the area. I can't believe it's still here. "Right here."

"Here? Under the cover of this tree?"

I lean against the rough bark. He takes a step closer to me. "Right here. I was fifteen. His name was Tahl."

"Tall?"

"Taaahaall," I say, exaggerating the syllables. "He hated when people called him Tall."

"Okay, so tell me about Taaahaall." He exaggerates the name the same way, which I think Tahl would hate even more.

"He was my first boyfriend." Realizing that isn't quite right, I bite my lip. "My only boyfriend."

"Uh-huh, go on."

"What else is there to say?"

Mason's smile is usually boyish, good-natured, and on the sweet side. But sometimes it heads into mischievous territory. Right now, it's downright wicked. This smile revs up my pulse and causes my toes to curl. I can barely stand still as if I've absorbed two pots of coffee. I freaking want to take a snapshot of this smile and keep it in my pocket anytime I need a jolt of caffeine.

"You haven't told me anything about the actual kiss. How was it?"

"Long. Long and a little traumatic."

He frowns. "Traumatic?"

"It's not what you're thinking. His lip ring got caught in my braces. It hurt. It took us a while to figure out how to separate without permanent damage."

Mason's shoulders shake with laughter. "Oh shit, Shenoy, that's gotta be the worst kiss in the history of first kisses."

"Maybe. Tell me about your first kiss."

"Nah, that's not what I signed up for."

I punch his arm. Ouch. "Don't double standard me."

"Fine." He sighs and takes a step back from me. "It was amazing."

Figures.

"I need details."

"I was fourteen the first time I kissed a girl. But it was the kind of kiss I'm gonna remember vividly even when I'm eighty. We were on the beach. I was lying on my back. The sunlight was so bright it filtered down on her like a halo. I thought she was an angel. She knelt over me. Her hair fell against my chest. When she leaned down, I wasn't sure what she was doing. I couldn't even breathe. Then she kissed me."

Why did I ask for details?

"Sounds like the best kiss in the history of first kisses."

"Maybe. At least an honorable mention. It's definitely the best kiss I ever had." He jerks his head toward the coastline. "Will you walk with me?"

"I'd love to."

We both throw off our shoes and walk toward the water. We leave deep footprints as we walk in the area straddling the water and sand. Our arms touch a few times. We're quiet, though. The white peaks of crashing waves contrast against the dark waters, making the Gulf look magical in a way. I walk deeper into the water until my ankles are covered. My feet sink into the wet sand.

"What are you thinking right now, Kiran?"

"I want to go for a swim."

He points at me. "Do you have a suit on under that?"

"Does it matter?" I turn to him. "In the last few years, I've forgotten what it means to take a risk or share parts of myself. I've been content to make excuses for my sabbatical from life. But the truth is there has only been one person holding me back. That person is me."

I take his hands in mine. "I was in a car accident. It happened a week after my eighteenth birthday. My mother had just bought me my first car. We were going out to eat, and I wanted to drive. I insisted on it. There was a rainstorm. We hit some debris on the road. The tire went flat. We spun around and crossed a lane. Thank God, there weren't any other cars around. But that also meant no one saw us land in the ditch. When I came to, there was glass everywhere. It wasn't just in the car. It was inside of me, all along the side of my face and body. My mom's side hit the embankment. The pressure of that collision killed her. I was trapped in there and helpless. All I could do was scream. I screamed for over three hours, begging her to wake up or for someone to help us. I screamed so much I couldn't talk for over a week. Sometimes I can still hear myself screaming."

He wraps his arms around me. It's a good, strong hug, the kind that makes me feel safe. I need this hug. I've needed a hug like this for a very long time. "Oh my God, Kiran. I'm so sorry." He wipes my tears.

"Thank you."

"It wasn't your fault. It's called an accident for a reason."

I nod. "It's taken me a while, but I believe that now."

"Were you okay? I mean, I see the scars, but how bad off where you?" Mason's voice is a whisper, but I hear it. It calls to me as loudly as the waves.

I want to stop talking now, but I can't. This is not a story I ever tell. I only have the courage to tell it once. "I was air-lifted to Tampa for emergency surgery. I had internal injuries. Papa and Linda flew down. They stayed here for six months while I recuperated. After, I moved to New Jersey permanently. I couldn't do all the things I did before. I couldn't even remember simple things for a while. There was a lot of rehab and then even more surgeries. I missed the entire second half of my senior year of high school. I had to withdraw my acceptance to Iowa. Eventually, I took the GED test. For the last three years, I've been hibernating, a complete cave dweller. I hardly leave the house. That's why I chose online classes. I withdrew from all my friends even though they tried to keep in touch. I'm still a mess."

He touches my cheek. His hand feels comforting against my skin. I haven't been touched in so long. I'm not even sure I can rationalize this. It's not sexual. There is no questioning where it will lead or what it means. Right now, it's comfort and exactly what I need. I lean into his hand and close my eyes.

"Are you in pain still?"

"Not unless I twist my body in a strange way."

"Like climbing over a fence."

"Yes, like that. The scars immobilize some movement, but I can do most things now."

"You fought your way through a really rough road. You have to be proud of that."

"Proud? I haven't driven a car or surfed or even gone swimming since it happened."

"But you want to go swimming now?"

"Yes, I think I do. Very much."

He lets go of my hands. "Okay, me too." He grips his shirt and pulls it over his head. His chest heaves with each breath. Even in moonlight, his blue eyes shine bright. His jeans come off next. He stands before me in nothing but black boxer briefs. I swallow, taking in his lean, sculpted body.

Mason takes a step toward me. I follow suit. Only a sliver of air is between us. The wind picks up and causes an annoying strand of hair to brush against my face. I think he's going to tuck it behind my ear. Instead, he unclips my barrette. With a hand on each side of my face, he kisses my forehead. The kiss is tender and pure. His hands slide lower until his fingers fiddle with the bottom button of my shirt. Seeking permission, he gives me an assessing look. I nod.

He undoes the button. Then a second, and then a third. His fingers shake, or maybe that's my body reacting. I never imagined being comfortable enough with anyone to expose myself. I can count the days I've known Mason Cutler on one hand. Yet there is a freedom between us I've never experienced with anyone else.

He gently pushes the fabric off my shoulders. It flutters away. My breasts heave in the simple white bra I'm wearing. He gazes at my body.

"You're beautiful, Kiran."

His fingers ghost over my skin. They slide along the biggest and ugliest of all my scars. A long, straight line that runs down my stomach.

"This is surgical?" he asks, not taking his eyes off it.

"Yes. They filleted me like a fish."

He falls to his knees before me. He kisses that spot. Once. Twice. Three times. My legs shake, but not from any kind of pain. He grips the button on my jeans. Before he undoes it, he looks up, seeking permission once again.

"Take them off, Mason."

They fall to the ground. Besides my panties and bra, I'm naked. Naked and not afraid for once. He stands. He places a finger under my chin and tilts my face until our eyes meet.

"Ready for that swim?"

"Yes."

He takes my hand and leads me into the water. It's chillier than I thought. But it could have been arctic, and I wouldn't mind. The waves crash against us, threatening to push me to the ground. Mason holds me tight. The water comes over my waist. It's dark and cool. Maybe it even breaks my self-imposed shackles. The moon is vibrant against the water as if the two are kissing.

When the water reaches just below my chest, we stop. I turn to him. He smiles softly. This time, he does tuck the strand of hair behind my ear.

I place a hand on each of his hips.

"One day we'll go surfing together," he whispers.

"I'd like that."

"One day I'll take you to the revolving restaurant on top of the Wilshire, and we'll have ourselves a nice dance."

"I'd like that too."

"And one day, I'm going to kiss you under a full moon."

"Make that day today, Mason."

He leans in. I expect him to go straight for my mouth, but he doesn't. He kisses my temple. Then he moves across to trace the shell of my ear. A shiver races up my back. He moves slowly until his lips brush against mine. He's all hard, lean muscles, but his lips are surprisingly soft. The kiss is gentle like a loving caress. He builds the pressure slowly, as if coaxing me. I ache for more. My teeth scrape against his upper lip. A groan comes from the back of his throat. He lifts me up. I wrap my arms around him and press my body against his. The kiss advances, becomes more aggressive. More passionate. Needier. More predatory.

He sucks on my bottom lip. I open my mouth. His tongue tangles around mine. He tastes of sweet mint. I moan as he tightens his grip on me. How can I feel so free when I've just surrendered?

When we break apart, he leans his forehead against mine. I'm happy he is breathing as hard as I am. His smile is two parts sweet boy and one part wicked, naughty man.

"I changed my mind, Kiran."

"About what?"

He runs his thumb across my swollen lips.

"That… That right there is the best kiss I've ever had."

"Best kiss ever," I agree.

Chapter 7

Mason

The girl has been through hell and back. Now I understand her fear of confined spaces, her panic attacks, and why she's hidden herself away. It's a shame because I think she's got a lot to offer the world. I'm honored she chose to share the tragedies in her life with me.

Last night, all we did was kiss, but it felt more intimate than anything else I've done with a girl. I'd be lying if I said I didn't want more. There was that moment when the elevator opened on her floor. She looked at me. I'm certain the longing on her face mirrored mine. But I didn't voice my thoughts. I sensed from the beginning that whatever crazy ride we're on, Kiran is the conductor. The last thing I want is to damage her trust in me.

I zipped my mouth before I could ask to go to her room. She didn't offer. She stood on her tiptoes and kissed my cheek. We said good night. Her hair was dripping wet. Watching her make her way down the hall, I shifted with the elevator doors as they closed so I could catch a last look. Why? Because I didn't want to miss a fucking thing, that's why.

We hadn't made any plans for today. When the knock at my door sounds, I hope it's her. I roll out of bed. I'm awake and...oh, fuck. I've got a Mason Cutler erecter set going on. I need to take care of my morning wood.

Shit.

"Who is it?" I call. If it's the cleaning lady, I'll ask her to come back.

"Kiran."

Not sure if this is good or bad. Good because I want to see her. Bad because I don't really want her to see me, at least not in my present condition. "Coming."

I wish.

Loose shorts. I know I have a zillion pairs. Why can't I find just one? I rifle through my stuff, but come up…short. Finally, I just wrap a towel around my waist. It's tented like there is a pole in the middle. Hell, there *is* a pole in the middle.

Her eyes go wide as she takes me in. "Hi."

"Hello, Kiran." She's wearing a faded Steely Dan T-shirt. The girl is nothing if not eclectic, but it's the fitted shorts about two inches past her thighs that capture most of my attention. It's the most skin she's ever revealed. One glimpse of her golden legs, and I'm a goner.

"I woke you. Sorry."

"No apologies, Shenoy. I needed to get up." The way the sun streams through the window tells me I've slept through my alarm. Something I never do. I missed my morning run.

"Hungry?" she asks.

I could feast on her right now.

"I could do with a meal."

"I'll wait for you down by the lobby. See you in twenty?"

"Make it thirty."

Hell, I really need forty, but thirty will do. Thirty, I can work with if I shower and jerk off at the same time. Sometimes, a man's gotta multitask.

Showered, shaved, and morning wood tamed, I go down to the lobby. I find Kiran looking over all the tourist pamphlets along the entrance wall. They advertise just about every tourist venue Jasper and its neighboring cities have to offer from ghost ship tours to Zeppelin rides.

"Anything good?"

She almost drops the pamphlet. "A few things. Probably nothing I'll do."

"Show me what you got there."

"It's silly." She clutches the paper tighter in her hand.

"Give it over, girl."

She hands it to me. It's an advertisement for a place in town that offers indoor skydiving adventures.

"Really?"

"I've always wanted to sky dive."

"Me too. I might get trained later, but it would be nice to do it for fun."

"This isn't real. It's simulated."

"Doesn't have to be." I pick up the brochure next to it. One that advertises real sky diving.

"That's inching up the danger scale." She chews on her lower lip. I've never seen anxiety and excitement manifest at the same time, but that is the expression she offers me.

"You're right. We should stick to something safer." I hold up her brochure.

"You'd go with me?"

"You bet."

"Let me think on this." She grabs both brochures and shoves them in her bag. "Do you mind if we go out to eat? I want to see Sam."

"Sure thing."

We head to a restaurant Kiran recommends. We sit outside on a table covered by a huge orange umbrella.

"What are you getting?" she asks, reading the menu closely.

"Fish and chips, you?"

She throws down the menu. "Do you have them with malt vinegar?"

"Is there any other way to eat fish and chips?"

"Not in my book." She licks her bottom lip.

I chug water to distract myself. "Are you getting it too?"

"It sounds good, except I'm really in the mood for chicken strips."

"Well, you've got a tough decision ahead of you."

She cracks a smile. "Or I could get the chicken strips, and you get the fish and chips, and we split them."

"Kind of a red neck version of surf and turf, wouldn't you say?"

She laughs. "Maybe."

"You've got yourself a deal."

The waitress approaches us. I almost have to cover my ears when the girl shrieks. "Kiran!"

Kiran looks up. "Sidney, how are you?"

"Fabulous. It's so freaking good to see you." I think this girl's voice is permanently dialed to max volume. "How are you?"

"Great."

"I can't believe you're in town. Why didn't you tell me?"

"I didn't tell anyone."

Her gaze dart over to me. Kiran shifts in her seat. "This is Mason."

"Oh, your boyfriend. So nice to meet you."

"No," Kiran says a little too loud for my liking. "We're friends. We just met at the hotel. You're working here?"

"Just over the summer. Trying to make some money toward school. You could have stayed with me. My mom would have loved to see you again."

"Sidney, it was a spur of the moment trip. I'm sorry." Kiran clasps her hands. There is an awkward silence.

"You guys were friends in high school I take it?" I interject with an obvious question to fill the void.

"Yeah, really good friends," Sidney says. "Once."

I need to give them some time alone. I stand. "Hey, I'm gonna head to the restroom. Kiran knows what I want."

At least what I want to eat. When I come back, they are still chatting. In fact, Sidney's taken my seat. But Kiran seems more relaxed now. I throw a few quarters in the old-style Pac-Man machine by the entrance to give them more time. I scan the top ten all-time high scores. Miss Kiran is number eight on the list. It doesn't take long for the ghosts to clobber me. When I come back, our drinks are on the table.

"Sorry about that," Kiran says.

"No big deal. I was playing Pac-Man."

"Am I still on the board?"

"Yeah, number eight."

She pouts. "I was number one."

"You want to reclaim your title?"

She shakes her head. "I'll let someone else keep it."

"Yeah, you might give a thirteen-year-old a real hit in the self-esteem department."

"Never."

I take a sip of my drink. "How did you know I wanted ice tea?"

"You never said. Just a guess. It's what I ordered too. It's really good here. It's sun-sweetened. Did I make a good choice?"

"Yeah, much better than the blow job you ordered for me."

"You don't like blow jobs? I'll remember that."

I choke on my drink.

"You okay?"

"Correction, I love blow jobs. Just not the drink."

"Okay."

"To recap, Mason loves blow jobs."

A woman at the end of the table glares at me.

"Good to know," Kiran says, placing her napkin on her lap. She's fucking smirking too.

"You're naughty."

Her cheeks turn crimson. "Who me? You're the one shouting how much you like blow jobs."

"True."

Sidney sets the bill down. Kiran and I both reach for it at the same time, but I'm a lot quicker.

"Don't even think about it," I warn.

"So I'll see you tonight?" Sidney asks.

"Yeah, it'll be fun."

"What's tonight?" I ask when Sidney leaves.

"Karaoke."

"Really?"

"Sidney says a lot of our friends from high school are in town, and everyone's going to be there tonight."

"Cool." I'm a little sad I won't see her tonight. But I'm happy she's going out.

"Would you be interested in coming with me?"

I'm not interested in karaoke. But Kiran... Kiran is a whole other story. "Sure."

"Yeah? For some reason, I don't think this is your thing. It might not be fun for you."

"It's not my thing, but if you're there, I'll have fun."

We go to the bookstore and spend a few hours with Sam. Sam isn't emotional, but he claps her on the back. I think it's his version of a hug. The three of us talk about books. I don't think I've ever seen her this way. She's completely in her element, confident and excited, bordering on elated. It's like witnessing a flower in bloom. I imagine Kiran in college pursing her true dreams. She will thrive at Iowa.

"Mind if I go into that store?" she asks when we leave.

It's a woman's clothing store. The word Boutique painted across the glass in flourishing gold letters makes me grimace.

"Shopping?"

"I just need to get one thing."

"Um... It's never one thing. I know for a fact."

"Oh yeah? You go shopping with girls a lot?"

"As a matter of fact, I do. Or at least I did. Dana does her own shopping now, thank God. But I had to take her to buy school clothes until high school. She's a tomboy, but she still took forever." I shudder at the memory of standing outside the dressing room doors while she tried on a million outfits.

Kiran gives me that sweet smile. "You're a good brother, Mason."

I think I'm blushing.

"You're a good man," she says a little quieter.

Definitely blushing.

"Fine, Shenoy. You win. Let's go." We head across the street. "What do you need to buy anyway?"

"A bathing suit. I didn't pack one. I don't even own one anymore. It's time to change that."

I shoulder bump her. "Done with the skinny dipping?"

"I didn't say that."

She slips into the store before I can respond. Not that I had a response. I was right.

It's more than one item she picks up. The sales lady offers to help, but Kiran refuses. I can see she's rushing, taking items from their hangers without even trying them on.

"Take your time, Kiran. I don't mind."

She tries on a few outfits. They show more skin. She looks damn beautiful in every one.

I zip up the white sundress for her.

"Is this weird?" she asks, twirling around in it.

The hem is a few inches above her knees. It shows off her long shapely legs. She pairs it with red cowboy boots. Red fucking cowboy boots. Fucking hotter than any high heel. At least to this boy, they are. As if I needed another dose of Kiran Kryptonite. She always looks beautiful to me, but in this dress… In this dress, she looks downright edible. In a way, the outfit is like her, innocent and unique and a little bit naughty.

"Not weird at all. It looks like someone made it just for you."

She doesn't believe me. I walk into the room with her and close the curtain. I turn her toward the mirror and stand behind her. With my mouth hovering over her ear, I whisper, "I wouldn't lie to you, sunshine. Just look at yourself. And if I could let you borrow my eyes so you can see what I do, I would. But I can't, so you'll have to really look this time."

She stares at herself in the mirror, her beautiful mouth pursed in contemplation. "You're right. It makes me look good."

"You make it look good."

"Thank you. I love the eyelets. It's a bit old-fashioned, but they are my favorite thing about this dress."

I don't have a clue what she's talking about. "What are eyelets?"

She takes hold of my finger and traces it around the circular cutouts at the waist. She takes a sharp breath as I mimic the same motion with my other hand. Turns out, I really like eyelets myself. There's a hint of vanilla in her scent today. It's driving me crazy.

"I'm going to get this. And the boots too."

"Good."

"Now leave so I can take it off."

"Not so fast, girl. You still require my services." I move her hair aside, imagining those soft silky strands brushing against my flesh. I run my hand up her back for no other reason than I want to touch her. She chews on her lip. I have an urge to chew on it too. I unzip her dress. It's slower this time, less mechanical. The sound of the tongues and grove of the zipper is audible as it comes apart. Her shoulders tense. Another part of me tenses too. Her bra straps are thin. One falls to the side. I adjust it... with my teeth. She leans back until she is against my chest. I have an urge to kiss her again. To rip this dress I love stitch by stitch, one eyelet at a time, until it's a pile of shreds on the ground. Then take her against the wall in this very confined fitting room until I finally relieve some of this pent up hunger that's left me a starved man.

"Finding everything okay?" the saleslady says. I jerk back like a boy caught hiding Penthouse in his bible at Sunday school.

"Yes. We're all set," she blurts out.

When we leave, I'm carrying a pile of shopping bags. But I don't mind. In the car, she holds up the bathing suit she picked. It's aquamarine; the material shimmers against the sun.

"I used to have a suit this color. I loved it."

Yeah Kiran, I remember that suit.

Chapter 8

Kiran

Sidney pounces on me when we arrive at the crowded karaoke bar. She's elevated from happy to giddy, courtesy of a few starter rounds. I introduce Mason to the faces I remember. Sidney is quick to jump in when I hesitate.

"I'll fetch us drinks," Mason says.

I shiver as the warmth of his hand leaves the small of my back. After some awkward small talk and a brief explanation of what I've been doing for the past three years, I start enjoying myself. At first, Mason being here made me nervous, what with all my different worlds colliding. I shouldn't have worried. He's got an amicable personality and makes friends easily. Of course, all the girls salivate over him.

I am one of them.

Yeah, I'm definitely head over boots attracted to Mason Cutler, but beneath all the flutters in my tummy, there's a sense of comfort. Even here, in this bar surrounded by people I haven't hung with in years, it's easier to digest with him by my side. The few people who look away when they see my scar barely register on the scale of self-consciousness I'm usually lugging on my back.

He orders us Mojitos because they have fresh mint leaves at the bar. The most important ingredient according to Mason.

"There's Tahl," Sidney says, jumping up from her chair and sprinting to the door.

Funny how tastes change. Back in high school, guys with piercings and emo dispositions, who were versed in the proper techniques of applying guy-liner, were my catnip. Now, not so much. Tahl looks the same except for the huge gauges in his ears and the vine tattoo crawling up his neck.

Mason leans over my shoulder. "Is that *the* Tahl of the lip-ring debacle?"

"The very one."

After he exchanges hugs with Sidney, Tahl makes a beeline for our table. "Hey babe, how are you?"

I give him a hug. "Good. Missed you."

"Me too, babe. Me too. I wasn't even going to come tonight, but Sid said you'd be here, and I had to see you."

As I pull away, his lip ring gets snarled in my hair. "Wait," he says.

Instinctively, I run my tongue over my teeth to make sure they are all intact. We both crack up, a gut-busting laugh. He manages to dislodge us without snatching any of my hair out.

"That lip ring gave me nightmares. I can't believe you still have it."

"The ladies love it." He wiggles his brows, the left one pierced. "But not as much as this." He sticks out his tongue. There's a metal stud in the center.

"That had to be painful."

"Sometimes a little pain makes the pleasure last longer. Know what I mean?"

I'll take questions I'd rather not answer for six hundred, Alex. "Sure."

"Can't wait to catch up with you." He grins and drags a hand through his mop of dark hair. "I'll even remove my lip ring."

"Why do you need to remove your lip ring for us to catch up?"

"Just making an offer." "He steps back and takes a look at me. He lets out some kind of woo sound. "You look amazing, babe. That is some dress."

"Thank you."

"I love the eyelets on it," Sidney chimes in.

"What are eyelets?" Tahl asks.

Before I can respond, a strong arm hooks my waist. Mason's other hand shoots out between Tahl and me. "I'm Mason Cutler. Nice to meet you."

Tahl winces from Mason's grip. "Sorry, man, I didn't know."

Mason smiles, his grin too wide, edging toward predatory. Not the type of smile fitting a casual handshake. "Well now you do."

Tahl gives us a weak smile, or maybe that's pain on his face. "All caught up."

What did I just witness?

Whatever Tahl now knows, I wish I did too. Did Mason just imply we were together? Or am I reading too much into it? Maybe he realized how creepy the conversation was getting and just wanted to rescue me.

I tell myself to shut up before I analyze the exchange backward and forward and sideways. Either I've drunk too much or not enough. I let it go as a new round appears. Everyone starts talking and laughing, rehashing crazy stories.

"Everyone has to sing," Sid announces, plopping down a huge three-ring binder in front of me.

"Um...what?"

"It's a rule."

"Whose rule?" I ask.

She smiles the old Sidney smile, complete with matching dimples. "My rule. See, I promised I would sing."

"What does that have to do with anyone else singing, Sid?"

She holds up her beer. "The liquid courage helps, but I'll only have enough confidence to pull this off if everyone else does too. I suck at singing but a promise is a promise."

"I didn't promise."

"But you'll do it to support me." She pouts. Toddlers and puppy dogs would have a hard time competing with Sidney's pout. But I'm on to her.

"You think we'll suck so it'll make you look better."

She giggles. "Pretty much." Then she turns to Mason. "This girl and I have known each other since kindergarten. The first day of school we wore the same shirt. Is it any wonder we became besties?"

"What shirt?" Mason asks.

"It had a big-ass white horse on the front with a glittery pink horn and the caption, *all horses should be unicorns.*"

Mason winces. "I can see it."

"Say what you will, but we bonded over unicorns and later, Harry Potter. Although, Kiran was always off about who the hero was."

"Oh yeah? How so?"

They are talking about me like I'm not present. I give Sidney a warning look. She ignores me.

She jabs her thumb in my direction. "She had a crush on Draco Malfoy, this one."

"You're kidding," Mason says.

"Look, I always thought he got a raw deal. I mean, his dad was an asshole."

Mason gives me an amused smile. "Were you into bad boys or just dudes with daddy issues?"

"Neither. I always root for the underdog. There was more than one in those stories when you think about it."

He knocks his glass against mine. "True."

When Mason goes up with Tahl to get another round, Sidney seizes the moment. "What's your deal, Kiran?"

"You can't make me sing, that's what."

"Not that. We'll put that on hold for now." She jerks her head toward the bar. "I mean, what's the deal with you and that smoldering shot of hotness over there?"

"Smoldering shot of hotness?"

"It's a technical term." She puts a hand on my shoulder like she always did when she wanted me to pay close attention. "Sweetie, he's a cup of hot toddy and a cool, smooth glass of Southern Comfort rolled into one."

"Sorry to disappoint. There isn't a story."

"He's into you."

"We just met," I say, trying not to admit just how drunk off Mason Cutler I really am.

"I think he's great."

"He's more than great. The trouble with Mason isn't falling for him. That's easy. It's the getting back up after part that worries me."

"Some falls are worth it. We all need a little trouble in our lives. We're better off for it."

"So you're not going out?" Jordan Adler chimes in.

"No."

"Cool. I can ask him out."

In my head, I jump on the table and make it clear I claim him like a freaking lioness. In reality, I'm silent.

What can I even say? Not that she asked me for permission. The reality is I have no hold on Mason. I can't prevent someone else from asking him out. Things are so much simpler in the animal kingdom, but this isn't *National Geographic*. He's free to roam wherever.

"Sure." I manage to mutter the simple word through gritted teeth.

Sidney gives Jordan a dirty look and opens her mouth to let her have it. This girl always had my back. Nothing has changed. I put my hand on her shoulder and shake my head.

The boys come back with drinks. Mason switched to beer but got another Mojito for me.

"You had the strawberry margarita, right?" he asks Jordan, setting down the glass.

"Oh yes, thank you." She bats her eyelashes so hard she might just fly away. Wishful thinking.

"Which song are you doing?" Tahl asks.

"I'm not," I say. "What about you?"

He takes the huge book from me. "Let me see. Maybe something by The Cure."

"Are you singing, Mason?" Jordan asks.

He shrugs. "I'm not much of a singer either. Unless you count the shower or the car. Then I'm Grammy good."

She laughs, her lashes fluttering in sync. "I'm sure you're a rock star everywhere." Everyone has that one mean girl in their group. That frenemy who always puts you down while acting like your best friend. Jordan Adler is mine. She hasn't changed a bit. It's exciting to see everyone, but she is one person I could do without. She snaps her fingers. "We can do a duet. It won't be so bad, Mase."

Mase? His name is Mason. Don't come up with any special nicknames. It's not cute. I struggle not to roll my eyes.

"Duets aren't really my thing."

"We can just pick a song and sing it together then." This girl is relentless.

"That's a good idea," Mason says.

Jordan's face lights up like the Rockefeller Center Christmas Tree. I lower my head and find a very interesting spot on the table. "How about it, Kiran? Want to try that?"

What? He wants to sing with me?

Before I say anything, they call Sidney's name. She hops to the stage. We all clap and holler in support. "This is for my bestie, Kiran. It's good to have you back, sister."

I doubt anyone knows why she dedicated this song to me. I burst out laughing because only Sidney could put it all in twenty/twenty perspective as she belts out Taylor Swift's "I Knew You Were Trouble."

She does a damn good job too. When she finishes, I give her a standing ovation and blow her a kiss. We haven't been in touch in three years, but the ties that bound us are not broken. They aren't even torn in the slightest.

I barely get a chance to compliment her before she informs me it's my turn. I shake my head and hold my hands out in protest.

"You wanna sing together, Shenoy?" Mason asks. "I'm game if you are."

"I suck."

"Me too, but who's judging? I'll even let you pick the song. No boy bands, though."

"Well, that's a deal-breaker, Cutler."

He leans in closer to me. His voice is low, each word laced with passion. "C'mon honey, let's make some music together. Maybe neither of us can sing worth a lick, but there isn't a doubt in my mind that we have a harmony of our own making."

Either I've drunk too much and am dizzy, or this man has literally made me swoon. Know why I love boys who read? Cause they can say romantic shit like that.

"Hey, I'll go up there with you if she doesn't want to," Jordan offers. "And I've been told I have a great voice too." She bends toward the table to give Mason a nice view of her cleavage.

"Thanks, Jordan, but Mason and I are going to give it a shot."

Three very strong mojitos, arm-bending friends, the threat of a mean-girl attack, and his encouraging smile is a good a recipe for a bad mistake.

I tap a title on the laminated page. "You know this one?"

He smiles. "I'm familiar. You sure you want to do that one, though?"

"Yeah, why?"

"Just confirming." His blue eyes twinkle as his smile inches toward wicked.

When we get up there, it hits me with the first note.

Mason is a liar.

He can sing. His voice is deep and masculine and oh so seductive. I almost drop my microphone as the notes wrap around me. I hum at first. He waits for me, but I have no voice. I can barely stand on my shaky legs. Billy Currington's "Must Be Doin' Something Right" is already high on the sexy, but hearing Mason sing it renders me speechless. Thanks, Billy Currington. Thanks a lot for writing a song so freaking hot it might just cause me to spontaneously melt. Did I really pick a song that talks about the complicated navigations of a woman's body? Did I really ask the boy who makes my heart sputter to sing it with me?

I sure did.

When Mason takes a step closer to me and tucks a strand of hair behind my ear, I hear a chorus of sighs from every girl in the bar. I swallow, focusing on his ocean blue eyes. God help me, I could strip right now. I hum along, but there is no way I can compete with his voice.

When it's over, there is a huge applause. At least I think it is huge. My heart is pumping so loud it drowns out all the other noises.

He steps closer still until we're almost touching. "You hardly sang. You hung me out to dry."

"You held your own." I reach out and touch his cheek to convince myself that this surreal experience is actually happening.

Guess what?

It is.

When we come back to the table, more people have joined.

"This isn't my drink," I say, pointing to the pink concoction where my seat is.

"It's mine. I moved us around," Jordan says, coming up behind me. Is she still here?

"You sang like a rock star," she says, clapping Mason's arm. "I love that song." She glares at me. "I even know all the words."

"I pretended I was in the shower the whole time." He grins at me. I'm glad he didn't say that while we were up there or I would have started imagining him in the shower too.

She plops down in my seat. "Are you sitting?" she asks Mason. "There's a chair over there for Kiran."

"Why don't I move that chair over here," he says.

Jordan, ever so bitchy, takes care of that idea. "There's no room."

"Jordan," Sidney says, standing up. I love Sidney, but I don't need her to stand up for me. What I really want to do is go back to the hotel with him. But tonight is about spending time with friends I haven't seen in a long time. If that means dealing with Jordan Adler, it's a small price to pay.

"No worries, I don't mind sitting in his lap."

Mason's arm comes across my waist. In that simple gesture, he squashes all the hope in Jordan's eyes.

"Nice problem-solving, sunshine."

I hate the idea of squashing anyone's hope. But in this case, I'll make an exception.

Chapter 9

Kiran

We get into the rickety elevator. I push the button for my floor.

"You forgot to push my floor," he says when the doors close.

"No, I didn't." I lean back against the cool interior walls of the elevator. I've caught him off-guard. He's surprised, but in a good way. I mentally fist bump myself for the way I handled it.

"Thought you'd never ask. But one question."

"Yes, I'm a virgin," I blurt out.

"How drunk are you?" he asks at the same time.

I'll take stupid things Kiran Shenoy blurts out for three hundred, Alex. Oh look, I got the Daily Double.

Yeah, real smooth. "Drunk enough to blurt out something very stupid."

He takes a hold of my arms and moves them away from my face. "Wasn't stupid."

"I just figured you should know." Every sentence feels like I'm backing up a bus and running over myself again.

"I already guessed."

"Oh, it's pretty obvious, huh?"

"Yes."

"I'm not drunk. You wouldn't be taking advantage of me in any way."

The doors open. He gestures for me to step out first or maybe just step out altogether. He follows me. The keycard reader doesn't work for three scary tries. I let out a deep breath when the light finally turns green.

Eureka. We're in.

I turn around and throw my arms around him. His hands settle on my hips. He walks us back to the bed. His mouth covers mine in lusty kisses. Kiss. Kiss. Pause.

With a deep breath, he buries his head in my shoulder.

"What is it?" I ask.

"Let's talk."

That doesn't sound good.

"Okay."

We sit on the bed. "I don't think we should, Kiran."

"Why?"

"This is your first time. It needs to be special."

"You are special, Mason."

He smiles and takes my hand. "Thank you. You're special to me too. But I can't make you any promises, Kiran. I don't know where my life will lead me. You're important to me. I don't want to ruin your first time. I don't want you to have regrets."

Is it normal for two people to have conversations about sex like this? I have no point of reference. Either way, he's sliced through my buzz.

I shift away from him. "What was your first time like? Oh wait, let me guess." I tap my finger against my lips. "I bet the heavens opened up and sun shone down on the earth while a choir of angels sang you into climax."

His rueful smile does nothing to temper me. "Is sarcasm your second language? You speak it fluently."

"Only conversationally. Seriously, what was your first time like? I want to know."

"It was awful. I was fifteen, and I had no idea what I was doing. We were in the backseat of her car, all cramped and uncomfortable. I wasn't very attentive either. The poor girl didn't enjoy herself. This makes me sounds like a complete dick, but I was thinking of another girl the whole time.

"That is a dick move. Who were you thinking of?"

He's quiet for a while. "Scarlett Johansson."

I lob a pillow at him. I aim for his head, but he catches it before it makes contact.

"Is that who you'd be thinking of with me?"

He clasps my hand. He probably suspects I'm about ready to smack him. "Never, Kiran. I promise you I would not be thinking of her."

I shift and bring my legs to the floor. "Well, that's a relief."

"I'm more into Jennifer Lawrence now."

I lob pillow number two. This time it smacks him right in the head. Score.

"I'm joking," he says.

"It's not funny. You tell me this is a big deal; then you make jokes. You're just full of dick moves."

He rubs the back of his head. "Yeah, I am. I'm sorry. It's just my way. I always try to defuse a situation with a joke." He takes a deep breath and shakes his head. "But this…oh, fuck it. I have to tell you something, Kiran. I'm afraid how you'll take it. But I don't want there to be any secrets between us. It's been killing me not to tell you."

Something wrenches inside my gut. Maybe it's all the dead butterflies that were fluttering around just a moment ago. He has a girlfriend. I should have guessed. I feel numb and nauseous all at once.

"Kiran?" He touches my shoulder. I react with a jolt.

"What is it? Start talking already."

Mason inhales a deep breath. "When I was fourteen, we came here for our annual family vacation. In fact, that was the last year we came here. I had this really fucked-up notion that I was going to teach myself how to surf. I went to the beach real early one day. A wave overtook me. My feet got tangled in a patch of seaweed. I don't remember much except for this girl in an aquamarine swimsuit. She came out of nowhere and pulled me to the shore. Then she kissed me."

I blink, trying to reconcile what he is saying. The image of the man before me does not match the memory he is talking about. It all comes together in one bright flash. I am his first kiss. The kiss on the beach. That was me. "Um… I was giving you mouth to mouth resuscitation. You count that as your first kiss?"

"The kiss of life. Best kiss of all."

I'm not queasy anymore or angry, but I am sad. "Is this why you wanted to hang out with me? Some kind of payback? Paying it forward by saving the poor girl who once saved you? Is this your fucked-up version of being a good Samaritan?" My questions are sharp, at odds with my tone. Defeat rings out loud and clear in my voice.

"No." He cups my face and turns it so we're looking at each other. "But I knew this is where your mind would go. Yes, I recognized you that first day in the elevator." Mason's hand slides down my arm. He rubs the heart-shaped birthmark on my wrist. "I remember this especially. Remember you holding my hand. I remember this mark on your wrist." When he looks up at me, his smile is pure. A few butterflies awake from their coma. "You were the girl who literally wore her heart on her sleeve. I wasn't sure if you were real or something I imagined. A symptom of bad shellfish. Why the hell did you run away? No one believed me when I said a sea angel saved me."

"You actually said the words 'sea angel'?"

"Scout's honor, I did."

"I was still grounded from sneaking out for the Bon Jovi concert. I wasn't supposed to leave the house, but the waves called to me. I couldn't stay away."

"So you really didn't recognize me? I'm a little offended."

"It all happened fast." I take in his chiseled face and muscular body. "Plus, you've had a couple of growth spurts."

"Yeah, I look different."

"So do I."

He tucks a strand of hair behind my ear. "You're older but still gorgeous. Look, it wasn't love at first sight or anything, but I did have a stupid, mad crush on the brave girl who saved my life." He leans closer and kisses me on the temple. "You know what? I'm pretty smitten with the courageous, beautiful woman she grew up to be too."

Exhausted from his revelation, I lay back on the bed, "Why didn't you tell me? You had a million chances." I pound my fist into the soft mattress, angry it barely made a sound. "I even told you the story of me saving you. You didn't even tell me then."

"I was afraid it would change things between us." He exhales. "Does it?"

"I'm not sure."

"I want you, Kiran." His voice is low, the cadence dripping with need. If lust had a rhythm, it would be Mason Cutler's voice. "What do you want right now? I hope it's me."

"What about that whole spiel? The first time should be special. I can't make any promises to you."

He tilts his head. "I will make it special for you. As much as I can. I had to tell you everything first. My conscience was as heavy as a lead balloon, sunshine. You said you liked my honesty. It drove me crazy that I was lying to you, or at least omitting the truth. As far as the future goes, that's all true. I can't make you any promises. Right now, I'm not interested in looking beyond the horizon. Tomorrows are always uncertain. Tonight is about this boy." He places my hand over his heart. It's beating wildly. "And the beautiful girl he met. The one who makes him feel things he didn't know he was capable of. Things his cynical mind didn't think existed in the real world. Now, you tell me what you want."

I don't answer. His arm circles me. He kisses me, softly at first. The kiss builds as if he's trying to convince me. It's working. But an annoying voice keeps interrupting the moment to tell me this is pity, not passion. I break us apart before I can submit to the temptation.

"Kiran—"

"I'm tired. You should go."

His bright blue eyes widen. "But…"

"I need to process this. We really shouldn't do this, considering we're never going to see each other after we leave here."

His hands fall. His expression is ripe with frustration, but behind that I see the inkling of sorrow. "This is one time I hate being right." He kisses my temple. The bed lifts as he stands. The room is colder now, more dark and lonely.

He opens the door, turning back once. His stare cuts right through me. "Don't get lost in your own head, Kiran. If you need someone to help you find your way out, you know where I am."

I sit there for a minute contemplating what I've done. I relive the moments we've shared. Although I can count them in minutes and hours and days, my brief time with Mason Cutler is immeasurable. He saw my battered body and nothing disgusted him. On the contrary, he made me feel beautiful. I shared parts of me with him that I had locked away long ago. Along with the stunning façade, he is sweet and funny and humble to a point of self-deprecating.

He even has regrets about thinking of someone else his first time.

Wait? The epiphany hits me over the head like a rogue boulder. There is only one obstacle to my happiness.

Me.

I stumble from the bed and run into the hallway. He's in the elevator. The thirty odd feet of carpet stretching between us might as well be a million miles. "Who was the girl?" I call out.

"What girl?"

"The one you were thinking of the first time you had sex?"

The doors start to close. He makes no move to open them. As they frame his body, he smiles softly. "It was you."

The door shuts.

Sometimes a girl's got to fight for her own happiness. I head toward the staircase. A fast walk becomes a full-out run. I spring up the two flights of stairs to his floor.

I'm breathless when I get there. I stand in front of the elevator waiting for the doors to open. This elevator is slower than a herd of tranquilized snails. There is no way I missed him. But the doors stay shut. Maybe he didn't go to his room. Maybe he went somewhere else.

"Fuck!" I say, banging my head against the metal.

"Kiran?" The strong masculine voice spiced with southern molasses spills through the metal doors.

"Mason? What's going on?"

"I'm stuck in the elevator. Are you on my floor?"

If I didn't think it would add peril or permanent injury, I'd pry open the doors with my fingernails.

"I had something to say to you. I have to say it now."

"Wait—"

"No, don't interrupt me, Mason. I have to get this out while I have the courage. I don't even care if there is a stupid door between us. Just listen. You're right. We're two people who found each other. Maybe we were even meant to find each other at this crossroads in our lives. I don't care about tomorrow, and I'm over yesterday. I want the now. I'm tired of always second guessing myself. You asked me what I wanted. I didn't answer you. Well, this is what I want." I suck in a deep, courage-inducing breath. "I want to rip all your clothes off and fuck the hell out of you."

Silence.

Was it too much?

"Um Kiran, I should tell you I'm not alone in here. The elevator picked someone up between floors before it got stuck."

"What?" Please tell me you're joking, Mason. It's three in the morning. Who could be in there at this hour?

"Hello Kiran, your language is so colorful these days."

"Mrs. Waters?"

Mrs. Waters, former tenth grade English teacher. Current front desk clerk. Witness to my most embarrassing moment. And trust me, there have been plenty.

"I'm staying here while my apartment is being repainted. I couldn't sleep so I thought I'd take a turn on the roof. Fresh air helps."

"Oh."

"This elevator is ornery. We're having the maintenance man look at it tomorrow. Don't worry, the doors will open in a second."

"That's great." My voice is high enough I wonder if I inhaled some helium.

Why are we still talking? I should run away and hide, preferably under a huge rock.

As promised, the door squeaks open. Mason, ever the gentleman, gestures for Mrs. Waters to get out first.

She offers me a tight smile. "It's not my floor, but I think I'll take the stairs the rest of the way."

"Probably wise," Mason says. "Probably what I should have done," he mutters below his breath.

"And Kiran?"

I force myself to look at her.

"Yes, Mrs. Waters?"

"Remember what advice I gave when we got our brand new textbooks at the beginning of the school year?"

That's a weird question. "You said we should protect them with a sturdy book cover."

She looks between Mason and me. "Keep that in mind, dear."

Okay, did my tenth grade teacher just tell me to use a condom?

I want to slither to the ground. The solid sound of the metal door closes, leaving Mason and I alone in the dimly lit hallway of the tenth floor.

"You can laugh. I give you permission."

He places a finger against my chin and lifts my face. "I would if I wasn't so turned on right now."

"You're kidding."

"You just declared you want to rip my clothes off and have your way with me. Honey, I don't think I've ever been so damn horny and embarrassed at the same time."

"Why are you embarrassed?"

He takes my hand and presses my palm flat against his chest. Then he slides it down his body until it's pressed against his groin. His very hard groin.

I cup him, shocked by how much there is to cup. "Is that you?"

His smile inches up, as do other parts of his body.

"Don't look so innocent, sunshine. This is me under the spell of you."

He grabs my hips and pulls me against him. I thread my fingers in his hair. He walks me backward until I'm against the door of his room. He fumbles in his pocket, and all the while his mouth slides up my neck. I would have fallen when the door opened, but the security of his strong arms keeps me upright.

He kicks the door shut. Mason tugs on my zipper. I reach backward to help him. I love the white eyelet sundress, but right now I don't care if he rips it to shreds.

"This fucking dress has been driving me nuts all night. Pure torture, this fucking dress."

The dress falls. I silently pat myself on the back for wearing my prettiest bra, even though it clashes with my panties. He traces the curve of my bra and then the pattern on the cups. I'm not sure if I wish there were more polka dots or less. My breasts perk at his gentle touch. Just when I'm about to demand more, he unhooks me. He takes off the bra. Licking his lips, he stares at my naked breasts. I wonder what crazy sensual thing he'll say to me.

"I like your boobs," he says. We both laugh. "Sorry, I wanted to come up with something better, but you're doing things to me that make it hard to hold a coherent thought."

"Mason, I love what you said. Right now, the last thing I want you to do with your mouth is talk."

His eyes darken. "Amen to that."

I yank at his T-shirt until he catches my drift and shucks it off. I trail my fingers down his hard chest, feeling every rise and fall of the hard muscles on his waist. I trace the inked letters on his side, wondering again what those words refer to. He takes out his wallet. He fumbles until he finds a golden square. He tosses it on the nightstand. His jeans come off next. His large hands feel warm and massive against my trembling body. They stop at my panties. He hooks a finger on each side.

His mouth travels down my body, punctuating each part of the journey with a hard wet kiss. He falls to his knees.

"What are you doing?" I ask, although I have a pretty good idea.

"Sit," he growls, pushing me onto the bed. "You're mine tonight, Kiran. I aim to have my fill of you. Do you understand?"

I nod. I sit. I get lost in the command of his voice. He spreads my legs and kisses each of my thighs. The anticipation is almost too much. I squirm as he presses his lips against me. I fall back when his tongue darts out. I cry out when he begins thrusting said tongue inside of me. I'm caught somewhere between the small gap of agony and ecstasy. I lean on my elbows to take in the sight of his beautiful head between my legs. I run my fingers through the soft strands of his chocolate and honey-colored hair. Mason moves inside of me with sureness. He picks up on my cues. When I moan, he increases the speed. When I moan too hard, he slows down to let me catch a breath. Then we're on the marathon again. I can see the finish line.

Fisting his hair, I scream, "Mason, I want you inside of me."

He lifts his face up. "Where do you think I am if not inside of you? Are you not enjoying this, sunshine?"

"I'm enjoying it too much. I don't want it to end here."

He kisses my belly. "Kiran, I'm not a one-trick pony. I promise it won't end here."

"I want you to enjoy yourself too."

His smile could melt icicles. "Silly girl, what am I going to do with you?"

I don't know, but I really want to find out.

"What would ever make you think I'm not enjoying myself? I've been wondering what you taste like for a while now. You taste like fucking peaches. Do you know that?"

The sultry cadence of his rich voice leaves me teetering over some false edge. "No, can't say I did." I fall onto my back in sweet surrender. "Please resume."

"With pleasure. But just so we're clear about things, I need to explain something to you. I'm no expert, but I have more experience than you. I'm going to use every scrap of knowledge I've picked up regarding the female body to please you tonight. Then I'm gonna learn you from the top of your hair to these pinky toes right here." I giggle when he pinches them. "See there, you're ticklish. Good to know."

"What do you mean learn me?"

"I'm going to learn your body. I believe I've figured out what makes you tick. Kiran Shenoy. Now, I aim to discover what makes you hum."

It's you—beautiful, sweet, wickedly delicious you.

I let out a soft moan that translates into "yes, please." Luckily, he requires no further communication and buries his head between my thighs again.

If I thought he skirted the line between agony and ecstasy before, I find a new word for the space I'm in…blissful. Mason is unrelenting. His finger enters me as his tongue flicks my nub. He pleasures and teases me at the same time.

Know what's better than one finger? Two fingers.

I can feel the heat of his breath, the wetness of his talented tongue, the softness of his hair against my thigh, the thrust of those long fingers. I fist the bed sheets with crazy desperation. There is so much going on inside me, and I cannot control any of it. I don't want to either. My body shakes all over. I arch my back, close my eyes, and call out his name.

When I open my eyes, he's beside me, watching me. "Peaches," he whispers before he sucks on his fingers. My throat goes dry while other parts of me get wetter. I'm drenched and parched at the same time. His lips brush against mine, leaving me craving more.

I cup his face and pull him closer. "Kiss me again."

This kiss is more passionate, almost aggressive. He parts my mouth. His tongue tastes like sweet mint and beer and…peaches.

We're both breathing harsh, short breaths when we pull apart. "Damn, you're tight."

"Isn't that good?"

"For me, yeah. It's fucking awesome. For you, though… It might hurt a little for you. If it does, you tell me, okay?"

"I will."

He holds up the golden packet. At first, I think he's shaking it as he's trying to open it. Then I realize his normally steady hands are just shaking in general. I grow confident knowing I'm having a similar effect on him.

I still his hands and take the packet from him. "Let me."

"Thank you."

I tear it with my teeth. He takes my wrist and kisses the underside, pressing his lips against the pink heart on my flesh. He drags my hand down his body until it reaches his erection.

"Touch me, please."

Unsure at first, I grasp him. My movements are reluctant and cautious. I squeeze him. He sucks in a deep breath.

"I'm doing this wrong, aren't I?"

He kisses my temple. "May I show you?"

"Please."

He places his hand over mine and moves us up and down his shaft in slow, steady strokes. I kiss his chest and start working my way down to him. He stops me.

"No, baby. Not that."

"You don't like it?"

He manages a laugh, although it's strained. "There isn't a man on God's green earth that doesn't love that. But if you do, I'll lose control. Right now, I'm hanging on by a thread."

He rolls away from me. I watch as he glides the condom down. There is something so erotic about watching him touch himself. "You ready, darling?"

Darling? It's not a word I'd ever accuse of being sexy. But in this moment, spoken by this cowboy as he straddles me, it has to be the most provocative word in the whole dictionary.

I wrap my arms around his neck. "Yes."

His entry is slow. He watches me with each inch of his advance. I gasp when he breaks a barrier. It's painful for a second.

"You okay?"

I nod, unable to articulate just how okay I am. He nibbles on my earlobe and whispers in my ear. "Damn, you're so tight, Kiran."

He rears his head up and closes his eyes, his face wincing with each thrust. I may lack experience, but I'm pretty sure this shouldn't be painful for him. Then it occurs to me why it is.

I tug on his hair, pulling him toward me. "You can move faster."

"Yeah?"

"Yes."

He grins in relief. "Oh, thank God."

Then he's no longer slow thrusts and soft kisses. He's hard, long, deep propulsions that leave me breathless. I cling to him. He grips my leg and brings it over his hip. I call his name in harsh guttural pleas.

"Let go, baby. I need you to let go."

I do.

Everything tightens as a current takes hold of every cell. I try to memorize the moment, the feeling of it, of him, but I'm too far gone to rationalize any of it.

He thrusts inside of me the whole time, his grunts getting louder and more desperate until he buries his head in my shoulder.

I wrap my arms around him. I don't want to let go.

Ever.

Chapter 10

Mason

The early afternoon sun streams through the window, casting soft shadows on the wall. She fell asleep in my arms. Not really a position I find comfortable, except I don't mind. Last night I made love to this woman. In many ways, it was a first for me too. There is a connection between us I can't explain in a rational way.

My only goal was to make it special for her. But I wanted her so much I might have gotten a little selfish at the end. Her soft plump lips are curved, almost in a smile. I'd woken up early to go for a run. When I laid eyes upon her, I just wanted to stay in this warm bed with her head on my shoulder. Her leg drapes over my hip, and her silky hair falls across my arm. The room smells of her. I breathe it in, wishing I could bottle up the scent. Or better yet, the feel of her soft, curvy body against mine as the sun's warmth cascades over us.

I stroke her hair. She murmurs something in her sleep.

"Morning sunshine, it's time to get up."

"Already?" She sidles closer to me.

God help me, I want her again.

"Yeah, Sleeping Beauty. Daylight's a wasting and I want to do something with you today."

Her smile grows. "Already?" Her hand goes lower under the covers.

I grab her wrist. I kiss each of her fingers. "Naughty girl."

"If I'm naughty, then you're completely indecent, Mason."

"True. But that's not what I meant when I said I want to do something with you." I glance at the bedside clock.

She frowns. "Then what?"

"Parachuting. The brochure says the place doesn't require reservations. But we should head out there soon. You want to try it, right?"

Her eyes blink open. She chews her lower lip. "Not anymore."

Can't say I'm too disappointed. I could explore her all day and not come up for air. Except I really want to make some kind of special memory with her. "Why not, Shenoy? You seemed excited about it when you were checking out the brochure the other night."

"I was, but I changed my mind. I don't want to do the simulated thing anymore."

I trace her plump lips with my finger. "So plan B? We lay in bed all day until one of us cries uncle?" Say yes. Say yes. Say yes.

She laughs. "That's a nice idea, but um… I have another option."

"Well, don't keep me in suspense."

Her deep brown eyes light up. "Let's do the real thing."

"The real thing?"

"Mason, will you jump out of a plane with me?"

There's an invitation you don't get every day.

When I don't respond, she nudges me. "Say something."

"I've never been excited and disappointed at the same time. Let me get used to this fucked-up emotion combo." I fall on my back. "Okay Kiran, let's take a leap together."

As if we haven't already done that.

* * * *

I call the airfield to make sure they can get us in. Luckily, they still have a few openings. I book us a time. We have a few hours so, of course, we spend them wisely. Then we both decide we should eat something. We head to the café in the hotel. We eat a light breakfast. Well, she does. She orders a fruit plate and granola. Or as I like to call it, bird feed. Me? I'm a growing boy so I go for the all-you-can-eat eggs, bacon, and hash browns.

I lick my lips when she holds up a peach wedge. She tortures me by nibbling on it.

"You gonna share that?"

A slow flush covers her cheeks in a pink glow. She pops it into my mouth. I close my eyes and chew slowly.

"It's good, isn't it?"

I raise an eyebrow, my fingers twitching. "It's the second best thing I've ever tasted."

The pink blush turns crimson. Now it's not just my fingers twitching. I take a steadying breath. She sips her ice water. We both move past the urge.

When we get out to my car, she stands by the passenger side. I grasp her shoulders. "I'll sit here. You go round to the other side."

"Was that peach laced with acid? The other side is the driver's seat, Mason."

I'm not even sure where the idea came from. I hate being a passenger in a car, especially when it's my car. In fact, I've never let anyone drive it besides Dana. And that was on rare emergency occasions. Here I am offering it to Kiran and hoping she'll take the challenge. "It's time you drove again. Your license is still up to date, right?"

"Yes, but…"

"We can take a few rounds in the parking lot until you're comfortable. If you're not, I'll drive us to the airfield."

"You trust me with your car? I haven't driven a car in three years."

"You trusted me last night." I tilt her face. "You've got this, darling. But you need to trust yourself. We're about to jump out of a plane. That was your idea. You can handle a car."

I expect her to reject the idea. Instead, she simply nods and walks around to the driver's side. I throw her the keys and follow. She takes her time adjusting the mirrors and getting familiar with my used sedan.

"How do you move the seat up?" she asks, looking around for some automated button that doesn't exist. "I feel like I'm on a sled."

"On the bottom. You have to pull."

She groans, trying to adjust. "It's not moving."

I bend and pull the lever. She slides, almost crashing into me. "It's stubborn sometimes. Is this comfortable?"

"Uh-huh."

I pull down the seatbelt and click it into place. I tug on it a few times. I have no idea why, except I just want to be in close proximity to her a few seconds longer.

I take my seat as passenger before the urge to kiss her overpowers me. We're never gonna hit the damn road if I don't start behaving. She starts the ignition, tucks her hair behind her ear, and swallows down a deep breath. I turn off the radio. It takes her a few minutes to back out of the space. I keep my mouth zipped. The last thing she needs is a distraction.

"I'm going to circle the parking lot."

"As many times as you need, sunshine."

She grips the wheel so hard I wonder if I'll have to pry her fingers off. She's cautious. Okay, she's slower than molasses in February. Part of it isn't just nerves. She's treating my cheap, rusty car like it's a BMW. She stops for pedestrians a city block away. She goes over a speed bump like she's tackling Everest.

"You're doing fine, Kiran."

"Am I going too fast?"

I shoot up in my seat. "Actually, you can pick up the pace."

"So too slow is your official critique?"

"I'm saying go at a pace that's comfortable for you. We're not on a city street or anything. But just so you know, I saw a turtle race past us."

She laughs and pushes down on the accelerator. "Funny, Cutler."

"Just saying."

"This car drives well."

"Thanks. It's done a good job for me. I'm working on rebuilding a Trans Am. Of course, I've been working on that since I was sixteen."

"A hot rod, huh? Is it hard to find parts?"

"It is, especially when you're trying to find original stuff. The car's gonna be smoking when it's done, but I want to make sure it turns out right. It's special to me."

"Why is it special?"

"It's a project my dad started before he passed away. I've always planned on finishing it."

She pats my leg. "I bet it's going to be gorgeous."

I wish she could see the Trans when it's done. I'd love to take her for a ride. "Hands on the wheel, Shenoy."

She puts them back at ten and two. "I'm ready to go on the street now."

I pull out my phone. "I'll be your navigator. It's a forty-minute drive. There is an expressway involved, but I can route us a different way if you'd prefer."

"No, it's fine." She makes a left out of the parking lot with no difficulty. With each mile, she gains confidence. Her fingers loosen. She cranks down her window and puts on her sunglasses. The wind blows through her hair. "I can't believe I'm driving."

"And doing a good job too."

The traffic picks up. Out of nowhere a car switches to our lane and cuts us off. Kiran hits the brakes. I throw my arm over her body. It's a reflex I've only used with Dana.

"Fucking asshole," I mutter.

Kiran isn't fazed, though. She nods in agreement and keeps going, keeping a cautious distance from the car ahead of us.

"Why did you reach your arm out? You were covering me."

I laugh. "It's stupid. Not like it'll keep you safe if we crashed."

Fuck, did I just say the C-word out loud? Smart move, Cutler.

"Probably not, but it's not stupid at all. My mom did that too."

"Mama Bear isn't exactly the vibe I'm going for." I'm trying and most likely failing to defuse the situation with my crappy sense of humor.

She smiles, her eyes on the road. I wish I could see them instead of the dark shades. Her eyes are expressive. Sometimes they reveal all the feelings she tries to hide.

"Thank you for trusting me."

"Kiran, you're doing really well. Hell, you could teach Driver's Ed, girl."

"Wow, Cutler. I'm already struggling between two choices regarding my future. Don't throw a third in there."

"Sorry."

She purses her lips. She's wearing some kind of strawberry gloss. I'm not even a fan of strawberries, but I suddenly have a die-hard craving for them.

"May I tell you something?"

"You can tell me anything, sunshine."

"I feel safe with you, Mason. That thing you did with your arm? It wasn't mama bear. It just shows how protective you are. The Marines are lucky to have you."

"Thank you. That means a lot to me. It really does. But I think we both have expelled enough sap to fill a forest of maples."

"I'll try to hold in my sap."

"Yeah, you do that." I swallow back something bitter that sinks into my gut. "Take the next right and get on the west on-ramp." She reminded me that as much as I want her to be mine, the reality is I belong to someone else. He's got a white beard, a pointy finger, and a tacky suit. His name is Uncle Sam.

She gets on the expressway without any issues. In fact, she even passes a couple of slower cars.

"You'll stay on here for eight miles give or take."

"You don't need to give me directions anymore. I remember this place. This is the way my papa took when we had to go to Tampa for my physical therapy. We used to pass it. I saw all those colorful planes."

"Now you're jumping out of one. Still up for it?"

"More than ever. You?"

"Call me a bicycle wheel cause, darling, I'm pumped."

"Can you turn on the radio?" she asks after the silence stretches a few miles.

"It won't distract you?"

"I think it'll help. I'm too focused. Know what I mean?"

"I sure do."

I flip on a station, but mostly we're getting static. I turn the dial slowly.

"Wait," she says. "This song."

I grimace, because the angst-filled lyrics and four-part harmony can only mean one thing: boy band.

"Mason, allow me to introduce you to the Backstreet Boys."

"I'd rather we stay strangers."

She pats my leg. "Give it a chance."

Not sure if I'll ever be a fan, but I gotta admit there is something about this tune that speaks to me.

"What's the name of this song, Shenoy?"

"'Helpless When She Smiles.'"

No wonder it rings true.

Chapter 11

Mason

When we get to the airfield, we're ushered into a room where we basically sign all our rights away. It's doesn't exactly invoke a feeling of security. I just scribble my signature. Chewing on her pen, she reads every damn form.

"Sign it, Kiran. We both know there is an element of danger. That's what makes it appealing."

"Yeah, but thinking about that in the abstract and writing down my next of kin on this paper are two different things."

"If you want to forget this, I would understand. No pressure."

"Not a chance. Just need a minute."

"Get out of your head, Kiran. Be here with me right now."

"There is no place I'd rather be." She signs her name in curling letters.

"Get the fuck out of here. Do you really dot your I's with a smiley face?"

She laughs. "Not since I was a teenager. I have no idea why I did that."

I put my arm around her and draw her close. "I like it. Even your name has a smile."

A woman clears her throat, interrupting us before I can kiss the pretty smile she gifts me. She clicks a remote to start an instructional video. Kiran pays close attention. Meanwhile, I steal a few sideway glances at her. Hell, I think she might just take notes. She gets excited as we watch all the footage of ordinary people zipping through the sky.

After that, we're directed to another room where we get rigged up in our jumping gear. She looks so damn cute in the orange jumpsuit. Me? I resemble a prison inmate.

We march ourselves out to the aircraft. She hesitates as we get closer. It's smaller than I imagined, and it looks like it's had more than its fair share of miles. She stops completely and closes her eyes. She tilts her head toward the sun and mouths something. Maybe a prayer?

"I'm sure it's sturdy, Kiran."

"You are?"

I gesture to the aircraft. "Look at it this way. Lindy flew a plane this size when he crossed the Atlantic."

"It probably *is* this plane."

I chuckle, although she may be right. "Kiran, it's passed every regulation. I did some research during the drive. They have a very good reputation."

"Yeah, of course it's safe." I'm not sure if she's affirming what I've said or trying to convince herself. "Size doesn't matter."

"Not when it comes to this."

She cracks a smile. "You're right."

"About size?"

She punches me in the arm. "About the plane." She shakes her hand out. "Are you made of metal?"

"Flesh and blood as far I know."

She arches her brow. "And very hard bones."

Those are kissing words. She takes a step toward me. She holds her hand up, palm facing me. I'm confused until I realize she wants a high-five. Not exactly the gesture I was thinking of, but I'd never leave her hanging. I slap her hand. "Let's do this, Shenoy."

We meet our instructors. They go over the same safety stuff as the video. We take seats on the floor of the aircraft. The plane rises higher into the air, the roaring engines making it impossible to talk. Not that I have much to say. Adrenaline is coursing through every vein. I'm about to jump out of a plane with this girl. That's amazing. Fuck, I met a girl who actually wants to jump out of a plane. That's really amazing.

My excitement dampens a bit. The reality of this experience is much different than what I envisioned. For instance, I knew we'd each have to tandem jump with someone else since neither of us had any skydiving experience. But is there a reason Kiran's guy strapped himself to her before we even took off? I get him giving her last minute instructions, but why does he need to whisper them in her ear? I wager his Spanish accent is fake too. No one rolls their R's that much. His name is Lorenzo. On our paperwork it has only one R. Yet, the way he introduced himself, it's more like six. Who the hell needs that many R's in their name?

Kiran takes a rubber band from her pocket. The way Lorenzo is staring at her is driving me crazy. She's quiet, lost in her own thoughts. He says something to her. Kiran laughs. Okay, he's comforting her. Chill, Cutler. Eight thousand feet and climbing is no time to pick a fight. She doesn't look uncomfortable. She isn't asking you to save her. This is all me and my own insecurity. I realize that, but no matter how hard I try, I cannot unclench my hands. This guy could be in the running to be a future boy band member. Bet he can dance and sing at the same time.

"Are you okay, Mason?" She thinks I'm freaking out about the fall.

I've already fallen, sweetheart. "Just fine."

Today is a day of introductions. It takes me a few seconds too long to name this emotion, probably because I've never experienced it. At least not to this degree. A hurricane swirls dregs of anger and uncertainty inside me.

Hello, Jealousy, it's really shitty to meet you.

"It's gonna be over soon, man," Lorenzo yells at me. "When you're touching the clouds, nothing compares."

Yeah, Lorenzo? Well why don't you feel up a few clouds and take your hands off Kiran? "Hey, buddy, is there a reason you have to practically hug her?"

"What?" he says, cupping his ear.

"You really need to be that close?"

"This is the right position."

"For jumping out of the plane. We're not jumping right now, are we?"

"I'm going over the instructions."

"We both watched the video." I look back at my guy who's sitting ten feet away from me flipping through a magazine. "Obviously, it's not necessary."

Lorenzo snaps his fingers at the other guy. "Larry, why don't you harness yourself to him? He's nervous."

Fuck you, Lorenzo.

"Do you want to strap on, right now?" Larry asks.

I wince at the phrase.

"Negative. We'll wait till the last minute." I turn back to the guy who's got my girl in his arms. "That wasn't my point, man. And you know it."

Kiran's mouth drops. She cranes her neck to stare up at Lorenzo. "Can I take this off?" she asks, tugging on the restraints that have them pasted together.

"Only for a few minutes," he says, giving me a hard eye-roll before unclipping her from the harness. "We're almost there."

She crawls over to me and sits up on her knees. "What are you doing, Mason?"

"Making an observation."

She puts her hands on my shoulder. "Well, stop making observations. I don't know what you're thinking right now, but you need to get out of your head this time. And while you're at it, you might want to consider not pissing off the guy who is in charge of my parachute."

She's right. The guy wasn't completely professional, but he wasn't making her feel uncomfortable. I'm the one doing that.

"I'll try to behave."

Her lips curve. She looks toward the window. It's all sky out there. She turns back to me. Her nerves are gone and she's almost giddy. "We're really doing this."

"We are, sunshine."

"Come back now," Lorenzo of the rolling R's yells.

Larry gets into position behind me. Before we can get strapped, she kisses me. It's a light quick peck. I pull her back for something deeper. I was right. Strawberry lip gloss. Strawberries never tasted so good. "I can't wait to fly with you."

"Me either."

When she returns to Lorenzo, he does all the things he's supposed to do, but without the unnecessary flourishes. In other words, fewer Rs.

They open the door. I slide up to take in the view. She does the same. It's nothing short of spectacular. There are patches of green fields and golden beaches and calming seas as far as my eyes can see. It's the kind of view that makes you realize how small we are while appreciating how stunning the world is.

"I can't believe I almost missed this to opt for parachuting in a building."

I can't believe I almost didn't come on this trip and missed her.

"It's time," Lorenzo announces.

He and Kiran go first. Her hand grips the sides of the aircraft opening. The wind whips strands of her hair in every direction. She turns to me once. Her smile is full of confidence and joy. I give her a salute.

She stares at the sky, her face determined. For some reason, I desperately want to put my arm over her body like I did in the car.

She leans forward. She leaps. My heart lunges as she disappears.

Now I'm freaked out. Not because I'm about to fall 10,000 feet. No, this isn't fear for me. It's fear for her. I can't see her. I don't know if she's all right. We move into position, but I forget the spectacular view and the intensity of what I'm about to do. Instead, I scan the skies below for her. I don't breathe again until I spot her. Larry taps my shoulder to let me know it's time. I fall. I inhale a lungful of cold air. I'm going about 120 miles per hour. But it doesn't feel that fast. It's surreal. I'm experiencing a slow-motion dream at terminal velocity. I can't hear a damn thing except for my beating heart. My skin tightens against the wind. It's a rush to be sure, but even in the midst of it, I never take my eyes off her. I only relax when she safely reaches the ground.

That, my friends, is the exact moment I realize I'm in love with Kiran Shenoy.

Chapter 12

Kiran

We're finally coming down from our high. Mason asks if I want to have dinner at the rotating restaurant in the Wilshire to celebrate. But I have a mad craving for a gooey cheese pizza. We grab one on the way back and head to the roof. We bring a bottle of red wine too, although neither of us thought to bring glasses. So we drink it straight out of the bottle, passing it back and forth between us.

The truth is, I didn't want to go to the Wilshire because I don't want to share him at all. The scales have shifted without my permission, and we've passed some kind of tipping point. I don't regret anything except I didn't spend every waking second with him. Now, all I can do is watch the seconds tick by, wishing like crazy I could arm wrestle the hands of time.

"Am I yelling?" I ask him.

"Don't think so. What about me?"

I shake my head. It wasn't until other people were giving us weird looks that we realized we were screaming every time we said something. I guess the adrenaline and noise screwed with our hearing. I'm so psyched about the experience I can barely contain myself. The skydiving was bucket list material. But Mason letting me drive his car and encouraging me the whole time was something I'll always hold in my heart.

I take a swig of wine and hand the bottle to him. "Let's go surfing tomorrow," I say.

"It's a plan." He slides lower in his chair. "Were you praying?"

"When?"

"You closed your eyes and mouthed something right before you got on the plane. Just wondering if you were saying a prayer."

"Actually, I was talking to my mom. I asked her if it was a bad idea. I do that sometimes. Ask her questions."

"Does she answer?"

"Not so far. I'm glad she didn't start answering today, though. She would have told me to keep my butt on the ground where it belonged. It's just this silly thing I do."

He turns toward me and takes hold of my wrist. He rubs the underside with his thumb. "Not silly in my book. I used to talk to my dad."

He lost his dad at such a young age. How did he manage to take care of himself, let alone his grandmother and sister? "What kind of questions?"

"Everything under the sun. My dad was a great man. He was the backbone to our family. You don't realize how devastating it is to lose your backbone until it's gone. I used to ask him if I was making the right decisions regarding Dana. If I should drop out of high school and work full time. If there's a better way. If I should put Gram in a home."

"Did he answer?"

"Not often. Once in a while I would hear his voice, though, especially concerning Gram."

"His mother?"

"My mother's mother. But he always respected her. She taught me a lot of skills too."

He speaks so highly of his grandmother and father. I wonder why he never mentions his mother. "What kind of skills?"

"I can tell you if a melon is ripe and how to properly plant a rosemary bush."

"Impressive. I'll remember that in case I need help with melons or…bushes."

He chuckles. "I'm your huckleberry."

"What happened to your mother, Mason?"

His mouth turns hard. "She had other priorities." I have no idea what other priorities could take precedence over your own children. Judging from the sharpness of his tone, I decide not to press. "I can't imagine what it was like for you to lose your dad and take over all those responsibilities."

"You're not the first person to ask that. Typically, I say we all do what we have to. That's my canned response."

"What was it really like? You can tell me." I take hold of his hand.

"At first, I was so angry."

"At who?"

"Everyone. At the doctors who couldn't save him. At cancer itself. Hell, I was even mad at him for up and leaving us like he'd had a choice. At my mom for quitting us. Even angry at Dana because she was so damn needy. When Grams got sick, I really fucking hated my life. On the outside, I did all the stuff the son of a great man like Joshua Cutler should do. But on the inside, I fell apart." Mason's mouth tightens into a grim line. "When I look back on all of it now, I realize how good I had it. If anything, I was lucky."

"Lucky?"

"Sure, Grams took us in. She needed us as much as we needed her. It wasn't a picture-perfect family, but we *were* a family. Dana and I might have ended up in the system if it wasn't for her. A lot of kids in our situation do. Yeah, I would give anything to have had a few more years with my dad. But I'm grateful for all the memories I have. What I really wish is that Dana had the years I did."

My lower lip trembles. I turn to look at the water below us so I don't give into tears. I want to go back in time, hug that brave boy, and make his world right. Then again, this beautiful man next to me is a product of those experiences. He grew up stronger and faster because of his heart ache. It's one of the reasons he is such a good man. Waves crash against the shoreline singing a sad melody. I take a small sip and hand the bottle back to him.

"You don't ask your dad questions anymore, Mason?"

He takes a long drink. He wipes his mouth with the back of his hand. "Just one, Kiran."

"What is it?"

"Do I make you proud? Never got an answer on that one."

I squeeze his hand. "I can answer it for you. You make him proud, Mason. You honor his legacy every single day."

He takes my hand and kisses my wrist. We watch the sun set over the water.

Chapter 13

Mason

I am hard. I mean explosive hard. Her luscious mouth is around my dick. Her hair brushes my thighs. Moaning loudly, I throw off the covers to watch her. I lift her long silky hair away from her face so I can see that beautiful fucking mouth in action.

We'd tried this the other night. She licked me like an ice cream cone until I couldn't take it anymore. Finally, I pulled her toward me so I could make love to her properly. Here is the amazing thing about Kiran. She picked up on the fact I didn't care for what she was doing. Not only that, she asked how she could improve. How to please me. I've never had a girl ask me that. It turns me on like crazy. I told her more mouth and hands and sucking. She's a quick study.

"Oh my God, baby. That feels really good."

I crane my neck back and suck air between my teeth. What a fucking beautiful way to wake up. My hips jerk reflexively. Shit. I expect her to stop. She takes it in stride. I run my fingers through her hair. She hums softly. I feel the vibrations in every vein and cell. Her hand is wrapped around my base. Every time she comes for air, she strokes me from root to tip.

She struggles to take me all the way. I want to tell her she doesn't need to. Except I can't speak right now. I can barely hold on. But as consuming as this is, I want us to both climax together. I need her in my arms.

"Come here."

She stops. Her mouth presses into the sexy kissable pout I love. She crawls up my body, the ends of her hair dragging against my flesh. It's taking mammoth strength for me not to come. I sit up and wrap my arms around her.

"Wasn't I doing a good job?"

"Best. Job. Ever."

"Then why did you tell me to stop?"

"We're not stopping. Just changing directions."

I cannot resist this power between us. It's tangible like the crackle of a thousand fires. I take her face in my hands and I kiss her crazy. She tastes like peppermint. It's delicious, but I've got a craving for peaches. When we come for air, her lips are swollen. So I kiss her more gently. I tug on her bottom lip. I work my way down her neck. She fists her hands through my hair. She leans up on her knees and straddles me. She brings her breasts right where my mouth is. I love how we're past the initial shyness. She tells me what she wants. And I aim to deliver.

I flick my tongue against her nipple and fondle the other one. I trace her opening back and forth. She's wet and ready for me. She gets up on her knees and rakes her fingernails down my back. We're in a dangerous position. It's so fucking good I'm liable to forget the condom. Her body quivers with my touch, responding to every action. This isn't just physical. This is an intimate conversation between us. Finally, I manage to tear my hands away and grope the nightstand. I knock over a bottle of water and the stupid alarm clock until I finally find the packet.

I hand her the condom. She takes it without a word. She slides down. Her hot wet mouth is over me one more time.

"You're killin' me, girl. Put it on already…please."

She smiles proudly. Yeah, girl, you manage to reduce me to monosyllabic incomplete sentences. Thankfully, she rolls it on.

"Get over here." I reach for her arms and bring her up to my lap.

Her eyes widen. "This way?"

I nod. "You can be in the driver's seat."

She looks unsure. I move her into position. She sinks down. My heart rate notches up as I'm wrapped in her warmth. I grip her hips and move her. It takes only a few seconds before she picks up the rhythm. She puts her hands on my shoulders for leverage. My grunts shift to growls. I bite into her shoulder, not hard enough to be terribly painful, but it will leave my mark on her for a while. The control I exercise in my life weakens when I'm with her. Hell, it disappears altogether. I hold on, fighting back the urge to go over the edge.

"Come for me," I say. It's more of a plea than a command.

She's not there yet. I recognize this. I grasp her hips and jerk inside of her. Each motion brings her closer. Her soft breaths transform to harsh pants until she tightens around me. Once she comes, I close my eyes and let myself follow.

We collapse into each other's arms, rocking back and forth in time to the tune of our chaotic heartbeats. I roll us over and pull out slowly.

"Be right back," I say, following each word with a kiss.

"I'll be here."

I head to the bathroom. I discard the condom. I wash my face and brush my teeth. God, I hope I didn't have morning breath. I grab a washcloth and rinse it with warm water. She lays completely naked on the bed, the filtering light of the sun casting shadows on her golden flesh. I sit on the edge of the mattress and run the washcloth between her legs.

"Surfing?" she asks.

"Yeah, but can we take a few minutes?"

"You want another round? That was pretty…vigorous. Round two might just knock me out."

I laugh. Hard to believe she can make me laugh after such an intense experience. "Me too, sunshine. I just want to lie next to you a little longer."

She scoots over and pats the area next to her. "Get in here then."

I lie on the bed. We're both on our sides facing each other. I frown at the indented mark on her flesh. The one I caused.

"I got carried away. Are you okay?"

She shakes her head. "I'm feeling exceptionally fine, Mason. It was empowering in a strange way."

"Empowering that I bit you?"

"Empowering that you were so turned on by me."

"I was. I am."

She smacks my chest. I trace the scar down her stomach. She tenses. Then God help me, she flinches.

"Kiran? What's wrong?"

She shakes her head. "It doesn't hurt."

"Not physically, but you dislike me touching you here."

She covers her face. "It's so ugly."

"I can't believe you think that." I kissed the long, neat line. She's still tense, but she doesn't stop me.

"This scar is beautiful, Kiran. I love it."

Her laugh is nervous. "You're kidding, right?"

"Serious as a Sunday sermon." I shake my head. "Do you think I'd joke?"

"No."

"Then what?"

"I have no idea why you would love a disfigurement. I hate it."

Of course she did. It is a constant reminder of the carnage in her past. I notice she winces sometimes when she stretches or twists her body a certain way. I do my best to watch for those signs when we're physical. It's not easy because I get lost in those moments with her. But the last thing I want is to cause her pain.

"It's not a disfigurement. There isn't anything ugly about you, Kiran. Not a damn thing."

"I had a consultation with a plastic surgeon. He won't touch the scar on my stomach but this one"—she gestures to her face—"this one he can remove."

She wears her hair in a way that covers the scar on the left side of her face most of the time. I understand her reason, but I still think it's a shame. She has such a pretty face.

"Do you want that? Would it make you feel better about yourself?"

"Honestly, I'm not sure. After all the surgeries, I'm squeamish about going under a knife again. Even if it's minor. You don't think I should do it, do you?"

"It doesn't matter what I think. It's not my decision."

"It's not your decision, but it does matter what you think. It matters to me."

I run my thumb across the underside of her wrist and watch as the small pink heart disappears under the pressure and comes back again. "If it'll make your life better, then you should do it."

"Is there a 'but' in there?"

"Yes." I hesitate because I completely get why she'd want to eliminate these reminders. "I hope my 'but' doesn't make me sound like an ass."

She laughs. "I'll be the judge of that."

I shift up. I want her to look at me. To recognize I am being sincere. "If this is about the way you feel about yourself, then do it. But if this is about other people's reactions, then I don't think you should."

"Why?"

"Why? Because fuck them, that's why." I tuck a strand of hair behind her ear. "Every scar you carry tells a story about you, Kiran."

She huffs, causing a strand of hair to blow off her forehead. "Yeah, a tragedy. A freaking train wreck."

"I read the story differently. To me, they speak volumes about your bravery and courage and survival. You are a survivor, sunshine. That's something to carry with pride." I run my finger down her belly across the straight deep vertical line there. "This scar here. I hate that it still hurts you, but I love what it represents."

"What do you mean?"

"This is where the doctors opened you up and mended you, right?"

"Yes."

"This is the scar that saved your life, Kiran. Why wouldn't I love it?"

"I never thought of it like that." Her voice is thick, cracking on a few words.

I kiss away the tears in her eyes before they fall. "Shit, I didn't mean to make you cry."

She narrows her eyes, completely at odds with the way her lower lip trembles. She's struggling to hold back the dam of emotions. Maybe she's even mad at me for breaking a few of her carefully constructed levees. "Oh, you didn't mean to make me cry? Then maybe you should stop saying things that are so sweet they spike my blood sugar."

"Yeah, okay. Have it your way. Your ass is too small."

She cracks a smile. "That's better."

"Your knees are knobby."

"Good."

"And don't even get me started on your nose."

She slaps her hand over my mouth. "Watch it, buddy."

I tickle her until she's laughing in hysterics. She falls on her back. I grab hold of her long legs before she can kick me. I don't retreat except to kiss the tip of her nose. "Your nose is perfect." I continue to tease her. The room fills with her laugher and sunshine. It's a song I will never tire of. "You're such a weirdo, Shenoy. Never had a girl ask me to insult her."

"Never had a boy…" She's laughing so hard she can't finish the sentence. I let up to allow her to catch her breath. I massage her sides where I tickled her the most.

"What were you going to say?"

Her smile falters. "Never had a boy who makes me feel the way you do."

Chapter 14

Mason

It took a while for Kiran to find her sea legs again. Or maybe I should say surfing legs. But once she gets acclimated, she's confident, chasing the highest and fiercest waves in an aquamarine one-piece. She offers them to me first. I decline. I'd just wipe out. She knows what to do with them. I do catch a few too, but they are toddler-sized in comparison.

I sit on my board in the middle of crystal blue water watching her with complete awe. She's graceful, her long legs manipulating the board with the slightest pressure and twist. It's almost organic, as if she is an extension of the turbulent water she glides on. I wasn't sure surfing was a good idea. It requires exertion and it's taxing. Hell, it's taxing on my body. The way she bends and weaves, there is no doubt this is painful for her.

I'm glad we're doing it. The way she works the board and cyclones through a wave, I am grateful to witness her in this element. There is a reason I suck at surfing. I always believed it was all about technique and physics. It's not. There is a creativity component. She's an artist, cresting waves the way birds rise in flight. She's completely focused and calm in the midst of chaos.

She lies on her tummy atop the board and paddles over to me. She sits and straddles her board.

"Impressive stuff, Shenoy."

"Thanks. Guess I remembered more than I thought."

"Muscle memory is the strongest memory there is."

She exhales a long breath, her face turned up toward the low dipping sun. "Thank goodness for that." She's still breathing hard.

"Tired?" I ask.

"Completely drained."

"Are you sore?"

She nods. "I have some pain pills back in my room."

"I've never seen you take any pills."

"I try not to, but I'll need them tonight and maybe tomorrow."

"So you're hurting something awful?"

She rubs her arms. "Yes, but it's a good kind of sore. When you first asked me to surf with you, it was so spontaneous. All I could think about was pain and fear. This time, I mentally prepared myself to work through it. Yeah, it hurts. Every muscle I own aches right now. But it's worth it to glide on the water and be completely free." She graces me with a bright smile. "I have no regrets, Mason. None." She chews on her lower lip. "Well, maybe one regret."

"What's that?"

"You won't be able to fuck me like a rock star tonight."

My cock jerks so fast I almost fall off my board. "Yes, I'll admit it is a disappointment. But just so we're clear, you're a rock star too, baby."

She tilts her head. Her lips curl into a sexy smile. "We do have a graphic sound when we're together."

"We're raunchy as hell. But tonight, let's go for something quieter. I'll get us take-out Chinese and a six-pack. We can crank up the television and find ourselves a classic movie to fall asleep to. What do you say?"

"Yes to Chinese. Maybe to classic movie."

"Maybe?"

"By classic, if you're talking Cary Grant circa nineteen-forties, then I'm your girl. But if your definition of classic is Sylvester Stallone circa nineteen-eighties, I'm hesitating."

"I was thinking more along the lines of a fine nineteen-nineties Bruce Willis vintage flick. The kind of movie that never goes stale."

She chuckles. "We're getting warmer. However, if we're going nineteen-nineties, then might I suggest some Cruise and Zellweger rom-com action with enough of a sports theme to please any masculine needs?"

"Baby, you got me at hello." I hold up my hand. She slaps it in a pretty decent high-five. "Nice negotiating skills, Shenoy."

"Nice compromise, Cutler. So the only thing I'll have to pass on is the beer. Not that you shouldn't pick up a six-pack for yourself." She rings out her hair.

I have no idea what she's thinking, but damn, I want to kiss the fiery crimson blush from the apples of her cheeks. "I'll get wine if you prefer."

"I'll stick to Diet Pepsi tonight. I can't drink on my medication."

Her statement reminds me she's tired. Not that I can't read it in her face or body. "Maybe we should head back?"

"Soon. Let's stay here for a while. At least until the sun starts setting. Do you mind?"

I kick my feet until my board is closer to hers. "Mind? It would be my pleasure to sit here with you, Miss Kiran, until every last cow makes it home. But are you sure you don't need a rest?"

"Not yet. I don't want to miss this."

"Me either." I reach for her hand and lock my fingers with hers. "Have you made any decisions about Iowa?"

Her smile brightens. "Yes. In fact, I called the admissions office this morning."

"When?" We'd been together the entire day.

"When you were sleeping. I woke up early and went to the roof. You know, before I woke you up."

"Best way I've ever woken up by the way. Did I thank you properly?"

"You did, and you're welcome," she says, her lips twitching at the corners.

"So? Don't keep me in suspense. What's the decision?"

"You're looking at an official student of the fall class. I'm going to Iowa. Isn't that great?"

"Honestly, I never thought I'd tell anyone going to Iowa is a great idea. But in your case, it definitely is. It's really amazing, Kiran. Congratulations." I put my arm around her and pull her as close as possible without tipping us over. It's a little awkward, but not uncomfortable. Never that.

"I'm taking charge of my life. I'm not a barnacle anymore."

I kiss the top of her head. "You never were."

She lays her head on my shoulder. We take in the sun's slow descent. I'm sure the sight is one for the photo album. Except I'm not scanning the horizon, waiting for this day to end. Just the opposite. I want it to go on forever.

Chapter 15

Mason

We never finished the movie. Somewhere between Tom Cruise's dickish antics and Cuba's killer money speech, we fell asleep. I wake early this morning to get in a run. The beach usually crowds in the afternoon, but today at six AM there are folks gathering in small groups, collecting shells and rocks. Under the circumstances, it wasn't much of a run. On the way back, I stop at the café to pick up coffees and some breakfast to-go. I'm gonna eat peaches in bed. And um… We'll have breakfast too.

"Care for a cup while you wait?" the waitress asks.

"Please." I flip my cup over. "Know what's going on at the beach today?" I ask the waitress as she pours the coffee.

"Oh, are they setting up already? It's our annual sandcastle-building contest. It's a lot of fun. I believe you can still register."

"Oh yeah?"

"Would you like an entry form? We have a few left. You just take it to the front desk after you fill it out."

It seems like a really silly thing to do. Not to brag, but I'm a damn good sandcastle builder. No, fuck that. I'm an architect. So yeah, I'm geeked about doing this very geeky thing. I'm not sure what Kiran's take will be, but I hope she'll warm to the idea.

"Are teams allowed?" I ask her.

"Afraid not. It's individuals only," she says.

"Bring me two forms, please."

"You're not getting that prize, man. They might as well cut me the check right now," the guy in the stool next to me says.

"Check? How much is the prize?"

"Check is an overstatement. You get your picture in the local paper and a packet of gift certificates. Doesn't matter, though, cause that prize is mine."

I'm not a big fan of shit talkers, but I dig his self-confidence. It'll be fun to crush him. Then maybe I'll stomp on his sandcastle too. "We'll see about that."

I recognize this guy. He's the same one I saw the first day I checked in. The one who just got married and is staying in the grandiose sweetheart's suite. He wears a camo baseball cap with Army written in large gold capital letters.

"You still in?" I ask, gesturing to his hat.

"Contract ended a year ago. I didn't renew." Yeah, he's a shit talker, but he sits ramrod straight. I missed it that first day, but he has the same stoic look about him I recognize in all the experienced troops, officers, and drill sergeants I met during training. The ones who'd gone into battle and witnessed war firsthand. I couldn't give that look a name or a clear definition, except I respected the hell out of it.

"See any action?"

His fingers tighten around the cup. "More than my fair share, bro. Iraq mostly."

"That's rough."

"What about you?"

"The Marines. Just graduated boot camp." It feels surreal to even refer to myself as a Marine. But I'm allowed after making it through the most brutal months of my life. The crazy part is that's just the prep for the real test.

"You're in for a long ride, Devil Dog."

"So I hear."

He smiles and holds out his hand. His handshake is firm. "Rob Jorgenson."

"Mason Cutler."

"You know what Marine stands for, Cutler?"

I'm not about to fall for this one. "Yeah, I know. 'My ass rides in navy equipment.'"

"I was going for 'muscles are required, intelligence not essential.'" He laughs and claps me on the back. "Sorry man, I love all my military brothers regardless of branch." He gestures between us. "But when an army grunt meets a jarhead, there's gonna be some shit talk."

"Fair enough. After all, doesn't army stand for 'ain't ready for the Marines yet'?"

He nods at my good-natured rib. "Nice one, Semper Fi."

"Likewise. Got any advice, brother?"

He drums his fingers against the counter. "Avoid the Jambalaya MRE. You'll be in the latrines all day."

"Seriously, that's a real ration?"

"Yes, and its revolting. Wouldn't feed that shit to a junkyard dog."

"Noted. Any other words of wisdom?"

"Be prepared."

"Yeah, that was a constant theme in boot camp."

He shakes his head. "I'm not talking about preparing yourself for battle. The Marines do a good job making sure you're ready for any battle. I'm referring to coming home. See, the world doesn't stop for you, even if you are defending it. You come home, ready to resume your life. But the thing is, it's not the same life you remember. You wife's shacking up with Jody. And Jody is your best friend. Your mom's not doing so well. The factory in your hometown shut down, and everything is in shambles. It wrecks you."

"Didn't you just get married?"

"It's my second marriage. My first wife decided she couldn't deal. She said her life was on permanent hold."

"That sucks, man."

He shrugs. "At the time it destroyed me, burned my skull even more than the desert sun. But now, it's all good. Never thought I'd find someone else." He takes a sip of his coffee. "Turns out, I didn't have to worry about looking. She found me." He stands and takes out his wallet.

The food I ordered sits in front of me. I have no idea how long it's been there. I hold my hand up before he lays down his cash. "Your coffee is on me."

"Thanks, man. I'm still gonna kick your ass in the sand-building contest."

I conjure a laugh I don't feel. "Yeah, like I said, we'll see."

Chapter 16

Kiran

Building sandcastles isn't how I envisioned spending one of our days. There are only two left. But Mason was really excited about it. He told me how his dad took him and Dana to the beach in Charleston most weekends where he taught a young Mason the intricacies of fishing and the fine art of sandcastle building. How could I say no?

Also, he registered us and paid our entry fees so there's that too. As a former local, I remember this contest. It seems to have grown in popularity. Several hotels along the beach host it now. At least a hundred people scatter over the beach to stake claim to an area. There are old and young and very young. There are a few professional graphic artists and 3D specialists ready to get their sandcastle on too. Margie Fox from the local news station is here in her white pantsuit with a huge microphone ready to give a play-by-play.

Hoping he's not too invested in this, I glance at him. His face is stone-cold concentration, making it clear he's not deterred one bit. This is no frolic-on-the-beach, shovel and pail stuff either. There are rules and judges. We're each given a box with an identical set of tools. We are not allowed to use anything else. Although, we can scavenge the beach for organic items we wish to incorporate. Judging from the piles the rest of the contestants have in front of them, I doubt there is anything left. Everyone has to make some type of sandcastle within four hours. The judge's scores are based on design, creativity, and overall stability of the structure.

As soon as the whistle blows to signal the start, Mason grabs every one of his buckets and takes off for the water. A lot of people do. I choose to avoid the herd and organize my tools. There are buckets of various sizes, a few plastic Dixie cups, also in varying sizes, a couple of shovels, and a bunch of plastic tools that look like something I might use to frost a cake.

When he comes back, buckets full, he starts scraping the sand. Then he wets it down and packs it. He runs off again. This time he packs the buckets with sand. He does this several times. I'm exhausted just watching him. Who knew sandcastle building required so much stamina?

Meanwhile, I fill up my first bucket and dump it top down.

"What are you doing, Shenoy?"

"Um…building a sandcastle."

"Darlin', you have to level the area first. Otherwise, it won't be structurally sound."

"Oh." I pat down the ground.

"You have to get water, Kiran. It's essential."

"Fine." I pick up my bucket and start walking.

"Take all the buckets, baby."

I blow a frustrated sigh. "Mason, stop bossing me. I'm no Frank Lloyd Wright."

He chuckles. "More like Frank Lloyd Wrong, sunshine." His expression sobers when he gazes at me. "Sorry, that came out really…."

"Dickish."

"Was going to say mean, but okay. Look, I'm sorry I dragged you into this."

"You didn't." I gesture to the beach. "This isn't my thing, but I'm cool with it. As long as you quit being bossy and stop giving me unwarranted advice."

"Deal."

Mason isn't the only fanatic. The guy next to him is cut from the same rough, sturdy cloth. What's his name? Ah yeah, he's one-half of the Jorgensens. They checked in right before me. His wife is there too, shoveling sand into her bucket absentmindedly while she looks longingly at the tiki bar. I hear you loud and clear, sister.

Mason doesn't build his sandcastle the way others do. He takes the largest bucket, packs it, and then tips it over. He does this many times until he has several neat rows. He builds it up until he has five tiers. He fills between the tiers and runs a plastic paint stick around the edges several times until it's all smooth. The shape is a perfect rectangle of sand. It comes up just over my knees. It's cool, but it doesn't resemble a sandcastle.

"I don't understand your strategy."

"You will," he says in a cryptic way.

Mason takes one of the Dixie cups and tears out the base. He curls the bottom into a tight circle until it forms a round shape and packs it with wet sand. He places these on top of the ginormous rectangle. Then he makes a few that are rounder and longer. He takes the tool that looks like a tiny ice-cream scoop and makes a ball to go on top of each cone. They look like hot dogs with circles on top of them.

"What are you making over there, Marine? A house of dicks?" Rob Jorgenson asks.

I almost choke on the laughter.

"Why are you so interested in my dicks, Army?"

Rob opens his mouth to reply with some topper, but he stops when his wife gives him a sharp look. "Rob, there are children here."

Both men look contrite.

Mrs. J and I catch each other's glances a few times, both of us smiling, trying to be supportive, while our boys are planning a full-scale attack. It doesn't surprise me that Mason is competitive, but I have never seen him this focused. It's strangely erotic.

I finish my cottage-style sandcastle, although that's probably a stretch. It's more like a large, grainy mound. I ditch my shovel.

"Hi, I'm Melanie Jorgenson," the pretty brunette says, holding her hand out to me.

"Kiran."

She gestures toward Mason. "Is he yours?" she asks like someone would inquire if a child belongs to you.

"Yeah, I guess he is."

"Looks like our fellows are friends."

I wrinkle my nose. "Friends or foes?"

"Maybe both." She pats the sand off her shorts. "Want to take a break and get a drink?"

"Break? Isn't it almost over?"

She takes her cell from her pocket and holds it face out. "Still over two hours left."

I smack my forehead. "Yeah, I can definitely use a break."

She offers her hand to help me up. "You guys ready for a break?" she asks the boys.

"No breaks," they say in unison.

"Want us to bring you back something?" I ask.

They both grunt a no.

It's probably ninety degrees out here and Mason's been nonstop. He's dehydrated and probably starving. I'm starving, and he eats twice as much as me. "We'll fetch a few bottles of water and some fruit for you guys."

I'm not even sure if they heard us until I start walking away and Mason yells after me to get him a peach. I almost trip face down onto the sand.

Melanie and I order some luscious frozen mango and coconut infused concoction. We order a plate of nachos with extra guac. I drop the waters and fruit in my knapsack. After dropping off the boy's replenishments, complete with stern warnings they need to drink some water, we drag two lawn chairs over to our spot. Turns out, Melanie is a big fan of romance stories too. We bond over that while scarfing down a huge plate of nachos.

I watch Mason's creation slowly come to life. He made the solid mass first so he could chip away at it slowly, using the negative space. He blends the sand and water until it's as smooth as concrete. The curvy slide thing on one side of the structure transforms into an elaborate staircase. On the other side he's made an impressive drawbridge. The hotdog things become fancy turrets with arches in between them. There are several towers with long intricate bridges connecting them. He uses the chisel to carve even squares onto the walls until they resemble stone.

There's a passion in the way he works. The chiseled planes of his face are locked in stern concentration. His fingers smooth and bend the sand into a shape. I get lost in watching him.

Margie Fox and her crew stop a few feet from us. She relays a foreboding story of one of the 3D artists, a favorite to win, who had to bow out. Turns out, the shell he was using as the top of his five-tower design was home to an honorary crab. While the artist was getting more water, the crab in question found his house on top of a column of sand. He started crawling, dragging the heavy shell straight down the tower and causing a domino effect.

The judges start their initial rounds and narrow it down to ten people to continue. Shocker alert—Melanie and I don't make the cut. Of course, Mason and Rob do.

"Kiran?"

"Huh?" I turn to Melanie, realizing I totally missed what she's said. "Sorry, what?"

"I asked if you want to walk around and check out the competition."

It's not a bad idea. Besides, I need to pry myself away before I jump Mason and ruin his gorgeous creation. Rob's castle is impressive too, except it resembles a fort more than a castle. He's hard at work shaping a huge scaly dragon that wraps around the front. There are a few other entries that are decent, but I think it's between Mason and Rob.

Melanie and I stop in our tracks as a little girl huffs her way across the sand with two dripping buckets. Her arms are limp as if they might give out.

"Need some help?" I ask, stretching out my hand to take one of her buckets.

She pulls them back, her bright red pigtails flying at the side of her face. "I can't. I'll be disqualified if I accept help." She says disqualified without the Q, and it's just about the cutest thing I've ever heard. Her cheeks are covered in a mass of freckles. She has a gap in her teeth. She so freaking adorable I want to adopt her.

"Oh, sorry."

She moves on. Curious, Melanie and I follow. Turns out Mason and Rob do have some competition. Her name is Abigail Helms, and she's ten years old. Although her entry is not as intricately detailed as Mason's or as precise as Rob's, it's as lovely as the artist herself. The construction is simple, just three layers tall, each one a slightly smaller oval like a wedding cake. She's carved mermaids on the walls. There are small broken bits of coral and shells decorating the outside. The whimsical design tugs at the heart.

"Uh-oh, we're in trouble," Melanie says.

"Yeah, I think we are."

Abigail rolls sand and shapes animals to stand in front.

"Is that a horse?" Melanie asks.

"Think so." When Abigail rolls the tiniest pointed horn, I know exactly what it is. "It's a unicorn."

Melanie and I both ooh and ahh before we finally drag ourselves away.

I plop myself down next to Mason. His castle is nothing short of stunning. "Hello, my handsome knight. May I ask what princess are you building that for?"

He takes my hand and kisses the underside of my wrist. "This princess."

The judges make the rounds to pick the finalists. Just as I called it, Mason, Rob, and Abigail are the three finalists. They hand Mason and Rob gaudy gold ribbons. Mason promptly pins his on my shirt. He takes his sweet time, cupping my boob in the process.

I give him a good luck kiss. At this point, each of the finalists have a half hour to put on the finishing touches and last minute flourishes before a winner is announced.

"It's down to the gritty wire. Or as we like to say, the gritty sand," Margie Fox announces.

Mason and I watch as Abigail's mom pins her ribbon on her shirt.

He jerks his head in her direction. "You check her stuff out?"

"She's talented."

He stands to stretch. "I'm gonna see for myself."

When he comes back, I ask, "What did you think?"

He shrugs. "Her horses aren't to scale."

I place a hand on each of his shoulders. They feel stiff, so I rub them a little. "Firstly, they aren't horses. They're unicorns. Secondly, everyone knows the average unicorn is much larger than a horse."

"Is that a fact?"

"It is."

I take out a fresh bottle of chilled water. "Drink this."

"Yes, ma'am."

I stand on my toes and kiss him on the cheek before I take my seat next to Melanie. "You're staying in the Sweetheart's Suite, right?"

She nods.

"How is it?"

"Over the top and gaudy, but it's weirdly romantic. Hey, do you need any candles?"

"Why?"

"Because there are hundreds of them everywhere in the room."

"I'll let you know."

Melanie sits up in her chair. "I'm torn here. I'm rooting for my husband to win, of course, but the idea of a grown man beating out an adorable little girl seems unfair."

"I'm having the same dilemma. Plus, the poor girl has to take a break every half hour so her mother can slather sunscreen on her. It's not really fair."

Mason walks over to Rob. They talk for a bit.

"Wonder what's going on there?" I ask.

"More smack talk."

"Yeah," I agree, except I don't see any macho rivalry. It's as if they are conspiring. They shake hands after.

Mason's knees are pretty beat up from kneeling on the sand for hours. A few splotches of red cover his usually tanned skin. He resumes work on his sandcastle. He pauses only to take a drink of the fresh water. When he puts the cap back on, the half-full plastic bottle falls. I scream as I watch it crash onto the longest turret.

"Fix it," I yell, as if he needs the guidance.

Mason shakes his head and points down the shoreline. The judges are making their final rounds, clipboards in hand. He gives me a crooked grin and a one-sided shrug. "Too late, darling."

I'm so sad for him. He put so much hard work into this.

"Sorry you broke your dick, Cutler," Rob says.

"It's a turret. What happened to your giant cat?"

Rob shoots him the same cynical look. "It's a dragon, and I accidently crushed it."

The head and tail have fallen off the creature that was the main focal point of Rob's creation.

It's official, little Abigail Helms takes the top prize. We all clap as Margie Fox places a huge gold crown on Abigail's tiny head. It won't even stay straight. The girl dances around, fighting back a yawn. She falls asleep in her daddy's arms before the ceremony is even over.

Rob elbows Mason. "Too bad, Cutler. That crown would have looked good on you."

"Me? You're the one playing with kittens."

"Dragon, dude."

Chapter 17

Mason

I know what a lobster feels like when he's boiled alive. It's equivalent to spending four solid hours knee deep in gritty sand with the sun beating against your back.

The long, cold shower helps. But it's Kiran who brings me the magical cure by rubbing a healing tonic of cold, blue gel on my back and shoulders.

"Where did you get this?"

"Melanie. She said it works wonders."

"I have to agree."

I lean back and close my eyes.

"Mason, did you ruin your sandcastle on purpose?"

"The bottle just slipped. I'm clumsy."

"No, you're not. I watched you carve an entire building from sand today. You're not clumsy. But you are a very bad actor. A man doesn't just say 'oh, well' and move on if that wasn't intentional."

"How about we take a break on the grilling, Sherlock, and do a little more work on the massaging? You missed a spot."

She kisses me on the cheek. "You're a really good man, Mason Cutler."

"What else could I do, darling? Did you see that kid? She could barely stand. Maybe I wouldn't have won, but if there was even a chance, I could not in good conscience take that victory. I gotta be ten times the size of her."

"I don't care how many excuses you make. It was a very special thing to do. Rob did the same thing, right?"

"He took one look at her and ditched his shovel." My stomach growls. "Hey Kiran, I'm starving. Do you want to get room service?"

"Sure. I'll get the menu."

I can tell by the way she says it, she's disappointed. I pull her arms. "What do you want to do tonight?"

"You're tired. We'll stay in."

I crack my neck. "I'm feeling better. You've got healing hands."

"If you're sure."

"Positive."

"Then I have an idea."

"I'm up for anything as long as I get to eat and get my favorite dessert."

"And what dessert would that be?"

I kiss the corner of her mouth. "Peaches, of course."

* * * *

Kiran's idea was a moonlight picnic on the beach. It doesn't get more romantic than this. She's barefoot in a teal sundress that hugs every curve.

The discarded sandcastles still line the beach. She stops in front of mine. "This is the spot."

"In front of my damaged sandcastle?"

"Damaged but not destroyed." She takes out a blanket from her knapsack. I help her lay it out. She lights a few small candles and carefully sets them inside each opening of the castle. Against the sand, they cast a soft glow, highlighting each detail.

We purchased a couple sandwiches, drinks, and snacks from the café. I hold up her options. "Chicken salad or turkey?"

"Turkey please."

We chew on our food, lost in our thoughts, watching the flickering flames grow higher and listening to the music of crashing waves. I finger the strap on her dress. "This is a nice dress."

"Thanks. I wasn't planning to bring it, but I grabbed it at the last minute."

"Why not? It looks gorgeous on you."

"I haven't worn it since high school."

"Well, I'm happy it made its way into your suitcase." I move the strap and kiss her shoulder. "Now it just needs to make the journey to the floor of my room."

She feeds me a grape. "In due time, Cutler."

I hope that time is soon.

She stares at the sandcastle as if she's trying to memorize every line and curve.

"What are you thinking about?"

"Nothing, just picking out my room."

"Your room?"

She points to one of the still erect turrets. "You said you built it for me. So if this is mine, I want to live right here."

"The west turret, huh?"

"It'll be the sunniest place. It looks spacious too. Of course there are a ton of stairs to get there."

Her tone is wishful, and God, I don't know if I want her to stop talking or never stop talking. "What are you doing, Kiran?"

The candles flicker for a second before going out. She frowns. "I'm dreaming for a second. It's silly but..."

"I'll build you an elevator. It'll be a damn sight safer than the one at the hotel too." I don't care. I'll buy into her dream. Dreams are cheap. Hell, they're free, aren't they?

She's relieved I'm playing along and honors me with one of her luscious smiles and slight bow. "Thank you, good sir."

"So this room of yours... Is it spacious enough for two?"

She taps her lips. "Yeah, Mason, there's always going to be a space for you."

I swallow the thick lump that forms inside my throat. Pull yourself together, Cutler. I drag myself from the edge of despair and back into the beauty of this dream she's building for us. I pull her onto my lap. "I got a question for you."

"What?"

"How in the hell do you propose we pay for this gigantic castle? The utility bills alone will kill us, let alone the property taxes."

She laughs and wraps her arms around me. "Only you can be practical when we're talking about moving into a sandcastle."

"One of us should be."

"We'll figure it out, Mason. We'll make it happen."

I nod at Kiran's castle. "Or we can always move into your thing. It's a cave, right?"

She punches my arm. "It's a cottage."

"Oh, I see it now."

"You do?"

"No, darling, I'm sorry. It really looks like a cave." I angle my head to sneak another peek. "Or maybe a large, soft, lopsided—"

"Mason!"

"What? I was gonna say cage. A lopsided cage."

She laughs, her mouth against my neck. "Let's dream a little bigger. I want the castle you built for me."

"Then it's all yours, princess."

"Just to set your mind at ease, I have a plan."

"Yeah?"

"I'll peddle my stories. If I don't make enough, then I'll sell jewelry made from seashells to the tourists."

"You make jewelry?"

She frowns. "No. I'll learn, though."

"That's reasonable. For my part, I'll find work at some garage."

Her head tilts. "Or you can always be a professional sandcastle builder."

"Is that a career option?"

"Why not? We're dreaming, right? There aren't any limits. We can live on the beach in a shack, and I'd be ecstatic."

"As long as it's got four walls and a roof to shelter us."

"And maybe a couple windows so we can look out at the world once in a while."

"Windows with heavy blackout curtains so we can shut out the world whenever we need."

"It's the perfect plan."

This is dangerous. I should have stopped us three dreams ago. Tomorrow's our last day, and we need to face reality. Rob Jorgenson's advice weighs heavily on my mind. It rings true because I've seen it happen firsthand. Now, there is no question Kiran would be faithful to me. This girl is loyal to a fault. But do I really want to hold her back from all the experiences she deserves? Even if she'd consider being with me in these uncertain circumstances, there are other worries too. I watched her jump out of a plane and almost had a heart attack. What the hell am I gonna do if I'm halfway around the world and she's in trouble? I couldn't get to her. I would lose my concentration, my thoughts all straying to her without my consent. I need every shred of focus, now more than ever. I am embarking on a journey that will lead me down paths unknown. Ironically, Kiran and I are not unlike these abandoned sandcastles. What we have is beautiful, but it's not meant to last.

She leans her forehead against mine. "I love you, Mason Cutler."

Is it more honorable to be honest or to lie to her? I have no idea. But hearing her affirm what I feel in my heart makes it impossible to hold back. Tonight, under the stars and next to the surf, we can dream. We'll worry about waking up tomorrow.

"I love you too, Kiran Shenoy."

Trouble is, love isn't enough.

Chapter 18

Kiran

We both stand in front of the door to the Sweetheart's Suite. There is a huge heart-shaped wreath of twined red roses nailed to the door. We turn to each other.

"Is this weird?" Mason asks.

"We won't know until you open the door."

We ran into the Jorgenson's when we came down for breakfast this morning. Melanie's sister went into labor so they had to cut their honeymoon short. Since the room was paid for and non-refundable, they insisted we take it.

I am a little skeptical, but ever since that first day, I've been curious what it looks like.

He inserts the keycard and opens the door. He gestures for me to enter first. My feet sink into the soft plush carpet as I enter. I blink several times trying to take it all in. This room is at least three times bigger than a regular room.

"This is so…"

"Tacky," Masons says.

I laugh. "Yeah."

"It looks like Cupid took a dump in here."

Although I would not have used that particular description, Mason does have a point. The walls are Pepto-pink adorned with pictures of beach sunsets. There's a tall, plastic palm tree with white twinkle lights in one corner next to a red velvet-covered loveseat. A section of the room is done up in black and white tiles where a heart-shaped Jacuzzi is embedded in the floor. A couple of free-standing Grecian style columns anchor the bed. The bed itself is massive and covered with enough pink petals to build a Rose Bowl float. Melanie is right about the candles. They are on every surface along with vases of silk flowers. At least the maids have been through and everything looks clean. It's just a lot for the eye to take in.

"Why would anyone stay here?" Mason asks.

"Because of that." I point to the bank of glass sliding doors that frame the ocean view. They take up the entire far wall of the room. The view from my room is amazing, but this one is nothing short of spectacular. Mason slides the glass door open. He takes my hand and leads me to the wide balcony with two chaises and a crystal blue glass fireplace.

I lean on the railing. He places his palm on the small of my back and lets out a low whistle. "This is nice. We can spend the night out here."

I shrug. "I don't know. The inside is gaudy, but I don't mind it if you don't."

"Whatever you want, sweetheart." He wraps his arms around me. "As long as I get to have you." He traces the shell of my ear with his tongue. I lean against his muscular chest as he kisses his way down my neck. His hands move up my sides and over my breasts. Even through my shirt and bra, they pebble with his touch.

My entire body quivers as he peppers kisses against my neck. Something hard pokes into my lower back.

"What's that?" I say, although it comes out a garbled mess.

"You really have to ask?" He slaps my bottom. For some reason, it makes me feel tingly all over. He rubs the area tenderly before he pushes himself against me. "That, darling, is what you do to me."

There are people on the beach below us. I'm no exhibitionist, but the way he touches me makes me forget about everything. Thankfully, my rational mind prevails. "Mason, take me to bed."

"Now we're speaking the same language." He picks me up.

I yelp in surprise. Then he crushes his mouth against mine so hard I fall into a trance. When he throws me on the bed, I bounce a couple times.

He sidles next to me and unbuttons my shirt with one hand while kissing each inch of revealed skin. His teeth grasp the cup of my bra and lower it. Mason's different tonight. He's rougher, his intense blue eyes growing darker with lust, his stance almost predatory. The real shocker is how much I love it. I get lost in his touch. I lay my head back and stare at the ceiling.

"Oh my God."

"What?"

I point upward.

He tilts his head. "Mirror over the bed. Perfect touch."

"It's awful."

He smiles. "Not so bad, peaches."

"I can't look at myself when we're…"

He fingers my exposed nipple. "You don't know what you look like when you come. I've seen it firsthand. It's a stunning sight. One I'd never trade. Not even for the most beautiful sunrise or sunset. So yeah, look at yourself in the fucking mirror, Kiran. See what I see. While you're at it, remember who's making you feel this way."

"How could I forget?"

He doesn't answer me. Instead, he works his way down my body and undoes my jeans. He slides them off in one smooth motion. I lean on my elbows and watch him discard his own clothes. His erection springs out of his boxers. He strokes himself, his eyes locked with mine.

"Take everything off. I don't want to see you wearing anything except a satisfied smile."

There's an edge to his voice, a command I obey. I reach behind my back to unclasp my bra. Then I hook my fingers into the side of my panties and bring them down my legs.

"Touch yourself, Kiran."

I can barely function. I squirm at my own touch. My whole body is overly sensitive. I slide my other hand over my breast. The slightest movement might set me over the edge.

"Make yourself come, Kiran. I'm gonna stand right here and watch you watch yourself."

"I want you, Mason."

"And you'll have me. But right now, I need you to do this for me." His voice still has the edge, but there is a plea in the command.

I stare at myself and roll my hips against the push of my fingers. I can't believe how slick I am. The mirror shows a girl I've never met. She's sexy and shameless. Her body is a bit damaged but beautiful all the same. I bite my lower lip and increase the tempo. I arch my back, completely lost in my own world. Of course, I still feel his presence, especially as his breathing becomes ragged. I've never made myself come before, not for lack of trying. But it's different this time. I'm self-indulgent and greedy for this pleasure. I take it all in, the reflection of a lusty girl on a down comforter as soft as a cloud surrounded by a hundred pink rose petals. I keep my eyes open as I lunge over the precipice. He's right. It's a beautiful sight.

His words replay in my head. *Remember who's making you feel this way.*

He was talking about me, not him.

I hear the rip of the condom one second before he's on top of me. Then inside of me. I cry out at the sudden attack. He stops.

He sucks in a breath. "I'm sorry, baby. I need you right now. Should I stop?"

I clutch his arms and move my hips up to deepen our connection. "Never. I'm yours."

His expression darkens with every thrust. I wrap my legs around his hips. I stare at the muscles of his back in the mirror. His sculpted ass. The flex of his powerful legs as he fucks me. He sucks and bites my neck. I grip a fistful of bed sheet along with a handful of rose petals.

"Mason, I lo—"

His mouth is on me swallowing the rest of the sentence.

Then I can't speak. At least nothing understandable. I let go again. We cling to each other, our body's slick, our breaths harsh, and our hearts pounding.

He lifts his head. I trace the curve of his smile with my finger. He pushes a strand of hair from my forehead and kisses me. It's so tender and completely clashes with the rough sex we just had. But it's exactly what I need.

He goes to the bathroom. I leer at his beautiful butt the whole way. When he returns, the bed dips with his weight. He lies on his back next to me. We both stare at the image of us.

"What do you think of the mirror now, Kiran?"

"It's cool."

"Just cool?"

"Okay, that was really hot. I totally get the lesson too, professor."

He laughs. "Lesson? I just wanted to witness you get yourself off."

I lean on my elbow. "Shut up, I'm on to you, Cutler, and what you were trying to show me."

"And what's that?"

I have no idea how to put all the crazy, passionate emotions into words. "The power was with me all along."

He quirks an eyebrow. "Baby, I'm gonna need some nachos for all that cheese." He bursts out laughing.

I feign being offended. For the love of Dorothy and her ruby red slippers, did I really just say that? I go to smack his chest, but his reflexes are sharp. He grabs my wrist before it makes contact and pulls me in for a deep kiss.

Once we calm down, I lay my head on his chest and listen to his heartbeat. I'm trying to live in this moment, but the room is drenched in amber light, signaling the sun's departure. I trace the words inside the inked star on his arm. "It means love."

"What does?"

"The words inside the star tattoo. I've been trying to figure it out. It always protects, always trusts, always hopes, always perseveres." I tilt my head, trace the star on his arm and the words once more. "I wasn't sure what the 'it' meant, but it's referring to love." I know those aren't just words. It's a code Mason lives by.

He strokes my hair. "Correct."

"Let's talk about the future."

"Okay, tell me all about Iowa."

"Not my future, Mason. Our future."

He swallows. There is something in his expression that causes the room to feel ten degrees colder.

"We don't have one." He slices through every shred of hope.

I push myself off him. "You can't mean that."

"Kiran, listen to me. You haven't been living for the past few years. I'm not going to deny you any experiences."

"You won't. I love you and you love me. I'll go to Iowa and you'll go to the Marines. And we'll be fine."

"We won't. We've only known each other for what? Eight days."

"So you don't love me?"

"I didn't say that."

"Then what the fuck are you saying?"

"Calm down, Kiran. Let me explain myself. We're on vacation in this tropical paradise and what works here doesn't translate to the real world. Do you know how difficult it is to have a long distance relationship with someone in the military?"

"I don't know, but it doesn't mean we can't try."

"Thirty days a year. That's what I get for leave. It's not enough."

"I'll take thirty days. It's enough for me. We can write and e-mail and text and call and—"

"It's not enough for me. We're not pretending to live in a sandcastle on the beach this time. I can't dream with you anymore."

"Shut up, Mason. Don't say anything else."

He doesn't listen. "What if you meet someone who's perfect for you? I know you. You'll keep those feelings locked up because you'll be scared of hurting me."

"I did meet someone who's perfect for me, asshole. The last thing I'm doing is keeping those feelings locked up."

He reaches for my hand, but I pull it away.

"Listen to me, Kiran, this isn't easy for me either."

"Oh, you're struggling with this, Mason? Because you seem to have it all figured out. Don't I even get a say?"

He shakes his head. "No, you don't get a say. The bottom line is I can't have you in my life either. I'd constantly be worried about you. Honestly, I need to be worried about me and Dana and the guys in my unit."

I squeeze my eyes shut, trying to hold in the tears, but they wrench free anyway.

"Don't cry. Please don't cry," he says in a raspy whisper.

Too late, Mason. I get off the bed and run around the room gathering my clothes.

"Where you going?"

"Don't worry about me. You have enough on your mind. There's no room for me."

I can't find my panties or bra so I just throw on my shirt and jeans. I finish buttoning the shirt as I walk toward the door.

"Don't leave."

"You left me."

I run down twelve flights of stairs and through the lobby. By the time I exit the huge revolving doors, I'm gasping for breath. I keep going anyway, jogging through deep sand, avoiding the bonfires and the live band. I walk across several hotels until I reach the fence. I climb it in my flip flops. It's only when I reach the other side that I let myself cry. I sob so hard I fall to my knees. I cry until I can barely catch a breath.

I flinch when a strong arm hooks around my shoulder.

"Leave me alone, Mason."

"I won't. I'm sorry I'm hurting you, but if you don't think I'm hurting me too, you're wrong. I'm slashing a knife through my gut."

"Then why?"

"Because this killer pain will hurt less than five lonely years."

He wraps his arms around me. I don't want to hug him back, but my heart is at odds with my head. The heart wins. I grab hold of him. I cry. He makes a muffled grunting sound like he's trying to keep it together. We do this until the sky darkens, illuminated only by stars.

I relax in his arms. I think about what he's doing. I don't agree with him, but I understand his sad rationale. Clearly, this is difficult for him too. These feelings are powerful, but it has only been eight days. We're both headed in completely different directions. Where he's going he doesn't need to carry any additional weight. I hate him right now. But I love him too. I want to protect him, and maybe that means I make a sacrifice.

So I'm going to soldier up and not make him feel any worse for this decision. Maybe we found refuge in the safe harbor of each other's arm. But we have to keep moving toward the path we've set for ourselves. He wipes my tears and tucks a loose strand behind my ear. "Will you forgive me?"

"Yes. We're both young, and we haven't tested ourselves. Life isn't fruity drinks and walks on the beach and dreamy sandcastles."

"Right." He exhales. "I want you to date other people, explore the world, and—"

"Cutler, if you tell me to find myself, I will punch you in the nose."

He manages a weak smile. "I was going to say be yourself. People will fall in love with you. It's very easy to do. I should know."

I kiss his cheek. "Don't take any risks you don't have to. When you're busy protecting the rest of the world, promise me you'll do everything to keep yourself safe. I worry you'll forget."

"I promise."

"This is unfair.

"It's a raw hand. But sweetheart, know this, I wouldn't trade these days for anything in the entire world. We just met at the wrong time."

"When is the right time?"

He shrugs. "Don't know. A year ago yesterday or maybe five years from tomorrow?"

"Nothing we can do about a year ago yesterday."

"No, we can't." A flash of surprise flickers across his face. "We can try for five years from tomorrow, though."

"What do you mean?"

"Let's make a pact. If neither of us has found anyone else and these feelings we have right now still exist in five years, then we will meet back here."

"That's a ridiculous plan."

"I know it is. But it's all I got. Just hear me out. In five years, you'll be done with school and into your career. You'll know what you want in this life. My contract will be over. I'll be able to offer you more than thirty days a year."

"What if one of us doesn't show?"

"Then the other one moves on. No hard feelings."

"Can I write to you?"

He shakes his head. "I don't think it's a good idea, Kiran. I really can't deal with bits and pieces of you. In five years, if it's right for both of us, I can give you all of me. Honey, I'll be wanting all of you too."

"You know I'll think the worst. What if something happens…?" God, I can't even finish the sentence. Thankfully, I don't have to.

He places a finger under my chin and lifts my face to meet his. "I'll make sure word gets sent to you."

"If I don't show up, you won't wonder what happened to me?"

"Of course, I will. We'll send a letter so the other one knows what happened. No hard feelings either way. If you've found happiness, then I'll be happy for you. You do the same for me, Kiran."

"How do you propose we send a letter if I'm not even allowed to write to you?"

He thinks about it for a minute. "We'll send our letters in care of the hotel."

"But if something happens to you..."

"I'll have Dana post my letter to you."

"Five years is forever."

"It's not, darling. For someone who's lived in a shell for the past few years, it'll fly by."

"First you compare me to a barnacle and now you make me sound like a crab."

He chuckles. "I was talking about me. It applies to both of us, though." He puts his hands on my shoulders and takes a deep breath. "So what are your thoughts?"

"It's a stupid idea."

"Never said it was brilliant. Just said it's all I got. Can you at least consider it?"

It is something...this plan of his. Some shred of hope to temper the pain in my heart. "Yes."

His smile is so bright and pure I have to match it. "Yes?"

"Yes, Mason. If things are right, I'll see you five years from tomorrow."

"Thank you." He kisses me. It's a tender kiss, soft and slow and passionate.

We both stand. The stars sparkle tonight. They look so close I bet I can reach out and pluck one.

"Is that the big dipper?" he asks, pointing to the constellation.

"It's there," I say, moving his hand. "See the star in the middle? The really bright one?"

"The North Star."

"Yeah, do me a favor, Mason. Look for it sometimes when you're out in the world. It's only visible in the northern hemisphere, and you can't always see it, but try to find it sometimes, okay?"

"Why?"

"Because I'll be looking for it too."

"Okay."

"Promise?"

"Cross my heart, darling." We both take in the amazing starry sky. I think this is the kind of night that inspired Van Gogh.

He takes my hand and leads me back toward the fence. "There's a heart-shaped hot tub waiting for us. We should get back, don't you think?"

Chapter 19

Mason

We talked and held each other all night. When sunrise came, we both left for our separate rooms to pack. Her flight's at ten AM so she's checking out early. I'm leaving when she does. There is no way I can stay here a minute longer without her. I do a quick check of my room to make sure I didn't leave anything behind. My phone rings just as I'm about to shut the door.

"Hey, sis, what's up?"

"What's the deal not returning my call? I left you a voicemail yesterday."

"Sorry I missed it. How's school?" Dana had opted to start in the summer and get a few prerequisites out of the way. The timing worked out for both of us to start a new course in our lives.

"Amazing. I can't wait to show you around."

The plan is for me to drive home, pack up the last suitcase, hand over the keys to the renters, and catch a flight to San Diego where I'll spend two days with Dana before reporting for duty. "Me too."

"So?"

"So what?"

"Do you hate me for forcing you go on this trip or do you realize how awesome I am?"

I glance out the window. Kiran is walking along the beach. The breeze plays with her long, dark hair. Guess she wanted one last walk.

"Mason?" Dana says.

I realize I've been quiet. "Sorry. You're awesome."

"You okay, bro?"

"Yeah. Why?"

"'Cause I didn't expect you to admit my awesomeness so quickly."

"I'm good, Dana. I had a great trip. I'll tell you all about it when I see you."

"Okay. Love you. Drive safe."

"Will do."

An hour later, Kiran and I are packed and checking out. Her teacher, Mrs. Waters, is working the front desk today. I try not to laugh at the way Kiran blushes.

"You sure you don't want me to drive you to the airport?" I ask her.

"I'd rather catch a cab."

I understand her reasoning. All we've done for the last twenty-four hours is say good-bye. It's in every kiss, every hug, and every touch. We don't need to continue that at the departure counter.

"We never made it to the revolving restaurant at the Wilshire," she says, staring at her keycard.

"It'll be the first thing on our list next time."

"Sure."

She's not convinced about the five-year plan. I wish I could show her it's not something I cooked up to appease her. I'm invested and sincere. I slide my room key to Mrs. Waters.

"How was your stay?" she asks.

"Good." Good isn't the right word. But right now, I'm too tired for anything else.

Kiran gives me a soft smile.

"It was so good I'd like to make another reservation." The words tumble out of my mouth without much thought, but it feels right. Especially when I see her smile brighten.

"That's wonderful. What dates?"

"Five years from today in the Sweetheart's Suite under the names Mason Cutler and Kiran Shenoy."

Mrs. Waters laughs nervously as if I'm joking. "I'm afraid I can't make a reservation that far out. The computer won't let me."

This won't do. I want a permanent placeholder for us like a bookmark in the middle of a novel. The story hasn't ended. To be continued. "We'll prepay. You can put it in the computer when it's time."

"I'm sorry, hon, that's not our policy."

I turn to the woman, her face kind but unyielding. "Ma'am, can you find it in your heart to break the rules just this one time?"

"I wish I could, young man. It'll be years until I can book your stay."

"I trust you, ma'am." I put my arm around Kiran and pull her close to me. "We both do."

She shakes her head. "Why you don't just call us in a few years?"

That would make sense. Except I want someone else to hold this date for Kiran and me in this moment. The plan doesn't seem as silly if it's written down somewhere.

"Mrs. Waters," Kiran chimes in, her voice low. "Jane Austen was your favorite author, right?"

The woman looks confused. "Yes, but what does that have to do with this?"

"Do you believe Elizabeth Bennet and Mr. Darcy would have gotten together without Mrs. Gardiner?"

Mrs. Waters removes her glasses and considers Kiran's question. They might as well be speaking a foreign language as far as I'm concerned.

"It's an interesting premise."

"My point is that Elizabeth and Darcy needed her to bring them together. Just as Mason and I need you now. So please, make an exception to the rules." She slides closer to me. "Be the hero in our story, Mrs. Waters."

The woman sighs. Not a frustrated get-the-hell-out-of-here sigh, but the kind of sigh girls make when they're thinking of something good. I almost want to high-five her. Instead, I put my arm around her and kiss her temple.

The woman rifles through a drawer forever. Finally, she takes out a sheet of paper. She slides it toward me. "You'll have to fill this out. I'll make sure it gets in the system as soon as I'm allowed."

When we're checked out and our future stay is in the safe hands of Mrs. Waters, I pull Kiran in my arms one last time and kiss her deeply. "I'll have to read Jane Austen because you really persuaded her."

She taps a finger against her lips. "*Persuasion* might have been a better example."

"What?"

"Nothing."

The cab she's called pulls up. I load her luggage in the trunk.

"Good-bye, Mason." She places her hand over my heart. "Don't forget what I said."

"I won't, Kiran. I'll look for the North Star, and I swear I'll protect myself." I tuck a strand of hair behind her ear and run my thumb across the birthmark on her wrist one last time. "And you don't forget either."

"I'll live my life. I'll take risks and have adventures. I won't be a barnacle."

"You're gonna do great things in this world, Kiran Shenoy. I know it." I kiss her forehead. "Good-bye, sunshine."

"Good-bye, Mason." She closes her eyes. "Good-bye for now."

"For now."

I open the door for her. I'm struggling to keep it together. It's not until the taxi is out of my vision that I finally pick up my duffle bag and head to the parking lot and my car. I throw the duffle back in the passenger seat. A piece of the hotel stationery sticks out of the side pocket. It's folded into a tight square. I carefully unfold it. A small piece of twine adorned with tiny seashells falls out.

The note is written in her neat script. I close my eyes and take a deep breath before I read her words.

Mason, I told you I would learn how to make seashell jewelry so we can sell it to the tourists. Remember when we were dreaming? Don't forget to dream, okay? See you in five years. I love you. Be safe. Yours, Kiran.

She dotted the I with a smiley face.

I love you too, baby.

Chapter 20

Kiran

Five Years Later...

The feelings never died. I thought of him every day. I wasn't obsessed, but Mason Cutler's hold on my heart never weakened. Every cell in my body is at attention as I walk up to the check-in desk.

What if Mrs. Waters never made the reservation? Yes, because that's my biggest worry right now. I tell myself to calm down.

The hotel has had a serious makeover. Gone are the gaudy palm trees and dated wallpaper. The walls are a neutral sand color with nice pops of blues and greens. It all has an upscale beachy Zen feel. I barely notice it, though.

"May I help you?" the girl at the front desk asks. She wears a business suit that seems out of character here.

"I'm checking in."

"Do you have a reservation?"

"Yes. It's under Kiran Shenoy and Mason Cutler for the Sweetheart's Suite."

"We don't call it that anymore. It's been The Paradise Room for two years now." I prefer Sweetheart's Suite, but I keep that to myself. She rapidly punches a few keys on her computer. My pulse notches higher with each click. There is a large sign behind her with a photo of a colorful pail and bucket. It advertises Jasper's annual sandcastle-building contest. It's happening tomorrow. Deciding it's a positive symbol, I smile.

"Ah, here it is. I'll get your keycard."

Mrs. Waters came through for us. I want to thank her. "Is Mrs. Waters still here?"

"Afraid not. She retired a year ago. I'll need a credit card for incidentals."

I hand her my card.

More key punching. More heart pounding.

"Am I the first to check in?" I ask, my voice tinged with desperation.

"Yes."

Stop freaking, he'll be here soon. It'll give me a chance to take a shower. Tonight we'll go to the revolving restaurant at the Wilshire. That is if we make it out of the room. It's going to be just fine.

"There's a note here," the girl says. She squints at her monitor. "This is unusual. It says a letter arrived for you yesterday."

Something inside of me cries out. I close my eyes and let out the breath I'd been holding for a long time. Maybe I held it for five whole years.

After taking the note and my keycard, I walk toward the elevator on shaky legs. The elevator has been modernized so the car moves swiftly without any hesitation. Even the Sweetheart's Suite or The Paradise Room or whatever the hell it is now has gotten a makeover. Gone is the over-the-top décor. There is no mirror over the bed, no Grecian stripper pillars, and no plastic twinkle-light palm tree. In their place are more aesthetically pleasing, subtle choices. It doesn't matter, though. I don't have the stomach to be in this room. I drop my bag on the bed and head to the beach.

I find a patch of sand sparse of people. I sit, crisscrossing my legs, and run my hand across the letter. It's my name and the hotel's address written in block letters. There is no return address. Why did we agree on a letter and not an e-mail? This isn't a freaking Jane Austen novel after all.

But that was part of our pact. Not to exchange any information. I tell myself not to freak out until I've read it, but there are only two scenarios in which he'd send a letter. Neither of them is good.

One is that the letter I'm holding is the one Mason wrote and asked Dana to send if he didn't make it.

The other possibility is that he is fine, but the feelings aren't there anymore. Maybe he's met someone else. Maybe he never loved me at all.

Either possibility would be devastating. Before I rip open the envelope, I say a prayer it's the second. The second would mean he's alive.

I open the envelope. The sheet inside is just a few paragraphs long and typed.

Dear Kiran,

First, let me say I am fine. I made it home just fine.

Thank you, God. I clutch my heart, all the tense muscles relaxing for the first time since I arrived. I sit straighter and read the rest.

My hope is you didn't come and this letter is moot. But if you are reading it, then I am so sorry. I've met someone. It happened a couple years ago.

I wish we'd come up with a few more stipulations regarding our plan so I could have saved you this trip. You were right. The plan was stupid. But that's who I was when I met you—young and stupid and too idealistic for my own good. All I can do is apologize to you.

Don't for one second think I didn't mean all the things I said to you. You're an amazing person and I'm thankful you were a part of my life. The days we spent together will always hold a special place in my heart. We were under the trance of amazing sunrises and rolling waves and full moons. We did have quite a few drinks in there too. The point is eight days in the sun isn't enough to make a life. I hope you'll forgive me and understand. Actually, you have to forgive me. You owe that to me because you agreed. No hard feelings if one of us doesn't show up. So please remember that and don't hate me.

Sincerely,
Mason Cutler.

The ink smudges as salty tears fall on the page. I have a good, long cry, the kind that wracks my entire body and leaves me gasping for breath. He met someone. He's happy. I'm relived he's all right. Relieved and heartbroken and angry. Why did he type it? It's so impersonal.

I can't stay here. I have to leave on the next plane bound for New Jersey or anywhere close to it. Everywhere I look there is a memory of him. Of us. I head back to the room to retrieve my unpacked luggage.

The girl at the reception desk looks worried when I approach. "Is something wrong with the room?"

"No, it's fine. But I'd like to check out."

"Already? You just checked in."

I slide the keycard to her. "Something came up." I turn to leave.

"Wait, let me get you a receipt."

I'm about to tell her I don't need one when I see an older lady approaching me.

"Hello, Kiran."

She has more gray hairs now and walks with a cane. "Mrs. Waters, I thought you retired."

"I did, dear. I came to see you. That little speech you gave has stayed with me through the years." She looks around and back at me.

I bite my lower lip to stop it from trembling.

Her smile disappears. She puts her hand on my shoulder. "Oh dear, I'm so sorry. Your young man isn't here then?"

I shake my head, afraid if I say something the tears will start up again.

"Would you like to get a cup of tea?"

"I have to take a rain check. I'm actually leaving."

"I thought he'd be here for sure, considering all the confirmations."

"Here's your receipt," the clerk says. I take it from her and stuff it in my purse.

"Bye," I tell Mrs. Waters, giving her a light hug.

"Good-bye Kiran."

I'm almost to the revolving doors when her words replay in my head. I turn and scan the area for her. She's still by the receptionist desk.

"Mrs. Waters?"

"Yes, Kiran."

"What did you mean when you said the confirmations?"

She holds a hand over her ear, indicating she can't hear me. I'm being rude yelling a question at her across the room. I leave my suitcase and run over to her.

"You said you thought he'd show considering all the confirmations. What did you mean?"

"It's nothing. I'm just a silly old lady, a little too enamored with love stories."

"You're not silly. Please tell me."

"He'd call every year around this time to check on the reservation. Sometimes I'd pick up the phone. When I didn't, he'd ask for me. Each time we chatted he would remind me who he was. Why he thought I'd forget, I have no idea." She arches a silver brow. "He is quite handsome, your young man."

I don't correct her that he's not my young man. Her expression sobers at what she's said, and she places her hand over her mouth. "I didn't mean…"

"It's all right. When was the last time he called?"

She thinks about it for a few seconds. "A year ago."

"Are you sure?"

"I remember because I told him I was retiring. He wished me luck. I let him know anyone at the hotel could confirm his reservation in the future. He said he wouldn't need another confirmation, since he'd be here himself in a year. He was always a pleasure to chat with and so polite."

I hug her again, longer this time. "Thank you."

* * * *

When I arrive at the airport, the lady behind the counter also punches in a ton of keys as she searches for a flight back to New Jersey. None of this makes sense. Mason's letter said he met someone a couple years ago. Yet, Mrs. Waters said he called just last year. The letter itself was typed and impersonal. Plus, he dismissed our time together like we were under a spell. Yeah, maybe we were idealistic and young, but it wasn't a dream. It was real. All of it.

What does it matter, though? Maybe I'll cheat and do a Facebook or Google search for him. I'll get the nerve to ask him one day, but that doesn't feel right either. I need to see him. I need him to tell me to my face. Short of searching every small town within a forty-five-minute radius of Charleston, I'm not sure how to do that.

"I found a flight," the girl says, breaking into my chaotic thoughts. "It's boarding in an hour, though, so you'll have to hurry."

"Great." I rifle through my purse to give her my credit card. The receipt from the hotel falls out. I grab the crumpled paper. The answer to my dilemma stares back at me in crisp twelve-point Helvetica font.

Mason's address is on this form. His home address. It's possible he doesn't live there anymore. Even if he does, who just shows up unannounced after receiving a break-up letter? Who does that?

The woman behind the counter clears her throat. She's holding her hand out for my credit card.

"I actually need the next flight to South Carolina, please." I guess I do that.

"You said Newark."

"I changed my mind. I need to go to Goodrich, South Carolina, or at least the closest airport to it, which I believe is Charleston."

She sighs, touching the neat bun on top of her head. "Are you sure this time?"

"No." I hand her my credit card. "But that's where I need to go."

She looks at me like she's trying to figure out where my straightjacket snaps up. Thankfully, she starts pecking buttons again.

* * * *

I waited at the airport for six hours for the next flight. I had a layover in Atlanta. The Charleston airport is quite a distance from the town of Goodrich so I opted to rent a car. But it was four in the morning so I waited another four hours for the rental place to open up.

I finally get the car and start driving toward Goodrich. Then the map app on my phone loses connection a few times, but after two wrong turns, I straighten myself out. By the time I pull up to the craftsman style house on a quiet, pristine, tree-lined street, I'm not nervous. I'm too tired to be nervous. I've been traveling over twenty-four hours.

The house is as sound and masculine as Mason. There's an American flag flying high on one of the beams. An old-fashion white swing sways on the porch. Wind chimes jingle an ominous song that reminds me what I'm here for. I ring the doorbell and take a deep breath.

The girl who answers is gorgeous, tall, and shapely from her pixie blond hair down to her pink tennis shoes.

"Are you here for an interview?" she asks.

"Interview?"

She has freckles and dimples. They just notch up the cute factor. "For the companion position."

"I'm for that," a lady says. I turn back. I'm so lost in my head I didn't even notice a cab pulled up behind me.

"I'm Dorothy Shue. Don't tell me you scheduled two interviews at the same time." Dorothy doesn't seem old except for the way she carries herself, as if she's walking on quicksand. She looks like she's just sucked on a raw lemon or two.

"No," the girl answers. "Please come in."

"Does Mason Cutler still live here?" I ask.

Dimple girl smiles. "He sure does."

And you're his girlfriend.

Before I can say anything else, Dorothy interrupts us. "Should I tell him to wait?" She points to the cab.

"I thought you drove. That's one of the requirements."

"I do. Just don't have a running vehicle at the moment. We can discuss the details." She yells at the driver to wait for her. She stops at the foot of the stairs and expels a heavy sigh. "These are a lot of stairs."

I go down the steps to where she is. The dimple girl does the same. This is awkward. Here I am with Mason's new girlfriend helping this elderly woman up the stairs. In all the millions of ways I pictured this moment, this never came to mind.

"Make yourself comfortable, Dorothy," Mason's girlfriend says, gesturing to the long beige couch in the living room. Dorothy drops her bag on the floor. I wince when it lands with a loud thud. What does she have in there? Bricks?

"I can use a drink, sweetie," Dorothy announces, followed by a loud huff.

"Certainly," the girl says through gritted teeth. "I'll fetch you some water."

"I'd prefer ice tea."

"I can make some."

"Well, you should hurry." She points toward the open doorway. "The meter's running."

The girl mutters something inarticulate. Then she turns to me, her eyes narrowing. "I'm sorry, who are you?"

"I'm here to see Mason," I say. Why am I even going through this? The proof of his letter is standing right in front of me clad in a vintage Ramones

T-shirt and cut-off jeans. When did I become that desperate girl I despise? I know all her forms—stalker, hussy, pathetic, home-wrecker wannabe.

The girl's blue eyes suddenly widen, and her jaw drops. "Kiran?"

So Mason told her about me. They probably laughed over stories about the silly girl who gave him her whole heart after just eight days.

I hold out my hand for a handshake. It's just my way of saying I give up and you win.

She throws her arms around me in an awkward hug. "I'm Dana."

My body shakes with relief as the tightly constrained muscles ache with the release of tension. I return her smile. Oh, this is Dana, Mason's kid sister. I should have seen the family resemblance. Her hair's lighter than his, but she has the same crystal cut blue eyes.

"Dana, he told me all about you. I feel like I know you."

"Same here, Kiran."

"Is he here?"

Her smile falters as if she's trying really hard to keep it in place. "Um… Yes, he's in the backyard by the shed with Molly."

Oh, Molly.

Just when the cut in my heart eases, the knife turns into a machete.

"Does Molly make him happy?"

Why the hell did I ask that question? I must enjoy torture.

"Sure. She's amazing."

Dorothy taps her foot, reminding us both she's still there. "Unless you plan to reimburse me for the cab, I'd appreciate if we can get on with this."

"Sorry, ma'am. Just hold up a minute, please."

"It's okay," I say. "I'm going to go now. I'm sorry I disturbed you."

She follows me out. "Did he tell you about Molly?"

"Yes, he told me he found someone. I thought for a second that was you."

She wrinkles her nose. "That's gross."

I make my way down the steps. "Good-bye, Dana. If you can do me a favor and not tell him I came here, I'd appreciate it."

"Wait, Kiran." I turn in time to witness Dana jumping off the porch, over all six steps. I'm still in shock with that little maneuver when she moves in front of me. "Don't you want to see Mason?"

"No. I should get going."

"Don't tell me you came all this way just to leave," Dana says. "Go see him for yourself, but don't leave here without at least saying hello."

Dorothy mutters something. I'm not sure what she says, but it's loud enough to come through the open door and down the front path. Dana sighs and points to the house. "I have to take care of this. He's around back."

Leaving it clear the decision is mine, she heads up the steps. I lean on the rental car for a minute contemplating. I'm drained, but how can I walk away? I'm here now. If I see him with her, then I'll accept this and move on. It'll be the last proverbial nail in the coffin that is our relationship.

I walk around the house. I stop in my tracks when I see him on the paved patio. He's sitting on a lawn chair, outside of a very large shed, drinking a beer. My heart leaps at the sight of him. Stupid heart. He looks the same. His light brown hair still has strands of honey and cinnamon, but it's on the longer side. He has sunglasses on, but even in a sitting position, I can see he's still long and lean. A golden retriever lifts its head as I walk toward him. I look around for Molly, but she's nowhere to be found.

"Is she here?" he asks, not even looking up. He sighs. "Let's get on with it."

"Hi, Mason."

His face clenches. The bottle in his hand shakes. "Kiran?"

"I wanted to see you."

"Didn't you get my letter?"

"Yes."

"Then I don't understand why you're here."

"Would I be a douche if I asked you to take off your sunglasses? I feel like I'm having a conversation with myself." It's something he said to me once.

He takes them off, folds them, and places them in his shirt pocket. God, his face is still beautiful, all chiseled planes and two days past a shave.

"How did you get my address?" He still isn't looking at me.

"Does it matter?"

"Suppose not." The dog must sense his frustration because it sidles closer to him. He pets her. "It's okay, Molly."

I almost laugh. Molly is a dog.

"Are you really with someone else?"

"Kiran, we made a deal." He looks at his beer as if it's some interesting object he just can't put down.

"Fuck the deal."

"What do you want me to tell you? I don't want to be with you. Isn't that enough? You really are a glutton for punishment, aren't you? Obviously, you still have all those self-esteem issues. You need a therapist, Shenoy, not a boyfriend."

My legs almost give out. But he wants me to run away. I refuse and stand my ground. "Don't talk to me like that, Mason. We don't talk to each other like that. Can you at least look at me?"

He doesn't look at me. Instead, he laughs. The sound of it is so bitter and cold it sends a shiver up my spine even though the air is heavy with humidity. "What did you think showing up here was going to accomplish? Wait, let me guess. You wanted to hear it from me, right? Because the letter wasn't enough?" His questions are flung at me, tiny sharp accusations that pierce my skin.

I nod, my finger nails biting into the flesh of my palms.

"Answer me," he says. He isn't yelling, but somehow that makes it even worse.

"Y-yes."

"Okay, listen up real close, girl. I'm only gonna say this once more. I do not want you. I never did. What kind of fucked-up person waits five years for someone else?"

"I do." I point to myself. "This fucked-up person does, but not anymore. Good-bye, Mason."

"So long, Shenoy. Don't come back here."

I should run, but I don't have the strength. Voices and random thoughts echo through my head. He barely looked at me. Molly is a dog. He called every year to confirm the reservation. Are you here for the companion position? The letter was typed. He thought I was Dana at first.

Oh. My. God.

I turn around. "Why didn't you tell me?"

He rubs his temples. I see the cracks in the façade. A few tiny, white scars crisscross the hard planes of his face. There are dark circles under his eyes and the golden tan of his skin is gone. He's at least three shades paler. "Tell you what?"

"You're blind." I run back to him and bend down. I touch his hair. He flinches. "Mason, did you think this changes anything for me?"

"It doesn't matter if it changes anything. I'm blind, but on this issue I am seeing clearly. I don't want you because I don't want you. There doesn't have to be any other reason than that. So please, let me go and live my life." The dog barks at me. "You're upsetting my dog."

"I'm upsetting you. Just talk to me."

"I did talk. I wrote you a letter. I told you in person now too. I've talked an awful lot. Trouble is you're not listening to me. Please just go. Leave me alone."

My legs almost give out when I stand. Walking away from him is the hardest thing I've ever done. When I round the corner, I hear something crash.

"Hey," Dana says as I open the door to the car. "You saw him."

"Yeah." I curl my fingers around the door handle.

"What now?"

"I'm headed back to New Jersey."

"I'm sorry, Kiran. I thought he told you the truth in his letter."

"He didn't. When did it happen?"

"About ten months ago."

"A roadside bomb? IED?"

"A human bomb. Mason didn't have a chance. It detached his retinas. He was about two months away from coming home when it happened."

I close my eyes tight, trying to keep it together to voice my next question. "Is he in pain?"

"No. Well, not physically at least. What did he say to you?"

"It doesn't matter. I shouldn't have come here. I should have respected his wishes."

She crosses her arms. "You don't want to be with him because he's blind. The way he talked about you I thought better of you."

The last thread of sanity snaps inside of me. "Shut up. You think this is why I'm leaving? I've spent almost twelve of the last twenty-four hours on a plane. I haven't slept in three days. I've said a prayer for him every single night for the past five years. I had no idea if he was all right, but I kept the faith, performed my vigil, and did everything he asked of me. He's been blind for ten months, and you can't even give me ten minutes to get used to it before you fling accusations? Just so you know, this is not my choice. It's his. What do you suppose I should do, huh? Force him to feel something he doesn't?"

"I'm sorry. I forgot."

"Forgot what?"

"Mason is a dick."

God help me, I actually laugh, which transforms into a sob. "I have to go."

How many times can a person be told to get out before they listen?

Somewhere inside the house, Dorothy yells, "Can we please get on with this?"

Dana sighs. "This woman is going to be the death of me. Let me get rid of her, and we'll talk."

"I've said everything I need to."

"You have to be exhausted, Kiran. Don't get on another plane. Stay the night. Not in town. The fleabag inn is the last place I'd recommend. But there's a really nice Wilshire in Charleston. It's close to the airport. I'm sure they have rooms this time of year. Just check in, and we can meet for drinks at the bar. Say around eight?"

I consider arguing with her, but I am tired. Every bone in my body aches. I can't handle another plane today. Also, I still have a few questions.

"Wilshire at eight."

Chapter 21

Kiran

I order a glass of wine. Dana orders a beer. She's wearing a T-shirt that says *Pluto is not a planet. Get over it.*

We both stare at each other, waiting for the other to go first.

"Is Mason alone right now?" I ask.

Dana plays with the label of her bottle. "Yeah. He can be alone."

"So he's had rehab?"

"A lot of rehab. In fact, I think he overdoes it. He also had a two-week course with Molly. They matched them."

"They fit well together. Why did you want to meet, Dana? Mason told me he doesn't want anything to do with me."

"I guess I didn't want you to leave like that. I'm really sorry it didn't work out and for what I said to you. Mason told me about the pact y'all made. The idea sounded so stupid to me."

"I know, right?"

She roars in laughter. "I'm sorry. For what it's worth, I did think it was romantic. Mostly illogical, though. Then again, I live on the cynical side of the equation."

"Cynical side?"

"I'm a scientist."

"Is there a chance he'll ever see again?"

"If he eats a lot of carrots."

"Are you really making jokes?"

"Sorry. It's in poor taste, I know. It's just been hard. We've both been trying to keep our sense of humor, even though it's twisted. It's highly unlikely he'll see again. The retinas are detached. They cannot be repaired through surgery."

It's not until Dana hands me a napkin that I realize I'm crying. I take a long sip of water and try to stifle my feelings so I can ask her the rest of my questions. She's patient. After a few deep breaths, I manage to speak, although my voice comes out thick and hopeless. "If Mason is self-reliant, why does he need a companion?"

"The companion deal was my idea. His stubborn ass still argues with me. It's a companion, not a babysitter, I keep saying."

"Why does he need one, though?"

"I might need to go away for a while."

"You're a marine biologist, right?"

She gives me a confused look. "Yes."

"Mason told me you were going to school for it."

"I graduated and found a great job in San Diego. When I got the call about Mason, I quit my job. Mason lived with me for a while in Cali until the renter's lease was up. He wanted to move back to Goodrich. He said I should have stayed in San Diego, but there's no way I'd leave him. I found work as a hydrologist in Charleston."

"I'm not sure what that is."

She waves her hand. "Most people don't. I perform research experiments to find ways to eliminate water pollution."

"That's impressive."

"It would be if we could get more funding or lobbyists or anything. As of right now, I perform the research and write papers. Tons of papers that I'm sure make very lovely fish wrap."

I want to interrupt and ask what this has to do with the companion position, but I wait for her to continue. She takes a long drag of her beer. "That might all change, though." Her blues eyes twinkle with excitement. "I've been invited to go on an expedition to Antarctica."

"Antarctica?"

Her dimple deepens as she smiles wider. "Yeah, isn't it amazing?"

"Not to me, but I'm happy for you. Why Antarctica?"

"It has most of the Earth's fresh water, and the ozone is almost depleted. It's a marine biologists dream and also a nightmare because the news is never good. Anyway, I'm able to study the effects on the indigenous fish and macro fauna there. It'll provide some vital data about what we're doing to our water. Or at least I hope it will. Without water, there isn't an Earth. No blue means no green. So unless we want to live like the people of Mars, we need to get our act together."

"Um, Dana, there are no people on Mars."

She lifts up her bottle, holding it out in a mock toast. "And that would be my point."

I recognize the same enthusiasm and wry sense of humor in both the Cutler children. Actually, I'm not sure if Mason has those characteristics anymore. But I can see why he's so proud of her. She has the energy of a hundred rabbits, a brain Stephen Hawking would find sexy, and a contagious passion.

"Wow." I hold out my glass for a real toast. "That's incredible. I feel really lazy next to you. I think my biggest accomplishment this year is doing my own taxes."

Dana clinks my glass. "Well, I've never done my own taxes so I'll drink to that. But I'd disagree. The article you wrote about the refugees won an award, didn't it?"

"How do you know about that?"

She shrugs. "Mason told me about it."

"Mason reads my articles?"

She gives a slight nod, playing with the label of her bottle. "He subscribes to online magazines and has an app on his phone that reads everything out loud. About the article, I thought you had an interesting take about losing your homeland and identity."

So maybe he read it by chance and wasn't seeking me out. Either way, what did it really matter? The man had made his feelings clear. Dana shifts in her seat. Clearly, she isn't comfortable revealing this bit of information about her brother. "Thank you. Tell me more about Antarctica."

"It's rare for someone my age to be invited, let alone raise the grant money. I passed it up at first. When Mason found out, he insisted I go. He pressured me so much I finally agreed on one condition."

"That he agrees to a companion?"

"You are smart, just as he said. The rest of that stipulation is that I get to choose. I'm afraid his stubborn butthole self is going to fire them before I even step foot on the boat."

I stifle a giggle. She called Mason a butthole. "How's the search going?"

"Horrible. We can't pay a large wage so we're getting the worst of the riff-raff. You saw evidence of that today."

"You mean Dorothy?"

Dana leans into the table. "I was so frustrated I told her I'd pay for the taxi on the condition she leaves straight away." She shakes her head. "My grams would roll over in her grave at my lack of manners and southern hospitability."

"But you have other applicants?"

"A few. I have to make a decision soon. I leave in a few days. I get we're not paying a lot, but it seems we should have better candidates. It's not like the job requires much, and it comes with free rent for a month. Don't get me wrong, I still think he needs someone there because all this is still new to him. But it's more for my peace of mind than anything. He's very independent. But he's also obstinate. He overdoes it. It would ease my mind to know someone was there to watch over him."

"Just watch over him?"

"That and keep the house clean, make sure he eats more than frozen TV dinners, drive him to the VA hospital in Charleston three times a week for his therapy." She counts off the duties on her fingers. "Oh, and show him where the North Star is."

"The North Star?"

She responds in a one-shoulder shrug. "Don't ask me why. I have no idea what his obsession is with that damn star. But since we've been back, he asks me to go out in the backyard with him and point it out."

The fire I've been trying to smother all day flares once more.

Do you walk away from someone you love just because they ask you to? A smart girl who believes in self-preservation probably would.

Maybe next time I meet a girl like that I'll ask her.

Me... I want to help him. In whatever way I can, even if it makes no sense.

An idea begins to form. I squash it like a tomato. It starts up again, growing wilder. I pull it from the ground like the unwelcomed weed it is. Still it grows. It continues long after Dana has said good night and I'm in my pajamas lying on the king-sized bed in room 203 at the Wilshire. The idea continues to beckon me while I eat a bagel from the continental breakfast. I actually scream at it to go away in the rental car on the way to the airport. Yet, instead of going the four miles to the airport, I turn around and go the forty miles back to Goodrich.

Chapter 22

Mason

"We have to make a decision," Dana says. She flips through a bunch of papers, shuffling them back and forth a million times.

I'm still reeling from Kiran's visit. All I want is to be alone in my studio. Not to mention Dana is frustrating the hell out of me with her endless babble. I reach out and snatch a paper from her. I hear the other ones fall to the ground.

"This one," I say, flapping it around like a white flag.

"You don't even know which one that is."

"I don't fucking care. They're perfect."

She takes the sheet from me. The paper starts to rip before I let go. "This is Jim. Remember Jim?"

"Of course I do. Nice guy. So we're all set. Give him a call." I move to stand. "Now that it's settled, I'm going out to the shed with Molly."

She grabs my arm. "Not so fast."

I hold back a frustrated sigh and sit my ass back down. "Dana—"

"Jim twitched the whole time he was here."

"Cut him some slack. He was nervous."

"Or he was on meth."

"He complimented Gram's tea set."

"Because he was interested in stealing it. I swear he was casing the place."

Damn, why did I have to pick Jim? All the lawyers in the white house couldn't defend that guy. The doorbell rings before I can come up with another argument.

"Another interview?" I ask.

"No. There isn't anyone else. I have no idea who it is."

Thank you unwelcomed solicitor for saving me. I shift, gearing up for Dana to walk away so I can make a hasty escape.

"Don't even," Dana says. "I'll be right back."

Dana says hello with a surprise in her inflection. The footsteps are soft, tentative.

"Who is it Dana?"

The sun's bright today, and it flows through the open door. My heart pounds as the steps grow closer. She still smells the same.

"It's Kiran," Dana says.

"What is she doing here?" I curl my fingers around the wooden armrests of the chair.

"Why don't you ask her yourself?"

"Hi, Mason," she says. "I'm sorry to come uninvited once more, but I hear you're looking for a live-in companion. I'm here to apply for the position."

I wonder if my ears are going bad too.

"Are you serious?" Dana asks.

"Yes."

"No," I say. "We're fine."

"We're not fine, Mason," Dana interjects. "I'm leaving in two days. We don't have anyone. Please sit down."

"Dana—"

"This is my house too, Mason."

I've done my best to make sure Dana is an independent woman, the kind who can stand up to any man. Right now I wish I hadn't worked so hard on that cause.

Kiran sits in the spot closest to me. It has to be her because Dana isn't as demure. She plops down, almost bouncing. Did my sister always exhibit the traits of a baby kangaroo?

"Are you crazy?" I ask, my voice quiet so Dana doesn't hear.

"Mason!" Okay, so I guess the baby kangaroo is closer than I thought.

"Hard to say. The jury's still deliberating," Kiran says.

I fight the smile. She has the same sense of humor, one flavored with a lot of salt. I hate her for this. For showing up just when I've gotten over her.

God, Kiran, it's so fucking good to hear your voice.

"Can you take leave from your day job?" Dana asks in her interview voice.

"I'm a freelance writer. I can work anywhere in the country as long as I have my laptop, which I do. Of course you'll have to understand this will be moonlighting for me. But I can set my own hours so it shouldn't be a problem to work around Mason's appointments."

"Excellent," Dana says.

"No," I say.

"What about your home?" Dana asks, completely ignoring me. "Don't you have to pay rent somewhere else?"

"I rent an apartment in Newark. My roommate will save my room and take care of everything until I return. She'll probably enjoy having it to herself."

I am pretending not to be interested on the outside. On the inside, I want to hear more. Ask her what she thinks of Goodrich, Dana. Ask her if she's had any relationships. Ask her... Oh fuck, what am I doing? Why the hell would Dana ask her any of that? More importantly, why the hell do I care?

"What about your stuff? You'll have to go home and get it, right?"

"I have a suitcase here. I can shop for what I need. My roommate can send me anything vital."

"So you can start right away?"

"Yes."

"And you realize we cannot pay you that much."

"I don't need a salary at all."

"No," I say again.

"Fine," Kiran says, "pay me if you insist."

"That's not what I meant," I say through gritted teeth. I sigh in exasperation. "She has no qualifications," I say in Dana's direction as if Kiran isn't in the room.

"She has the most important qualification, Mason," Dana replies, her voice huffy. "She cares about you. That's really all we need."

"Dana—"

My sister puts her hand on my knee. "Shuttie. Listen to me, butthole."

Butthole—a term of endearment I haven't heard since I was fifteen. It brings back such sentimental memories.

"Dana, get away from me. You stink." Yes, I've also reverted to my teenage self.

She sniffs. "I do not. This is my new perfume. It's organic and environmentally friendly."

"Organic? What do they put in it? Decayed fruit and rats?"

"No, that's just what I put in your dinner last night."

"I thought it was an improvement from your normal cooking."

She sighs, signaling we are done. Kiran is here. I can't keep changing the subject with my really awful comebacks.

"Listen to me, bro."

"Say your piece."

"Do you really want me to go on this trip?"

"Of course I do, Dana. It's a once in a lifetime opportunity for you."

"Then don't stand in my way. You promised you'd let me pick someone. I choose Kiran. I know this is awkward and weird, but I don't trust anyone else with you."

"You don't even know her." I wonder how Kiran looks as she hears this. I don't have to see her face to know how much I've hurt her. Maybe it's a good thing. "I don't even know her anymore."

"Doesn't matter. She still cares about you."

"What makes you say that?"

"She's here, isn't she? Look, Mason, if you don't go through with this, then I'll cancel the trip."

"You can't cancel. You've committed. You've accepted grant money."

"If the choice is going to Antarctica or leaving you with someone unstable like Jim or downright sour like Dorothy, then I won't go. My reputation will be ruined, but whatever."

Damn Dana and her extortionist arguments. She didn't need to go that far. My sister has been through hell, and I would never stand in the way of her dream. "You can go."

"I didn't hear you. Say it again."

"You heard me just fine."

"I know what you're thinking, Mason."

"That your perfume is crap?"

"That you'll tell her to leave after I go. I've got that all figured out too."

"Have you?"

"The reception will be spotty when we're at sea, but I'll be able to connect to the Internet once we reach port. Kiran will e-mail me every week with an update. If you fire her, I will fly back here and kick your ass."

This isn't lip service. Dana will really do it.

"Do you know how difficult it is to arrange emergency flights from an ice cutter in the almost frozen Ross Sea, Mason?"

"No idea."

"Me either, but it sounds ridiculously expensive. So don't make me do it."

"Are we done?"

Dana kisses me on the cheek. "Thank you." She claps her hands. "Where are my manners? We have a guest, and I haven't even offered her anything. I'm going to make us tea. Would you care for tea, Kiran?"

"I'd love a cup."

"Cool. Mason hates tea. Coffee, right Mason?"

"Affirmative," I say, although I'm really thinking of the bottle of whisky inside the liquor cabinet.

The kitchen door closes. Kiran's breaths are soft and steady.

"Why are you here?" I've asked the question so many times it's on auto-play in my mind.

"Because you're here."

"That's not an answer. I'm in an impossible situation."

"Maybe so, but here we are. You were there for me when I needed a friend. I'm trying to return the favor. I understand your feelings have changed. I'd be lying if I said it's not..." Her voice drifts off. She's struggling to finish the thought. "Difficult. But I can deal if you can swallow down that stubborn lump of pride and let me help you."

"That's it?"

"Yes."

"It's a stupid plan."

"It wouldn't be the first time I followed a stupid plan."

Chapter 23

Kiran

My stepmother, Linda, called me last night. She knows about the pact between Mason and me. There are only two people who know about the true extent of my eight days with Mason Cutler. Linda and Sidney. Linda because she kept commenting how much I'd changed when I came back. Finally, I broke down and told her. As a hopeless romantic, she thought it was a beautiful idea.

When I told her the outcome of finally meeting him again, she wept. She tried to comfort me, but in the end I had to console her. I spoke to Papa too, and told him I was helping out a friend and would be out of town for the next few weeks. It was the truth, or the closest to the truth I could disclose. He would freak I am even living with a boy, let alone whatever is going on here. Not that I even have a clue on that account.

Confiding in Sidney eased my mind. We renewed our friendship over the years. Also, she is one of the few people who actually met Mason. I needed confirmation he did actually exist and our eight days wasn't a figment of my over-active imagination. Sidney consoled me for two hours last night as we Skyped with matching bottles of wine.

Today, Dana shows me around the house. I spent the night at the Wilshire again to give Dana and Mason some privacy. She has decided to fly into the Falkland Islands early. Apparently, there are equipment issues and decisions she needs to be involved in. So today is the day I officially start.

There are many intricate details in the Craftsman house. Mason and Dana's grandfather built the home himself. I try not to salivate as I take in the built-in bookcases, but it's hard to pass up a shelf lined with leather-bound books without checking out the contents. Everything is immaculate and organized.

Dana clears her throat, drawing my attention away from the collection of Langston Hughes poetry. "You can borrow anything you want."

"What about Mason's appointments? Should we take a cab?"

"That'll cost a fortune. Besides the carbon emissions on those vehicles..." Dana shudders as if I've suggested mining for coal in her backyard. "You can use my car for any trips or if you just need to go out. Make sure you plug it in every night, though."

"It's electric?"

"A hybrid. Mason's car is in the garage too. But it's a freaking gas-guzzling stick shift man-car."

"Man-car?"

"He rebuilt a Trans Am from scratch."

Okay, hybrid it is.

He must have finished the car, the one he talked about the day we drove to the little airfield to jump out of a plane. I'm so proud of him and sad for him, since he can no longer drive it, but I barely have time to process it all. Dana talks a mile a minute. She walks into a large room off the living room. "This will be your room. Does that work?"

It has double French doors leading inside. On the far wall there is another set of glass doors leading out to the patio. "It's perfect. Is this a normal bedroom?"

"This is actually a study. When we first moved back in, Mason lived in here until he got used to the layout of the house. Then he moved back to his room upstairs." She points to a treadmill. "Do you mind if this stays in here? Mason uses it every day. We can move it out if you want, but I'd rather leave everything the way it is. Mason has it all memorized."

"I don't mind at all."

Dana opens a dresser drawer and hands me a black binder. "This is for you."

"What it is it?"

"A handbook of sorts. Its general instructions, a few interesting articles I've printed, the names and numbers of Mason's doctors. Oh, and my top ten list of dos and don'ts. That's very important."

I take the thick book. I open it to the first page, which is her list. "Always announce when you enter or exit a room."

Dana smiles. "These are things I figured out as we went along. Once I walked away to get myself a drink. I must have been quiet because he didn't know. When I came back he was talking to himself. It turns out he thought I was still there."

"It makes sense, but I never would have thought of it. I'll memorize these."

I follow Dana around the room as she shows me where she stows the extra sheets and towels. I pause at the few paintings on the far wall. They are garden scenes, the brush strokes broad, the colors intense. "Who painted these?"

"Grams. She used to paint, and she even had an exhibition once. I guess that's where Mason gets it from. He got her talent, and I inherited her bad teeth. The DNA gene pool is a bitch. Go figure."

"What do you mean he has her talent?"

Dana shakes her head. "I'm sure he'll tell you in time."

I blink my eyes at the black and white framed picture on the dresser. A gorgeous young woman with Dana's smile peers at the camera, a baby on one hip and a shotgun on the other. "This is her?"

"Yep. She was no gatherer woman. She hunted with the boys and managed to take care of a baby too. Not at the same time, of course."

"Of course."

Through the window, I see Mason and Molly come out of the shed. He feels down the side of the shed until he gets to the lock. He closes it and heads back to the front of the house.

"I guess we should get this good-bye going," Dana says.

"Sure."

She takes a few steps toward me. "Kiran, please take care of my brother. I don't say this to him as much as I should, but he's always been there for me. Everything I am, I owe to him."

"I will. I promise."

"Ready to go?" Mason asks, his tall frame taking up most of the doorway.

"Yes." Her voice chokes on the single word.

"Jesus, Dana, are you crying?"

"Just gonna miss your jerk face."

"I'll miss you too. Now pull yourself together. Those sub-zero sea creatures aren't going to study themselves."

She wipes away a tear with the back of her hand. A car honks on the street.

"The cab's here. Where is your luggage?" Mason asks.

"Still in my room," Dana says.

"I'll fetch it."

"Do you need help?" I ask.

"What I need are some good directions, please."

Dana provides them. "On the right-hand side of the door, there are two bags. One is a duffle with a strap. The other one rolls."

"Got it."

She turns to me once he's out of the room. "Rule number four is never leave anything on the floor. Not shoes or grocery bags or luggage. If you do have to leave something, let him know where it is. It's all a tripping hazard. Rule number five is to give detailed directions. If Mason's about to walk into something, words like 'watch out,' don't really help. Tell him what is in front of him and where things are."

"I'll remember."

She looks as if she wants to say more. She blinks her eyes.

I embrace her. "I'll take care of him. Trust me."

We round the stairs. Mason has no trouble with the luggage. He's as built as he ever was. In fact, I think he's even more muscular. No doubt this is due to the treadmill and weight set in the study. He takes her bags out to the waiting cab. He's not wearing sunglasses today.

He gives Dana a hug. "Take care of yourself. You call and text as much as you can, you hear me?"

"I will." She looks at me. "Thank you, Kiran."

"Welcome."

She tilts her head toward Mason. "Behave yourself."

"Stop harassing me. I'll be a perfect gentleman."

"I'm holding you to that promise."

Mason opens the cab door. "Godspeed, Dana."

Dana gives us a dimply smile. "Y'all know the saying 'I might be out of pocket because I'm on a sea cutter headed to Antarctica?'"

"No," I say. 'I've never heard that. Is that something people say?"

She smiles. "It's something I get to say. Thanks to you."

Chapter 24

Kiran

Mason goes back to the shed right away. I hoped for a conversation, but it wasn't going to happen. I spend the day going over Dana's rules and familiarizing myself with the house. Finally, I knock on the shed door. Mick Jagger is belting out "Memory Motel."

Why this song, Mason? Does it mean something?

The shed isn't really a shed. It resembles a little house complete with gray shingle siding and windows. Windows with dark curtains drawn shut. No one answers my knock. I close my hand into a tight fist and pound harder. The music stops, and the door creaks open. He peeks from behind it.

"I wanted to give you a heads up. I'm starting on dinner."

"You don't have to do that for me. I'm capable of feeding myself."

"I promised Dana I'd make sure you had at least one hot meal a day."

"I know how to use the stove. You'd be surprised how much I can do."

"I *am* surprised. That's not the point. This is just dinner. We're not renegotiating the Geneva contract. I'm making dinner for me, anyway. Don't worry, I would have made dinner for you whether you were blind or not." I bite my lip, wishing I could swallow back the last sentence.

His mouth draws into a thin line. Then he startles me with a laugh. "Well, since you put it that way, I can eat."

When he comes into the house, his shirt and jeans are covered with a gray dust. The shirt is tight against his frame, showing off his broad shoulders and muscular back. His jeans are ripped at the knees. His hair is unkempt but in a way that's completely sexy and touchable.

"You okay, Kiran?"

"Yes, why?"

"You're breathing a little hard. Are you doing something strenuous over there?"

"Just setting the table."

"How long till supper?"

"At least twenty minutes."

"Let me wash up."

When he comes down, he's freshly showered, smelling of mint and man. His dirty clothes are folded neatly in his hand. He takes them to the laundry room.

I back out a chair for him. He moves to the chair on the opposite side of the table. He holds it out. We're in some strange standoff, both of us standing with chairs in front of us.

"Oh, sorry, I wasn't sure where you sat."

He sits. I take the plate from the chair next to him and move it in front of him.

"Is lemonade okay?"

"Yeah."

I set the glass next to him, hard enough to make a sound. Sound is how he sees distance according to Dana's list. "It's chicken with broccoli rabe and a slice of corn bread."

He nods.

"Do you like broccoli rabe?"

"Yeah, it's better than broccoli Rick, in my opinion."

There are flickers of the silly boy I love within this wounded man. They are filtered rays of light in a dark room. "Did you steal that line from a ten-year-old, Cutler?"

"Nope. The credit for that genius zinger goes to me."

I take the seat I held out. His hands are flat on the table. His shoulders are hunched tightly. He's nervous. I'm not making it easier. He picks up a fork and moves the food around.

"Chicken is at six o'clock and the broccoli at twelve. The corn bread is between one and two. It's cut into a square. I already cut the chicken up for you."

"Thank you for the explanation, that's helpful, but don't ever cut my food again."

"I'm sorry. I just…"

"I understand you were trying to help. I appreciate it, but I can manage. I'm not helpless in all things."

"I don't believe you're helpless at all."

He doesn't reply. The clank of forks and knives punctures the silence between us.

"The shed is really cool. Who made it?" My voice sounds too enthusiastic, clashing with the somber mood.

"I did." He takes another bite of his chicken. I think that's all he'll say at first. He points to his eyes. "Before this. I'm not too keen on using power tools yet."

"Yet?"

"Last thing I need is to meet the business end of a table saw. Maybe one day it'll be different."

What? I want to cover him in bubble wrap and not let him out. I wave the silly thought away. He's trying to find a new normal without any light. It's something that's impressive and scary. My God, it's scary for me. I can't even imagine what he's going through.

"What are you working on in the shed?"

"It's hard to explain."

I drop the subject. The silence is almost oppressive.

"This tastes like Gram's cornbread."

"It is."

He drops it on the plate. "Come again?"

"I mean it's her recipe. I found a wooden box of index cards with recipes. I thought I'd try one. Hope you don't mind." I'd only made cornbread from the box. Doing it from scratch was not in the plan, but I wanted to make our first meal special.

"Mind? I'm grateful."

He takes a while to eat his food, savoring each bite. He asks for seconds.

"Have you always been able to cook?"

I'm happy we're having an actual conversation. "No. I muddled my way through it. When I went to Iowa, I was eating a lot of junk food. I figured if I wanted to eat something good on my budget, I should learn how to cook. So, I bought a bunch of cookbooks at a secondhand store and a cheap set of pans. I made a lot of mistakes at first."

"Mistakes?"

"I burned stuff. Tried to get a little too creative. Accidently used a tablespoon of salt when I needed a teaspoon. That sort of thing."

"Looks like you figured it out."

"Thank you."

"I lied to you earlier."

I grip my knees to keep my legs from shaking. Is he going to tell me he didn't mean those nasty things he said the day I came here?

"I don't use the stove yet. The microwave is more my speed. I'm afraid of eating something undercooked or burnt."

I'm silent. Upset with him for holding back. Upset with myself because this is hard and his words still sting. They ring in my head, opening up fresh wounds each time. Am I supposed to pretend he didn't tear off a chunk of my heart? Does he get a free pass to be an ass? But this isn't about Mason and me. This is about being there for someone who needs you.

"Aren't you afraid of burning yourself?"

"That too, I guess." He drums his fingers on the table. "How have you been, Shenoy?"

"Good."

"That's it? That's all you got? Good?"

How can you sum up five years in one succinct sentence? "What do you want? A synopsis?"

"A little more detail would be nice."

"You told me you weren't interested."

"My memory is intact. I never said that."

"You said you didn't care about me."

His hand slams on the table causing the silverware to jump. "Please, Kiran, cut me some slack. I'm trying to have a normal conversation in the most abnormal situation. Can you try with me?"

This is hard for him. I stayed to make it easier, but now I'm only adding to his difficulties. I decide to tell him about Iowa. Iowa seems neutral... like Switzerland.

"I graduated from Iowa. It was cold. Colder than I thought. It took me a while to get used to being completely on my own. I felt awkward the entire first semester. I was that puzzle piece that didn't fit no matter how hard you pressed it in place. I almost dropped out."

"What changed?"

"I got over myself and started seeing the puzzle differently. I found a group of friends. I started to speak up during discussions. I wrote some essays and short stories I was really proud of and read a ton of amazing books."

"That's great, Kiran."

Did you wonder about me over the years, Mason? The way I wondered about you every single day? "How were the last five years for you?"

"I liked being a Marine. It felt like I belonged to a huge extended family." He holds his hands up. "That's about it."

I want to ask him more, but it's clear he's not ready to talk in details. "Tomorrow, you have therapy, right? Dana gave me the schedule."

"Yes. It'll be a boring day for you. I have rehabilitation, and I see my psychologist. You don't have to hang around, though. It's too far to drive back here, but there's a lot to do in Charleston."

"I'll bring my laptop and work. Maybe we can do something together afterward, though."

"I'm not very social these days."

"We can just go for a walk, Mason. Maybe get some coffee."

"What is this, Kiran? Are you planning to help me get over my fear of driving? Are we gonna jump out of a plane together?"

I drop my fork. It clatters against the glass. His expression turns contrite. I see the apology written on his face before he even speaks. "Kiran, I'm—"

"Driving a car is definitely out of the question. But who says we can't jump out of plane?"

"Be strapped to some guy and not being able to see the ground would be difficult for me. I need to keep whatever control I can."

"What if it was me you were strapped to?"

"How would that work?"

"I enjoyed it so much when we did it, I got my certification. You can jump with me. If you trusted me to talk you through it and pull the parachute that is."

"You're kidding. You got certified?"

"Yes."

"I'll think about it."

I stand to clear the table. Remembering Dana's rule not to move anything, I'm careful to push my chair back in. She even marked the position of the couch with pieces of red tape on the floor in case it shifted.

"I can clean up," he says.

"I don't mind."

"You cooked. I'll do dish duty."

"Okay."

He feels around the table until he grasps my plate. I don't move. He's close to me. I struggle not to wrap my arms around him.

"By the way, I wasn't staking my place at the table when I backed out that chair."

"What were you doing then?"

"Holding the chair for you, Kiran."

Chapter 25

Mason

During the drive to the VA Hospital in Charleston, I suggest we listen to an audio book. Kiran agrees, although I sense she doesn't want to. I need someone else's voice in the car with us. Dana's car isn't very roomy, and I am already struggling not to touch her face or tangle my hands in her hair.

So we listen as a high-pitched British guy dictates a time-travel psychological thriller. I let her go through the downloaded books on my app. This is what she chose. Maybe because there's a hint of romance. I don't have the heart to tell her it ends badly.

I shift awkwardly in the tiny seat.

Kiran pauses the audio book. "Maybe you should move your chair back?"

"Wish I could. This is as far back as it goes. I swear Dana's car is made for elves."

She laughs. I wonder if her mouth is still as sexy as I remember. Does she still mouth the words when she reads?

"You do look cramped."

"It's funny the stuff you miss. I thought it would be those stunning sights like hiking in the Rocky Mountains or when all the Dogwood trees bloom or those beautiful sunrises we shared."

"You don't miss those things?" she asks, her voice as soft as a whisper.

"I do, but I remember them." I point to my head. "Up here. But I know there won't be any future grand sightings to add to that list. Mostly, it's the subtle things I miss. Not knowing how someone is looking at me or who's even around me. I wonder how Dana looked when I said good-bye to her. I'm missing so much...life."

"Dana was sad and excited at the same time. She was fighting a smile and a tear."

I nod. That sounded right. I could go on about this, but what use was it? What was the use in telling her how much I miss her smile? How sad it makes me that I'll never see it again. "I miss driving."

"It isn't much fun in my opinion."

"Well, if you're talking about this automobile, I'd agree. But you've never driven a custom-built Firebird, have you?"

"I've never driven any kind of sports car."

"It's more than just the utility of getting from one place to another. I experienced something each time I took a spin. There's a hypnotic power in the roar of the engine. There's a grace in the way the car takes turns or climbs a hill." I bet I sound foolish, going on about a car.

"I saw it in the garage. It's gorgeous."

"Thank you. I barely drove it and now I'll probably sell it. Doesn't make much sense not to. Dana wants nothing to do with it."

Her navigator app chimes in, interrupting us with directions.

"You can turn it off. I can tell you how to get there."

"You can?"

"Yeah, I know this area well. If you can tell me what street we're on, I can route us."

"May I ask you something?"

"Shoot."

"If it's too private, just tell me."

"Ask the dam question, girl."

"Can you see anything?"

"Yeah, I see some stuff. Usually, I can make out light and dark shadows. I can even see dimension if something is moving, like the cars on this road. I can't make out their specific forms to tell you make and model or anything, but I can see flashes of something zinging by us. If I'm lucky, I get some color too, shades of muted oranges and reds and yellows." I'm always grateful when I get to see color.

"When does it happen?"

It happened the day she came, although it wasn't exactly a happy day. I remember the sun was bright. I saw her, a slow moving shadow against a sky of yellow. "When there is a lot of light."

We pass through the tourist district. When she speeds up, I know we're in the business area of downtown. The small pothole we drive over tells me we're close. "Turn right after the park."

"Should I pull up to the building?" she asks after making the right.

"Not unless you need assistance. Pull into a parking space. I can walk."

"Sorry."

"Don't apologize. I get you're trying to make things easier for me. Thing is, I want to be as normal as possible as much as possible. That includes not being let out at the front of the building like a geriatric grandma who's had hip surgery."

"Okay, Cutler, I get it."

She parks the car. I open the door and feel the cement with my foot. I stand and stretch out right away, grateful to be free of the clown-mobile.

It's a long walk, and there are a few steps and curves along the way. Part of the sidewalk is covered with rosebushes. I've gotten really intimate with those thorns. Stone tiles separate grassy fields, and at one point there is a stone fountain right in the middle that you have to go around. At least I've never fallen in there. This walk from the parking lot to the building is paved with disasters waiting to happen, but I don't mind it. In the beginning I felt some small sense of accomplishment when I made it into the building without tripping or banging into something.

Kiran comes over to my side. Her hair brushes my arm. God, it's still soft.

Her laptop bag bumps me. She takes my hand and starts walking to the building, leading me along. I stop.

"I have my stick. I don't need you to lead me."

"I wasn't trying to lead you."

"Then what were you doing?"

"I just wanted to hold your hand."

She speaks softly, but the hurt in her voice is loud and clear. It amplifies six times over. I take my cane from my pocket and extend it. "Give me your bag. I'll carry it."

"I'm sorry I bumped you."

"That's not the reason I want to carry it."

"Then why?"

"Because I'm a gentleman."

"Oh, of course," she says, handing it to me.

I throw the strap over my shoulder. "Now give me your hand again." I hold my hand out, palm up. She places her hand in mine. Her fingers shake. I inch my hand up to her wrist. Her pulse beats some wild rhythm. I struggle not to pull her closer. Instead, I trace my thumb over the pink heart, the line and shape drawn from memory. I move up higher, my ascent much too slow and exploratory. Once I reach her upper arm, I encircle my fingers around her. There is more definition then I remember. Nothing that would cross into body building status, but her biceps are definitely more toned and carved. Maybe she'd always had them and I hadn't noticed? No, I had memorized her body during those eight days. This is something new, or new since then.

"When did you get guns, Shenoy?"

"Huh?"

"Your arms." I give her a squeeze. "You have some muscle."

"I've been working out." She flexes for me. "Just swimming and some weight training."

"It shows."

"Thank you."

We stand their awkwardly, me with my fingers curled around her arm.

"You can walk now, Kiran. I'll be a half-step behind you." I move the walking stick to give me some extra guidance.

"There's a curb ahead of us, Mason."

"Not for another ten feet. You really don't need to tell me that far in advance."

"How did you know?"

"I've been here a lot."

Just when I think I'm very smooth, I realize I've hit her leg with my stick. Shit. She doesn't even say anything. Not a yelp or an ouch or anything. Except I know I've made contact with her shin from the sound. It must have hurt because her body tenses. "Are you okay?"

Silence.

"Kiran?"

She sucks in a deep breath. "Fine. I'm fine."

"Girl, I know that hurt. I'm sorry."

"It was an accident."

"Did you nod when I asked if you were hurt?"

She laughs, the sound infectious. "Yes. Stupid, right?"

"Naw, a lot of people do that. It's natural." I retract my walking stick. "Let's try this again."

"Maybe you shouldn't do that."

"Kiran, it doesn't make sense for me to use it while I've got your arm. It's really not needed. I'll follow your movements."

"Aren't you more comfortable with the stick?"

"Yes."

"Then why?"

"It's good practice for both of us. The streets in some areas of Charleston can be narrow and crowded. They aren't suitable for a cane. It's probably not a bad idea for us to practice walking together. That is if you still want to take a walk after my appointments?"

"I do."

"All right then."

That is the short answer. The long and far more truthful answer is that I really want an excuse to touch her. I want to hold your hand too, Kiran.

Chapter 26

Kiran

We sit at the table with big steaming bowls of chicken and stars. Mason doesn't complain. In fact, he says it's a favorite. We're down to soup and bread. There are other things in the cupboards and fridge. Weird things such as jicama and seaweed tofu and agave nectar that I have no idea how to cook.

"Dana has some interesting taste in food."

He chews on a crescent roll. "Yeah, tell me about it. She's a health nut. Or maybe just a nut. Luckily, I have the local pizza place on speed dial and an app that will call them for me on command."

"We need to go grocery shopping."

"I'll pass."

I stir little noodle stars around the broth. "Besides therapy, when is the last time you went out?" Even the walk in Charleston only lasted one city block before Mason said we should turn around. He focused so hard on each step I didn't want to disrupt his concentration. So we didn't speak the whole way.

"Can't remember."

"Maybe you should. Isn't that what your therapist suggested?"

"I'm not comfortable with strange places yet."

"This is your local grocery store. You probably know it better than me. Besides, I'll be there." Didn't he trust me? The way his shoulders tense, I'm not sure. "We can bring Molly too."

"Why are you doing this, Kiran? I don't need you to fix me."

"I didn't realize you were broken. Are you really going to spend your life in a shell?"

His mouth tilts. "Girl, are you comparing me to a hermit crab?"

"If the shell fits. This is coming from a former barnacle, so get over it."

He drags a hand over his hair. I envy how it all falls back into place so beautifully, two errant strands fork over his forehead in model perfect form.

I stack our dishes to take them to the sink. I almost walk away and then remember I need to push my chair back in. *Never move anything.* Dana's warning comes back. I slide the chair into place with my hip.

"Why are you trying so hard, Kiran?"

Because you're worth it. "Because I want you to be happy."

"I'm not who I once was. You have to realize that."

"Yeah, not completely. Either am I. But it doesn't mean I stop caring about you or that I don't want to know the new you."

"The new me is an asshole. I don't feel like a..."

"A what?"

"Nothing."

"Tell me."

"I'm going to the shed."

This is becoming a common theme. If I push too hard, he retreats. "I'll go by myself then."

After I rinse our bowls and place them in the dishwasher, I do a quick check to make sure I've put everything away. He's left. Most likely, he's out in the shed doing whatever he does.

After grabbing Dana's keys and my purse, I head through the back door to the garage. I reach to hit the open button on the garage door, but stop myself when I spot the tall, lean shadow. Mason is running his hands over the image of the bird on the Trans Am's hood.

"Any requests?" I ask. I don't open the door. It's dark and hot in the garage. Tiny dust motes float around us.

"No."

"What are you doing out here?"

"Contemplating."

"Oh." I reach to hit the open button, but his deep, husky voice halts me.

"I'll go with you."

"I'm glad." I fist bump the air to celebrate my small triumph.

"Don't sound too happy. It's kind of a joke that going to a fucking grocery store is such a big deal."

"It is a big deal, Mason. Thank you for coming with me."

He shrugs, his smile tight and nervous. "I figure you might need me. I'm an expert at telling if fruit is ripe."

"I've never had my own personal fruit feeler-upper."

"At least I'm good for something." He says it sarcastically with self-deprecating humor that is part of Mason's personality, but his smile isn't genuine. There is nothing funny in the statement.

When I take a few tentative steps toward him, I bump into a ladder.

"Are you okay?"

"Yeah, just clumsy." My God, it's dark, but there is a little light peeking from the small window. This is barely a taste of his world, and I can't even manage to walk a few steps. How is he so graceful?

I stand close to him, blinking my eyes to adjust to the low light. "What were you going to say earlier? You don't feel like a...what?"

"Nothing."

"Say it. Tell me now. What don't you feel like?"

"A man."

"It's not true."

"You can't tell me how I feel, Shenoy."

"Can I show you something, Mason?"

"If you're going to give me some goddamn feel-good speech, you can save it, sister. I'm not in the mood."

"No speech."

I move a step closer to him until only a tiny sliver of a gap stands between us. I place a hand on each of his broad shoulders and gently work my fingers into his skin. His body doesn't relax, but it does feel less stiff. I work my way down his front. I skim the pads of my fingers over the soft, faded fabric of his T-shirt. His breathing increases. I reach his jeans and run my fingers over the muscles right above the button. The tempo of his breathing increases, matching mine. When I see the large bulge under the dark denim, I stand on my tiptoes and lean close to his ear. "Feel like a man now?" I whisper.

"Woman, I don't know if you are pure evil or a genius."

"Maybe an evil genius." I pull away before I get carried away. I've made my point... I think.

"Coming?"

"It'll take more than that," he mutters, following me.

I get another idea. I tell myself not to press my luck. Not to push too hard. Yet, I still go on.

"Want to take the Trans Am?"

"Are you fucking with me?"

"Swear I'm not."

"When did you learn to drive a stick?" he asks.

"Last week."

"What the hell are you saying, Kiran?"

I have no freaking idea, Mason. Just spouting off a stupid idea.

"Answer me, please," he says in that low voice I would follow anywhere.

"Ever since therapy when you told me how much you missed it, I've been watching every single YouTube video on driving a stick shift. I hoped it would make you happy to sit in the car again and feel the engine. Now that I think about it, it's the dumbest idea in the world."

He tilts his head. "You really think you can do it based on videos?"

"Yeah, the grocery store's only two miles up the road according to Google maps. It's up to you, though."

He walks right past me into the kitchen. Cursing myself, I lower my head. I should have quit. Why would he want to be a passenger in his own car?

A jingling sound snaps me out of my wayward thoughts. Mason shakes a set of keys at me. "Be careful with her."

"I will."

He whistles and calls for Molly. She comes running behind him. "We'll c'mon, girl. We don't have all day."

I sit in the driver's seat, adjusting and readjusting everything. Now that I am sitting here about to drive his baby, I'm nervous. He's placed so much trust in me. I pray my ten hours of YouTube tutorials are enough.

"You got this, Shenoy."

I wish he had the same confidence in himself that he has with me. The car roars to life. I drive slow and cautious until I get the hang of the pedals and clutch. I have to admit there is something empowering about driving a stick shift. A sense of control I enjoy. He places his hand on my wrist.

"Honey, you need to stop riding the clutch."

"Sorry." I lift my foot and curl my hands on the steering wheel.

We arrive at the grocery store unscathed. "Nice work, Shenoy. You're a natural."

"Thank you."

I notice the ice cream shop next to the grocery store. It has a huge red and white striped awning. The sign reads *The Creamery – Best ice cream in South Carolina. Maybe even the world.*

"Mason, is that the ice cream place you told me is better than Kirby's?"

"That would be it."

"Let's get a scoop."

He gives me a look that says no all over it. "Let's just get our groceries and go."

"Seriously, Mason, the closest thing to junk food Dana has is dehydrated pineapples. You can't expect a girl to survive on that stuff. I need ice cream."

"Okay."

The bells chime over the doorway. The air conditioning blasts, blowing the ends of my hair up as we enter the shop. The girl behind the counter turns toward us. Her rosy lips inch up in a huge smile...at Mason.

"Mason!" she shrieks, moving past the counter and running to him. "It's Lana."

She wraps her arms around him. He stumbles. Molly rushes behind him, ready to break a fall if needed. I grab his arm, but he catches himself.

"I missed you," she says, backing away. She smoothes down her pink mini skirt and adjusts her white tank top. Probably not a great idea to wear a white tank sans bra when you work in an ice cream parlor with subzero temperatures.

"Hey, Lana. It's good to see you too."

"Who is this cutie?" she asks, bending down to pet Molly. I cringe, wanting to yell out Dana's rule number eight. Never pet a service dog unless you have permission from the owner. They are at work, and the attention will just distract them from their duties. But I keep my mouth shut.

"That's my best friend, Molly."

Lana stands. Somehow she's wedged herself between Mason and me. She twirls a strand of her long red hair. "You're making me jealous." She laughs at her own joke, her hand against Mason's arm.

"Hi," I say to remind everyone I'm still here.

"I'll be with you in a minute," Lana says, turning her attention back to Mason.

"Lana, this is Kiran. She's helping out while Dana is gone."

Okay, a minute ago I was a sexy evil genius. Now I'm the girl helping out. I shouldn't be hurt by his description, but hurt is exactly what I am.

"That's nice." She gives me a side glance. "Bless your heart."

The phrase sounds more like a curse than a blessing.

She takes Mason's hand between hers. "How have you been? I called you, but Dana said you were busy each time."

"I'm fine."

"I'm so sorry, Mason."

"Thank you, Lana."

"In case you didn't know, you're still super hot."

He cracks a smile. Maybe Lana's direct approach was better than what I did.

"Um...thanks. I would tell you that you look great too, except well, you know."

She laughs as if he's the funniest thing since episode 19 of The Big Bang Theory.

"Hey, Mason!" A man in a long white apron comes toward us.

"Is that you Jeff?"

"It is."

"Thought I smelled trouble."

Jeff claps Mason on the back. They manage one of those almost-there embraces men do. Mason gestures to me. "This is my friend, Kiran."

At least he promoted me to friend status.

"Jeff and Lana's parents own the dairy farm that's the basis for this fine establishment," Mason explains.

"Lana, don't just stand there. Take their order," Jeff says.

"I'm gonna make Mason something special," Lana says. "Wait till you get a taste of what I'm serving." She twirls around, skirt flaring.

"Hold up a sec," Mason says.

"Yeah, sugar?"

Mason reaches his hands out and takes my wrist. "What would you like, Kiran?"

I glance at the board. "I'll have a scoop of the green apple ice cream."

Jeff raises his eyebrow. "You sure? It's a unique flavor combination. Don't get me wrong, I love it, but some of our patrons claim its way too sour."

"Sounds perfect." It will definitely fit my mood.

Jeff ushers us toward a booth.

"Cutler, you never sent me an RSVP. Are you planning to come on the fishing trip?"

"Sorry, man, I don't really trust myself around hooks just yet." He drums his fingers against the tabletop. "Or boats or large, deep bodies of water."

"I'll make sure it's safe. C'mon, bro, it's my birthday and I want you there." Jeff smiles at me. "Tell him he should go."

Mason shakes his head. "It's your birthday. The last thing you need is to be watching out for me."

"The last thing I need is not having my best buddy there." Jeff nods in my direction. "You can bring Kiran if it'll make it easier for you."

"Kiran doesn't fish." Mason tilts his head. "You don't fish, right?"

"Right, but I can watch YouTube videos on the subject."

Mason laughs. "Yeah, you are a quick study."

I decide to leave them alone to catch up. Obviously, Jeff is excited to visit with Mason. "I'll be right back."

I use the restroom. On the way back, I linger to check out the display of all the interesting ice cream flavors. Lana is preparing some complicated concoction for Mason.

"So, how do you know our Mason, or did you just answer an ad?" Lana asks in a way that makes it very clear "our" Mason is not my Mason.

"We've been friends for a while."

She lowers the visor on her head. "Can't be that long. He's never mentioned you."

"You know him well I take it?"

"Oh sure, my brother and Mase have been best friends forever."

I glance at the table a few feet away. Mason and Jeff are still chatting away. "They seem close."

"Mase and I are close too. We've been on and off since high school."

"Oh." Oh.

"Yeah. Even when he left for the Marines, we always got back together again."

Even though it's freezing in here, my insides are on fire.

She leans toward me, dropping her voice as if we're confidants sharing a secret. "I plan to ask him out again. I won't let his disability stop me."

I'm speechless… And suddenly I strongly dislike ice cream.

Lana has three huge scoops in a banana boat container. She spoons hot fudge on top. Despite all these crazy emotions, a warning shoots up like a red flare. "Excuse me, is that for Mason?"

"Yes," she says. "I'll get yours in a minute."

"No, it's not that. Mason can't have chocolate."

"Since when?"

"Since always. He's allergic."

She sets down the hot fudge ladle. "That's right. I forgot."

"What the hell, Lana. Are you trying to kill him?" Jeff asks.

"Calm down, man. It won't kill me. Just gives me a killer headache." Mason clears his throat. "It's no trouble, Lana. I'll just have a plain old scoop of vanilla if you please."

She throws her creation in the garbage. I would have felt sorry for her except she curls her mouth somewhere between a smile and sneer. She places a scoop of vanilla in a bowl. She does the same with my green apple.

I bring our bowls to the table. Mason takes out his wallet. All the bills are folded in different directions so he can tell the notes apart.

"Your money's no good here, Cutler," Jeff says, placing a hand over Mason's wallet.

"Let me pay you."

"No can do, brother."

They argue for a minute before Mason finally concedes. I place Mason's bowl next to him and hand him his spoon.

"Think about coming fishing, Cutler. It's only one day." Jeff glances at the Cuckoo clock over the ice cream display. "Man, I'm sorry, I'd love to catch up more, but I promised my dad I'd meet him at the farm."

"No worries," Mason says. "We'll talk soon."

"Yeah, for sure." Jeff turns to me. "It was nice meeting you, Kiran."

"You too."

Jeff gives Lana instructions to wash the back floor on his way out the door. She sighs before disappearing into the backroom.

"Mason, if you want to stay here, I can do the grocery shopping and come back for you."

"Why?"

"So you can catch up."

His expression is one of puzzlement. "Didn't Jeff leave?"

"Yes." I lean forward. "I meant with Lana."

"No thanks." He jerks his head toward the door. "Let's go outside and finish our ice cream. If memory serves, there are a couple benches out there."

"There are."

He slides out of the booth. "Well, c'mon, Shenoy. Ice creams a melting here."

We find a bench under the shade of a large oak tree. We sit close enough, mainly because the bench is small. I'm still wound up from the conversation with Lana. Not for the first time, I think I built up those eight days in my head.

Mason shoulder bumps me. "I can't believe you remembered I'm allergic to chocolate."

"Of course I remember. It's one of the saddest things I've ever heard."

He chuckles. "You did shed a few tears at the time. Thanks for looking out for me."

"Well, that *is* my job."

"Are you okay, Shenoy?"

"Fine."

"Why did you think I wanted to hang with Lana just now?"

"Because she's your ex."

"Ex? Where did you hear that?"

"From her."

"Is that a note of jealousy I'm detecting?"

No Mason, it's not a single note. It's a whole freaking symphony.

"It's just jarring running into your ex-girlfriend."

"She's not my ex. To qualify for ex status, you have to be going out in the first place."

"You never went out with her?"

"Maybe two dates back in high school. When I was home on leave a few years ago, we went to the movies with a whole group of people. I wouldn't count that as a date. She's my buddy's kid sister. That's all."

"Were there other girls?" I blurt the question as soon as it enters my head. I'm not even sure if I want him to answer.

"I had a few dates over the years."

"Anything serious?" I hear a horrible screeching sound inside my head. Probably, the metal on metal of broken down brakes that can't seem to stop the awkward questions.

"No. I didn't even go out with the same girl twice. Matter of fact, the only relationship I've ever had in my entire life would be the eight days I spent with you. If you quantify that as a relationship."

"Oh." Oh.

"What about you?"

I scrape the bottom of my paper cup with the colorful plastic spoon. I'm so unprepared to answer the same question I posed. "I did what you said. I lived my life and went on a few dates."

"Anything serious?" When I don't answer, he bumps me again. "C'mon, spill it."

"I had one relationship."

His mouth tightens. "How long?"

"About six months."

Mason takes out a plastic bag of treats and feeds Molly. "Who was he?"

"Are we really doing this?"

"In all fairness, you started it."

True. I take in a sharp breath. "His name was Vic."

"For Victor?"

"For Vickram. A friend at school set us up. She probably matched us because we were the only two Indians in all of Iowa. Or at least, it seemed that way."

Mason chuckles, but the sound falls flat and hollow. "Go on."

How much more detail does he need? "He was nice. Papa loved him."

"He met your father?"

"When Papa and Linda came to Iowa to visit me, they took us out to dinner. Of course, Vik had all the prerequisites that mattered. He was pre-med, well-bred, and wealthy."

"What happened? He sounds perfect."

I'm not sure how to answer. Do I tell Mason he never made me laugh? He didn't make my pulse hum with excitement? In short, he wasn't Mason.

"Maybe on paper he was perfect, but he wasn't perfect for me. The feelings weren't there. That was unfair to me. It was really unfair to him. So I broke it off."

Mason doesn't respond except to say we should get on with grocery shopping. We head to the store and fill up the cart. On the ride home, the silence is unbearable.

"Sam's selling the store," I say to fill up the empty air.

"Why? He loves running the store."

"Yeah, but he's decided to move on. He's moving to Seattle with his sister. He's selling it all, including the inventory."

"I hope whoever buys it takes care of his books."

"Me too. Sidney says hi by the way."

"Oh, yeah? You're still in touch?"

"We're closer than ever. She's getting married in a few months. I'm one of her bridesmaids."

"No kidding."

"No joke. I have a big poufy peach dress with a bow over the butt to prove it."

He smiles, a big hearty smile. "I bet you can pull it off."

"I don't think so, but it's what she wanted. The wedding is going to be at the Wilshire."

He's quiet for a while. Maybe he's remembering that promise he made to me the night we went swimming. *One day I'll take you to the revolving restaurant on top of the Wilshire Hotel, and we'll dance.*

"Do you remember Rob?" he asks.

"Rob, one half of the Jorgensons?"

"The very one. We exchanged info and kept in touch too."

I swallow something bitter. He kept in touch with Rob, but not me? Of course, there were reasons for that. Maybe not logical ones, but I had agreed to them nonetheless. "How is he? How's Melanie?"

"They're doing well. They have two little boys now."

"Wonderful."

"Are you okay, Kiran?"

No, I'm not okay, Mason. I'm pissed about the fucking years we lost. I'm pissed about the barrier between us now. The one he set up. Before I can rationalize myself off the ledge, something darts in front of the car. I slam on the brakes to avoid hitting the deer. The vehicle screeches. I scream. Molly barks. The deer prances as if it doesn't have a care in the world. Thank God there wasn't a car behind me, or there would have been a collision.

"Kiran!"

I pull over to the side of the road to calm down. I turn to him. "I'm sorry. A deer ran past us. We missed it, but I had to hit the brakes fast. The car is fine."

"Fuck the car. Are you fine?"

"Besides the fact I almost hit Bambi? Yes, I'm fine. Are you?"

He expels a low breath. "Now I am. You handled it well."

I look down. "Mason?"

"Yeah?"

"You can put your arm down now."

Across my body is Mason's arm. It's extended, straight and rigid, veins flaring, muscles flexing. It has to hurt. He must have held it up as soon as I began our screeching halt. Just like he did back in Jasper the day he let me drive that other car of his.

Mason, the protector.

Some things don't change.

Chapter 27

Kiran

I'm typing away, trying to finish my article when Mason appears in the doorway in black shorts and a faded Dallas Cowboy's T-shirt. Molly is at his side.

"Hey, mind if I use the treadmill?"

"Not at all."

"Sure? It sounds like you're working."

"I am, but I don't mind."

I shift my focus back to the screen. I'm writing a book review of the latest Nick Dorsey novel. Each sentence becomes increasingly more difficult. The small desk where I sit is only a few feet away from the treadmill. All I have to do is lift my eyes to see him. He starts with a slow jog. His steps are rhythmic, playing against the hum of the machine.

"I'm going to put on my ear buds," I tell him so he'll know if I'm slow to answer. I don't have to worry about him. Molly is right there standing to the side, alert and ready to jump behind him to break his fall if needed.

"Can you turn it on speaker?" he asks. "I usually listen to music when I work out, but my phone's charging right now."

"Any requests?"

"Something fast. But you choose the music, Miss DJ." He lifts his eyebrow. "No boy bands, though."

Figuring my workout music appropriate, I turn on my playlist.

Spoon sings "Do You." Mason increases his speed, the muscles on his arms flexing. I try to keep my hands on my keyboard. Panjabi MC and Jay Z rap "Beware." Good advice. Mason picks up the tempo. He loses the

T-shirt. Oh holy mother of beautiful boys. His body is ripped and toned in all the right places…which is everywhere. A sheen of sweat covers his six-pack abs. His shorts hang just low enough to reveal those indented V-lines around his hipbones.

There are new tattoos on his sculpted body. The bible quote still covers his right arm, but the star has more shading now. The Marine insignia adorns his right shoulder while intricate black spirals weave around the hard muscles on the right side of his waist.

Eminem advises me to lose myself. That's just what I do. Heat travels up my body. I press my legs together. My mouth is dry. My fingers trembling on the keyboard, I try to focus and ignore the hot as hell man in the corner of the room. But how? I know, I'll search for hysterical kitty videos. That will take my mind off Mason's Thor-like body.

My screen fills up with millions of hits. Kitties playing the piano. Kitties running in circles chasing their own tails, kitties doing back flips in midair, kitties prancing around in hilarious dance routines. After three minutes of watching kittens and their silly antics, I realize all the adorable kitties in the world can't distract me. My willpower withers away. I glance up once more.

Little Wayne and his friends remind me I'm a sucker for pain. No shit.

Mason increases the speed on incline. His honey-colored hair turns damp as he sprints. Beads of sweat gather at the corner of his forehead. He takes his discarded shirt and wicks them away. He grunts one of those ferocious, exertion-fueled man-grunts. I sigh. Molly gives me a sideways glance. Yes, she's on to me. She disapproves of my leering.

I disapprove of my leering.

I bite my lower lip so hard it will leave a mark. "Linger" by the Cranberries starts up. The song mocks me. He makes a face to indicate it's not his preference. Are all the songs on my playlist sexual? I switch it up, opting for my happy playlist. These songs are innocent and barely scratch a PG-rating. Sure enough, the first one is from the Sound of Music soundtrack. Julie Andrews muses about her favorite things.

"What the fuck, Shenoy?"

"What? I love musicals. Deal with it."

He lets out a frustrated groan. "Dealt."

I tap my toe to it. It's a good choice. After all, this is about as wholesome as I can get. I hum along, mentally patting myself on the back. Then I steal another glance like a thief in the night.

Solid tan muscles all drenched in sweat
Oh how gorgeous they glisten
Reminds me of a muscle that I have been missin'

A deep blue-eyed stare and a spanking that stings
These would be some of my favorite things
A warm husky voice and those strong but soft hands
Just waiting to quell all my lusty demands
Harsh breaths, flexing muscles, and big manly grunts
All of these things go straight to myyyyy...
Stop...stop...Stop!

"Shenoy?"

"Yes!" I scream, almost jumping from my chair. God, please don't tell me I spoke out loud. I desperately need some bleach to disinfect my dirty mind.

"Julie Andrews isn't exactly workout music."

Says who? "I can change it."

He slows down the pace. "I'm done, anyway."

Thank God, stop me before I move on to something really raunchy... like Mary Poppins.

Chapter 28

Mason

The day when my life changed and my world went dark started off normal. Or at least as normal as life is when you're deployed. I remember having coffee with my CO. Remember taking a morning run through the barracks. Remember going over drills. Remember playing horseshoes with the guys. But before any of those things, I remember waking up and staring at the pictures I taped to the bottom of the top bunk. It was a ritual I did every morning, an opportunity to look at all the people I loved to remind me why I was here.

There was a photo of Dana and me at her high school graduation, her in a blue cap and gown decked out with golden cords. Next to that was a photo of my dad and me building a sandcastle on the beach and another of us fishing. There was an older picture of my grandpa and dad when Gramps was being awarded the Silver Star for his heroic efforts in the Gulf War.

I always looked at her photo last. The one where I held her in my arms. I snapped it the night we had a picnic among the ruins of sandcastles. The night she told me she loved me. A night I thought about every night following.

If I'd known, had some premonition or inkling, that staring at the picture was my last chance to see her face, I would have taken more time.

Our patrol left in the afternoon on a routine humanitarian mission to deliver aid to the locals. Just another normal day in the desert among poppy fields and damaged buildings. The kids in the village all ran to our truck. They chanted, jumping up and down, while we unloaded bags of rice and cooking oil. A few bags of hard candy for the kids. A boy, no older than fifteen, asked for help with a stalled car.

Sure, I'll help you. I know my way around cars. He opened the hood. When I straightened, I noticed how much he was sweating. The way his hands shook when he shoved them into his pockets. Then my body flew back into the air as if I were made of straw or cotton. Shards of sharp glass and metal pelted me, piercing into my flesh and even my brain. Once in a while, I still taste the metal in my mouth and smell the distinct scent of dust and sulfur and toxic chemicals. Sometimes, I even hear the blast echoing in my ears, drowning out all the other noises.

Like now.

I wake up sweating. I tell myself I had a dream. But the sounds are still all around me. The air is disappearing. It's happening again. I am in the war zone once more. But I'm not alone. This time, she's with me. Oh God.

"Kiran!"

I throw off the covers. Molly is next to me. She rubs her fur against my leg to let me know she's there. Calling Kiran's name, I run to the stairs. Someone is shooting at the house or bombs are going off somewhere close. Whatever the fuck it is, I have to find Kiran, and we have to get the hell out of the house.

"Kiran!"

I almost stumble on the stairs, taking them way too fast for my own good.

Her footsteps are fast, coming toward me with hard strides. "Mason, I'm right here." She touches my arm.

My heart is liable to beat straight out of my chest. "We have to get out."

"It's okay—"

"Let's go," I yell. I feel her jerk back. "Now."

"It's fireworks, Mason."

Fuck.

Did I really just freak out over fireworks? The really pathetic part is even though she's told me what that horrible sound is, a sound I recognize, I am still going crazy.

She rubs my arms. "Hey, why don't you sit down."

I do. Right there on the third step. Molly brushes my side. Kiran sits next to me. I hate that she is seeing me this way, weak and pitiful. I bury my face in my hands.

"I'll be right back," she says.

"Where are you going?"

"To ask them to stop." Her voice is determined. "One of your neighbors is letting them off. I'm going to give them a piece of my mind."

It's almost laughable for her to think she'll make them stop. I reach for her. As much I hate her to see me like this, I can't stand the idea of being alone. "Stay with me."

"Okay."

Why the fuck am I shaking? I press my hands against my ears to drown out the noise.

She crawls into my lap, each movement tentative as if she's asking for permission. I wrap my arms around her.

"I'm such a loser." I didn't mean to say it aloud, but some thoughts cannot be jailed.

"You're the bravest man I know."

My response is far too cynical to be a laugh. "You're joking, right?"

"No. You thought there were bombs going off, and the first thing you did was come looking for me. If that's not brave, I don't know what is."

I bury my head in her shoulder. The pops grow louder, each one causing me to tense. She hums against my ear. Then she sings, her soft breath hitting my skin. It takes me a moment to recognize the tune. "Home." She's singing Daughtry's, "Home." My go-to, feel-good song.

I hold her tight, rocking back and forth. Maybe it's minutes or hours, hard to tell because she doesn't know all the words. One verse bleeds into another. I'm calmer. I even manage a smile when she messes up a line. She leans her forehead against mine.

"Are you smiling because I'm a horrible singer?" she asks.

"I'm smiling because you make me feel good."

I run my nose down her neck, inhaling the scent of jasmine and tangerines and Kiran. She's wearing a thin shirt and shorts. Her breasts are heaving against my chest. I drop my hands so they rest on the staircase in an effort to keep them to myself.

I fail.

I feel around until I find her ankle. I circle them and inch higher, traveling the journey up her long, long legs. She lets out a sound of pleasure that undoes me. I grasp her hips. She clutches my shoulders. I move up her sides. Her hair brushes against my face. I tangle my fingers through it several times.

"Your hair is shorter."

"About three inches."

"You use a different shampoo now, don't you? It smells of peppermint."

"Peppermint and rosemary."

I have to see her…all of her. There is only way I can accomplish that. I place my hands on the sides of her face. I have to touch her now. I slide my thumbs across her forehead, over her eyebrows, down her nose, and across her high cheeks.

"You didn't have the scar removed?"

"No. It's part of me now."

She's still for me, patient and calm, so I can take my time. I trace my thumbs over her lips. Those fucking delicious lips that put me under a spell. Nothing has changed. They're still soft and sensual and plump. She has that deep indented line that runs vertically down the lower lip. I remember kissing her there.

I want more of her. I want to tease and taste and touch. I want everything. The kiss is uncontrollable. I meant it to be soft and slow, but once I press my lips against hers, I lose it. The dance between us becomes aggressive. I crush my mouth into hers, holding her head with my hands.

I don't relent. I taste her mouth. I tug on her lower lip. I pull her hair. Blood pumps at an alarming speed through every one of my veins.

She gasps. "Mason—"

I keep kissing her, hard, much too hard to be pleasurable or passionate. It's an aggressive full frontal attack. My lips are chapped. Hers have to be bruised. I am being too rough. Too needy. I know this.

She pulls away from me, gasping. "Mason, please."

She shivers in my arms. Ever heard the sound of a tear roll down someone's face? Someone who means everything to you? I have. It tears me apart.

I hang my head in shame. "Jesus, I'm sorry. I don't—"

"Don't be sorry. I'm not."

"Then why the hell are you crying?"

"I wish I wasn't. I don't want this emotion right now, but it's here, and I can't stop it." She expels a double-sob in close succession, something only toddlers or folks who are truly emotionally drained do.

"Kiran, I can't see your face so you really need to explain to me what is happening with you."

"I didn't pine away for you for the last five years. I lived my life. But you were never far from my thoughts. I watched the news religiously. Whenever I heard about military casualties, I held my breath until they released the names. I died a million tiny deaths in the last five years. Every night before I went to bed, I prayed you were safe. I haven't reconciled it all in my head. Everything is happening so fast, the tears just came out." Her voice is quiet and cracks just about every other word. Even in this proximity I have to strain to hear her.

"And you're crying because of what happened to me? Who I am?"

A throaty sound comes from her as if she's shocked by what I said. "Are you really this blind? I just explained it to you. These are tears of joy. I am so fucking relieved you are safe, and I'm so angry with you at the same time. I don't know whether to keep kissing you or smack your head."

Running my thumb over her lips, I smile. "I vote for the first choice. That is, if I am allowed a vote."

I feel her mouth curve as I slide my thumb across it.

She kisses me this time, a soft sweet kiss. I don't move. I let her lead us. I understand she had no time to process this. I want to follow her. There is no doubt I frightened her earlier. I hate myself for it. I don't trust myself not to react like a savage beast again so I give her the control. Her fingers curl into mine. I squeeze her hand. Slowly, my mouth reacts, matching her rhythm. It's as if I'm learning how to kiss all over again. It's always been different with Kiran than anyone else, a feeling I cannot define except to say it makes me feel whole.

We kiss long after the last firework has blasted the sky.

At least, the ones outside.

Chapter 29

Mason

Jeff gave us a full tour of his boat. I'm surprised at how comfortable I am maneuvering around. Not that Jeff or Kiran will let me fall overboard or get caught in a sail. There are six of us on the boat. We set sail, heading to deeper waters where all the best fish stories start. Kiran is wearing shorts. I know this because the bench seat is narrow and my hand has accidently landed on her bare knee a few times.

Okay, maybe not so accidently.

She doesn't inch away. When I apologize, she just brushes closer to me.

Flirty Kiran is a dangerous thing.

We all have a long chat. Kiran gets an earful of our high school glory years and debauchery. There are a few of my more embarrassing moments in there too. The time my buddies and I took a shortcut to school by hopping a fence only to be met with the meanest junkyard dog on the planet is not a tale I enjoy hearing. Especially considering said mutt ripped the back pocket of my jeans and boxers clean off. I showed up to school reporting for first period breathless and bare-assed. Kiran laughs so hard she snorts, which in turn cracks me up.

Having a few beers with old friends while fishing are things I took for granted, but now I realize how special they are. I tell Jeff to man his boat and stop hovering over me. Hopefully, his sister will get the same message. Lana has never made it a secret she has a crush on me, although I've never returned the feelings. Despite moving away from her and every other non-verbal signal I can manage, she's right there every two steps. I swear she has more hands than an octopus.

I'm pissed she thinks my disability entitles her to put her hands on me, using the ruse of being helpful. I tell her in the most respectful way to cut it the fuck out. "Lana, you put your hands on me one more time, I'm blowing a rape whistle." Okay, so maybe not the most tactful of approaches.

"Um…sorry. Just didn't want you to fall. We on are water after all."

"I feel the railing."

"Will you teach me to fish, Mason?" Kiran asks, maybe to help extricate me from Octagirl.

"I'd love to."

We find a quiet spot on the port side. Several people offer to help us with our lines, what with Kiran being inexperienced and me being me. I refuse, though. It takes a while and Kiran has to help, but we finally manage to rig up our tackles.

"Thought we're supposed to use worms," she says.

"Shrimp are better in my opinion. I prefer live, but looks like Jeff went with frozen. It'll still do the job."

"That's a relief. I don't think I could handle wriggling worms. I'm having a hard enough time with this shrimp." She sighs in frustration, her pole falling to the ground.

I laugh as I imagine the disgusted look on her face. "Give it here. I'll set you up."

I pray I don't look like an idiot and hook myself. Like everything else in my new life, it takes a while to figure it out, but I finally do. Then I bait my own line. "You ready to cast off, Shenoy? Hopefully, we can lure ourselves a little dinner."

"Let's do it." She casts out. I follow.

"Now what?"

"Now we wait." I hold up my beer. She clinks hers against the glass. The waves are peaceful, almost lulling. The sun is low, casting an orange aura over everything.

"I read your book," I say, two beers later. "I enjoyed it."

"What?"

"In a manner of speaking. I have an app on my phone that read it to me."

"You're kidding. How did you even know I wrote a book?"

I shrug.

She bumps my shoulder. "Seriously, tell me."

"I cheated. I looked you up a few times."

"Yeah, I thought you cheated. Dana said you read my article too."

"I've read everything you've written. You're definitely following your calling, Kiran."

"Did you really enjoy it?" The question is full of nerves and self-doubt.

"I did."

"It wasn't successful. Only ten people bought it, and I'm not skewing those numbers. It's a fact."

I don't have the heart to tell her only three people bought it. I know this because I purchased seven copies for myself. "That doesn't mean it's not good, Kiran. Will you write another?"

"Not sure yet."

"You should."

"Tell me the truth, Mason. Don't lie to me."

I read the missing words in her sentence. Don't lie to me again. Don't send me fake letters and tell me you don't care about me. She's right. She deserves better. "I'll tell you it's not my typical genre, so I may not be the best judge."

"There is a conjunction missing in that sentence. Spit it out, Cutler."

"I liked it. I did. With that being said, I felt it was a little idealistic." I close my eyes, reciting the last line. "He takes her hand and leads her into the horizon toward an uncertain future, but they both know their love will overcome any obstacle in their path." I wondered, after reading that line, if that's what she wanted for us. What she wanted from me. What I didn't have the courage to do.

She chuckles. "Yeah, I suppose. But then again, I've always been a dreamer."

That's what I love about you, Kiran. "Thank you for coming with me. I know this isn't your thing."

"I don't want to be anywhere else."

I'm about to call out her lie when she squeals. An honest to goodness girly squeal. "I think I've got something."

"Well, hold on to it, girl."

She stands. Her feet stomp as if she's trying to gain traction. She's about to snap her line with all that moving. I reach for her hand. "Steady. Be steady."

"I can't hold it."

"You can," I say, my voice calm, almost at the opposite end of the spectrum to hers. "Pull back on the reel...slow."

I lean my chest into her back. Several pairs of footsteps head in our direction, signaling we've drawn a crowd. They yell out advice, one voice muffling into another.

"Quiet," I say. "She's got this."

Her body tenses. "I don't think I do."

"Relax. Let me help." I run my hands down her arms until I reach the reel. She doesn't move. We work together. This fish is definitely a fighter. It wriggles and squirms. We're patient, letting it tire. When I feel her tense, I take over the reel. When she relaxes, I hand it back to her. We're at it for an hour. When our catch finally emerges, Kiran shrieks in delight.

Jeff claps me on the back. "Congrats guys, that's gotta be the biggest Spanish mackerel I've ever seen."

"The way it fought, I thought it was a shark," Kiran says.

I laugh as I pull in our catch. "Honey, if it was a shark, we'd both be its dinner because it would have dragged us overboard."

Once we get it into the ice, I tell her to sit. I massage her arms and shoulders until I feel the tight knots unraveling. When we dock, we cook the day's catch over an open flame.

"Good job, darling." I polish off my plate.

She leans her head against my shoulder. "Couldn't have done it without you." Her sentence is interrupted by a yawn.

"What do you say we bid our thanks to Jeff and say our good-byes?"

"Okay, if you're sure."

"Positive."

The whole way home, we play old forgotten country songs and sing along. We're both tired, but it's that good kind of exhaustion. The kind that's ripe with accomplishment.

"Are you expecting someone?" she asks as we pull into the driveway.

"No."

"There's a car in the driveway."

"What kind?"

"A black car."

"I'm gonna need more specifics."

"A black car, stained with rust spots, and a broken taillight."

"Not what I meant, Shenoy."

"Sorry, Mason, guess we'll just have to find out because I probably couldn't tell the make and model in the daytime, let alone in the dark."

It doesn't take long to find out.

"Mason!" she yells. "We've been waiting for you all day." The voice is loud enough to penetrate through the closed windows.

"You recognize her voice?" Kiran asks.

"Yeah." I wince, wishing we could back out the driveway and keep on driving until we hit the ocean.

"Who is she?"

"A woman who once rented me space in her womb for nine months, and I've been paying back rent ever since."

Chapter 30

Kiran

Mason's mom is attractive, but it's clear from her wrinkled face and the way she carries herself she's had some difficult years. She has the same honey-colored hair as her children and Mason's blue eyes. She's wearing a low-cut dress and worn tennis shoes.

"What can I do for you?" Mason asks, as soon as he steps out of the car.

"I'm over here, Mason." She puts her arms out and takes a few steps toward Mason. He holds his hand up, gesturing her to stop.

"I know exactly where you are. Stay there."

"What kind of way is that to talk to your mama?"

"What do you want?" There is a cold sharpness in Mason's tone I have never heard before.

"To see my son." She blinks at me a few times. "Who are you?"

"I'm Kiran. I'm helping out while Dana is away," I explain, not wanting to put anything else on Mason's shoulders. He's tense, struggling with something deep and dark.

"And where is Dana?"

"In Antarctica," I say.

The woman gives me a sideways glance before she bursts out laughing. "Are you pulling my leg?"

"She's not," Mason answers. "It's been Dana's dream for at least ten years. Of course, you wouldn't know that."

The woman fidgets with her dress. "Now, now, son, no reason this can't be pleasant."

"Mrs. Cutler," I say, stepping between Mason and her. "Maybe you can come back in the morning?"

"Hardly, I'm only passing through." She knocks three hard, loud raps on the car window. "Gerald, get up."

I touch Mason's arm to let him know where I am. "There is someone in the car."

The man takes his time stepping out of the vehicle. He runs a hand through the few flyaway wisps on his head before making his way toward us.

"Come and meet your new stepdaddy, son." She holds up her hand to reveal a small stone. When Mason doesn't react, she puts her arm down. "Oh sorry, I'm still getting used to you not being able to see."

"Used to it? How did you even know?"

"I still have friends in this town, Son. I called as soon as I found out. Didn't Dana tell you? I wanted to visit earlier, but she said not to come. She told me you didn't want to see me.'"

"She was right."

Gerald takes a few steps forward, his face fitted with a smile that doesn't reach his eyes. "Hi, Mason, Carla has told me a lot about you." He reaches his arm out.

"He's holding out his hand," I say to Mason.

"I already knew that, Kiran."

I step back, unsure what my role should be. I want to tell this horrible woman to go away. All she's doing is stressing out Mason.

Mason sighs, dragging a hand through his hair. "You need to get back into your car and leave. Do not come back here again. You are not welcome."

"This is my mama's house," Carla says.

"You weren't welcome here when Gram was alive, and you sure as hell aren't now."

Gerald clears his throat. "Look, Mason, we've driven a long way. My car here is on its last legs. It pretty much broke down in your driveway. Carla and I are dog-tired. Can you just offer us a place to stay for the night?"

As if God, or maybe the other guy, is weighing in on this decision, it starts pouring.

"Great," Mason mutters heading toward the door. He unlocks it. "Well, c'mon."

When they bring in two large bags, I question if they are only staying one night. The bulky luggage lands with a thump a few feet from the door right where Mason can trip on them.

"I'll put these upstairs in Dana's room," I say, going to reach for one.

Mason grabs my arm. "I'll do it."

Carla stares at the steps. "I don't think Gerald can handle the stairs. He has a bad back."

"Oh, then why don't you stay in my room?" I offer. "It's down here." All I want to do is get them settled so Mason and I can go to sleep. This is the worst ending to the best day.

"That should work," Carla says.

Mason holds his hand out for one of the bags.

"It's heavy," I say handing it to him.

He lifts it, feeling the weight, before flinging if over his shoulder. "Jesus, what do you have in here, Carla? Bricks?"

"Just our stuff. We're moving to Georgia. Gerald found work there."

Rolling the other suitcase, I follow Mason. When I come out, the unwanted guests have taken off their shoes right in the middle of the foyer. I pick them up. "I'll just put these in the closet."

"Thank you, dear. Can you make us something to eat? We're starved."

Mason crosses his arms. "She's not a maid."

"Isn't she working for you?"

"She is my friend, and you will treat her with respect."

"I don't mind," I say, hoping it'll relieve the thick fog of tension that's taken over the house. I scramble toward the kitchen before Mason can object anymore.

He follows me inside. Yesterday, I attempted Gram's fried chicken recipe. It didn't turn out as expected, but it wasn't horrible. I take out the Tupperware with our leftovers and some macaroni salad.

"Are you okay?" I ask him.

He rubs his temple. "I don't want them here. But I don't feel right throwing her out. Either way, I'm going to apologize to you right now for anything she has said or will say."

"Don't, Mason."

"Where are you planning to sleep?"

"I'll be fine on the couch."

"No, you won't. Sleep in Dana's room tonight."

"It's not necessary."

"Sleep in Dana's room tonight," he repeats, his voice taking on a cold commanding tone I'm not used to. It's at odds with the way his fingers grip the countertop. I almost wonder if his prints will be on the stone when he lets go.

"Sure, I'll sleep in Dana's room."

I'm thinking of what else to say in this crazy moment to help him. He takes my hand and pulls me toward him. The embrace lasts for a while, as if he needs this. The rhythm of his pumping heart echoes in my ear.

"Why don't you go change?" I suggest.

He twists a strand of my damp hair. "Let me help you."

"I'm just reheating leftovers. It's no big deal. Go ahead."

"Okay. I'll be right back."

I take the chicken from the microwave when Carla waltzes into the small kitchen.

She takes a look at the plates I'm setting up. "Gerald can't have fried foods. Do you have fixings for a few sandwiches?" She opens the fridge before I can answer. "Here we go." She takes out some lunchmeat, tomatoes, and cheese. From the pantry, she takes a can of tomato soup. "I can fix our supper," she says. "That will be all, Karen."

"It's Kiran." I dump the chicken into the garbage.

Carla gives me an up and down stare as if she's noting every physical flaw I have. I cross my arms and lean against the counter. That's right, I'm not going anywhere. How did Mason grow up to be such a fine man when he was raised by a woman like her? Then again, Mason credits all his happy memories to his father, grandfather, and of course, Grams.

She throws the soup into a pot, leaving the can opener and the serrated metal lid on the counter. I pick up the trash and throw it out. I wipe down the countertop so it won't stain from the soup she's spilled. Carla takes the sharpest knife from the tack board over the sink and begins to slice the tomato. "How do you know my son?"

"We met when we were both vacationing in Florida."

She leaves the knife and cutting board on the counter. I wash them and put everything away. She starts on the sandwiches. I take the soup off the stove before it boils over.

She throws a plate in the sink. I rinse it and place it in the dishwasher.

She sighs, drumming her long red nails on the countertop. "What is with you? I said I can do this. You don't have to clean up after me. Mason made it clear you are not a maid."

My parents always taught me never to disrespect elders, but there is only so much a person can take.

"I'm not cleaning up after you. I'm trying to maintain a safe environment for Mason. His home should be safe." She doesn't seem to comprehend. "He feels with his hands. Leaving sharp objects lying around is dangerous." Not to mention, extremely inconsiderate.

"Mason has always been self-sufficient."

"Of course he is, but this is like hiding a bear trap in someone's living room."

She nods. "You're right. I'm sorry." Good, she understands. She turns to me once before taking the food to the living room. "Be a dear and clean that pot out. And grab us a few beers."

Gerald and Carla eat their dinner on the couch. Mason and I sit on the armchairs flanking them. All of us are drinking beers. I figured like me, Mason could use one.

"Why did you come here?" Mason asks.

"I wanted to see you, Son." She looks around the house. "You know, you should think about selling this place. It's free and clear, right?"

"Why would I sell it?"

"Houses are fetching a nice price in this area what with people moving father out from Charleston and all."

"And where do you suggest I reside?"

"There are so many marvelous communities for people like you, Mason. They have the most qualified staff." She glances at me with a disapproving stare.

"I'm independent."

"Well these places can cater to that."

He sighs. "I'm not selling the house. Is that what you wanted? Because even if I did, you're not entitled to a single cent."

"It was just a mere suggestion. That's not why I'm here, Son."

Every time she calls him son, he gets a little more aggravated. I wish she would stop.

Mason takes a long swig from his beer. "Why are you here, Carla?"

"It's mama. You call me mama."

"You were relieved of that title a long time ago. Now, what is it you want from me?"

"I wanted to see you. To make sure you're all right."

"Quit your crap, Carla."

"Listen, young man, don't talk to your mother that way," Gerald says, although his demeanor doesn't match his voice.

"Sorry. *Please* quit your crap, Carla." He tilts his head toward Gerald. "Is that better, Ger?"

"You're being very disrespectful," Gerald says.

Mason steeples his fingers. "You're right, Ger. My grams and daddy taught me better than this. I guess I'm taking after my mother right now. What are you on, Carla? Is it Oxy? Or is hillbilly heroin too expensive now? Did you downgrade to meth?"

"I've been clean for two years."

Mason claps his hands. One. Two, three solid claps. "Great job, Carla. Please forgive me, I'm fresh out of blue ribbons."

Gerald moves forward in his seat. She pats his leg. "It's all right. Let's just all calm down. Mason is angry right now. We have unresolved issues to work through."

Mason's mouth tightens into a straight line. "Unresolved issues? The JFK assassination is an unresolved issue." He gestures between them. "Us? There is no resolving this. Why are you here? Really? Do you need money?"

"No."

"Then what? Because there's no fucking way this is a social visit."

She takes her napkin and wipes the lipstick encrusted corners of her mouth. "I was hoping you'd let me have the Trans Am."

I gasp. Losing his stamina, Gerald melts into the couch. Carla wipes invisible crumbs off the table. It's Mason's reaction that is the oddest. He laughs. It's a harsh, guttural sound and quite possibly the hollowest laugh I've ever heard.

Mason shakes his head. "Aye, there's the rub."

I move to sit on the arm of his chair to be closer to him. I squeeze his arm to let him know I'm there. I'm not sure if I should go. This is a family matter after all. But I can't imagine leaving him alone with this vicious woman who is so ugly inside it's almost impossible to reconcile Dana and Mason are her children. He puts his hand on my knee. That's all the reassurance I need to stay right where I am.

Now that she's come out with her real reasons, she spits out each sentence in a fast frenzy. "I mean your father bought that car."

"He bought the chassis for us to work on. He always meant it to be my car."

"I'll give you some money toward the repairs."

"How the hell did you know it was running anyway?"

"I told you I still have friends here. I heard you've been tooling around with some girl driving it." Her icy gaze turns my way.

Mason drags a hand through his hair. "Now I remember why I hate this town. Too damn small in every way except for the huge fucking grapevine that cuts clear across state lines."

"Hear me out, Son."

"I heard you and, for God's sake, stop referring to me as your son. But just for the record, let me make sure I got it straight. You believe you're entitled to my vehicle because my daddy bought the chassis and a few parts?"

"Yes and…"

"And?"

Carla is quiet, wringing her hands. "I need a smoke."

"Not in my house."

She shifts to stand. "We'll just be outside then."

"Tell me first," Mason says with more force.

"Mason," I say, trying, rubbing his shoulder. "Let's go to bed. We're all tired."

"No, Kiran. I want her to answer me." The lines of his jaw harden. "I'm burning up with curiosity. I gotta know."

"Know what?" I ask him.

"Why the woman who hasn't seen me in over ten years, the one who gave up on her children when they needed her most, the one who doesn't have the decency to attend her own mama's funeral, comes here unannounced, delivered straight to my door by the devil himself. Why in the hell would a woman like this see fit to ask me for a favor?" He's not yelling, but each sentence makes me flinch.

I have no idea how she can respond to that. Maybe she realizes there is no excuse for her behavior either because she says the worst possible thing. "You're not using it, are you?"

I almost fall as I stand. "You—you—" Oh my God, I can't even form words.

Mason shoots out of the chair. I wonder for a second if I should block him or encourage him. I'm so angry. Instead of doing or saying anything to her, he swings his arm around my waist. "Calm down, Shenoy. You're getting a crash course in Carla, but I'm used to this."

"She can't talk to you this way, Mason. This isn't right."

"A lot of things aren't right in this world." He pulls me against his chest.

"What is that supposed to mean?" she asks, her eyes narrowing at us.

"Carla, maybe we should get to bed," Gerald suggests, taking her arm.

Carla jerks her arm away. "Not until Mason tells me no. Our car is on its last wheels, and we'll never make it. If you say no, Mason, I'll zip my mouth. I promise I'll leave it alone."

"Will you?"

"Yes."

"Will you leave me alone if I say yes?" he asks.

My heart breaks for him.

"Mason, I'm sorry about this. I've messed up more times than I can count."

"I don't want your sorry-ass apologies. Take the fucking car. I'll sign over the title. It's yours as long as you promise to be out of here at the crack of dawn and never set foot in mine or Dana's life again. Is it a deal?"

"Mason—"

"Is it a deal?"

"But—"

"Is it a deal?" He lets go of me. He holds his hand out like this is a real business transaction. "Shake on it or swear on a stack of bibles. Just tell me it's a deal."

She bursts into tears. Gerald puts his arm around her.

Sealing the deal, she shakes his hand.

I shut my eyes tight, trying to dam up the tears before they fall.

Chapter 31

Mason

I can't sleep. I listen for the sounds of Carla or Gerald stirring. I won't be able to sleep until daylight comes and they are long gone, at least past the county lines. Part of me wants to go to the shed. It's really the only place I feel truly relaxed, but there is no way I can go anywhere and leave Kiran alone with my womb donor and her current man of the hour.

Molly's food bowl is probably empty. I decide to go fill it. On the way back, I stop at the top of the stairs at Dana's room. The door's open a crack. I lean against the hallway.

"Mason?" she asks.

Great, as if meeting the fucked-up side of my gene pool isn't enough. Now I'm standing outside her door, a certified stalker, watching her sleep. Well, not exactly watching. Somehow, that makes it creepier.

I take a step inside. "Sorry, I didn't mean to wake you."

"I wasn't asleep." Her voice is lower than it should be, more distant.

"Are you sleeping on the floor?"

"Yeah."

"Why?"

Then I realize why. Sometimes, I can be a dope. "Shit, you probably hate the waterbed. I totally forgot about it."

"Didn't waterbeds go extinct in the nineties?"

I laugh, wondering how it's even possible to produce laughter right now. "Apparently, this is a holdover. Dana thought it would help her acclimate for deep sea diving. Don't ask me. She's just weird."

"I actually didn't mind the waterbed except for the temperature. It's freezing cold."

I rub the back of my neck. "Suppose I should have told you about the heat pump. I would have if I'd remembered."

"There's a heat pump?"

"Yeah, but it takes a good while to heat up." I take a few more steps, cautious because I'm not sure where she is and the last thing I want is to step on her. "Get up."

"Up?"

"You can sleep in my bed."

I hear her shift up. "You're sleeping on the waterbed?"

"Hell no. I'll sleep on the floor, thank you kindly."

"You don't have to give up your bed."

"Yes, I do. Get up."

She moves past me to my room. I follow behind. My door squeaks as she pushes it open. "There's room on your bed for both of us."

"Kiran, it's not a good idea."

She takes my hand and walks us to the bed. "Then I'll sleep on the couch."

"Sounds like a threat."

"It's not a threat. It's a question. Why am I up here, Mason?"

"The couch is uncomfortable. Now get into bed. I know you're tired."

"Not without you. We can sleep in the same bed. Just sleep."

Tonight, when I wrapped my arms around her, she was shaking, all furious with anger and ready to pounce in my defense. Somehow, that distracted me from my own anger. I am thankful she was there. Her presence calmed me.

But this? Sleeping in the same bed together is going to be anything but calming. We haven't been intimate since the intense kissing session. A part of me cannot resist her no matter how hard I fight the urges.

I'm falling in love with her again.

Fuck, who the hell am I kidding?

I never fell out of love with her.

"Stop being stubborn, girl."

"I'm stubborn? You're the one who isn't seeing reason. Besides, you're lying to me."

"About what?"

"The couch is super comfortable. I fell asleep on it the other night when we watched that movie, remember? You put the blanket over me. Why was it fine then and not now?"

"That's really good, CSI, but enough already."

"You're right. The couch it is."

I pull her back as she's walking away. "Wait." I sigh. "We'll sleep on the bed."

"Okay," She gets in on the side closest to the door.

"Slide over. I need to be by the door."

We both lie on the bed. The rain has come back. It hits all the angles of the house. I try to zone into the rhythm of it instead of the beautiful girl beside me.

"I love the rain," she says.

"Me too."

She squirms on the bed, her hair brushing against my arm as she gets comfortable. Goddamn girl, sit still, I'm trying to keep it together over here.

"I hate your mother."

Yeah, that's better. Talk about my mother. That's like ten buckets of the Antarctic sea dousing any arousal.

"I'm embarrassed you had to witness my family drama."

"Don't be. It just shocks me how good you turned out, Mason. I can't believe you gave her the car."

"Why not? She's right. I don't need it."

"But—"

"It's a small price to pay if it means not having to see her again, Kiran. I appreciate you learning to drive it for me. It meant a lot, but it's time to let it go."

"Still, it makes me so mad." Her slow, rich, velvety voice is closer to me. "That woman…well, she…she…" Kiran sits up. "Can't. Understand. Normal. Thinking."

"Yeah, she's changed. Drugs and desperation will do that." My jaw drops, replaying Kiran's sentence. "Girl, did you just call my mother a cun—"

She slaps her hand over my mouth. "I didn't say that exact word." She sounds contrite. "I'm sorry."

I pull her wrist and bring her toward me. "I'm not mad. But you need to understand, she wasn't always the woman you met tonight. Once, she was my mama. And a good one at that. The kind that headed up the PTA and attended every school function."

She rests her head on my chest. "What changed?"

"She lost the person she loved most. When my dad died, I think all the good parts of her went into the cold, hard ground with him. She started drinking more and taking sleeping pills every night. She decided to replace him with a revolving door of men. I sat back and just tried to get by. I took Dana to school and made sure she ate, but I ignored all the other shit. I was stupid, Kiran. I thought she'd just snap out of it one day. Have a fucking epiphany or hit rock bottom, but it never happened. It just got worse. Dana paid the price for my ignorance."

"What happened?"

"Football practice was canceled because the weather was calling for thunderstorms. I came home early and…" I can't even finish the rest. I can't go back to that awful day in the middle of July, only ten months after my father passed. "He was a nice guy too. Helped us with bills and even came to a few of my games. I thought maybe he'd help Carla find what she needed. She cared for him more than the others. That day, I realized he was the devil incarnate. After I beat the hell out of him, I called Grams. She drove all night and got us out of there. Not only that, she brought her shotgun and threatened to blow his balls off if he so much as came near her granddaughter again. Grams got Dana therapy and gave us a proper home. I don't know if anyone could have helped Dana more. I know this sounds fucked up, but in time, I might have been able to forgive my mother for those horrible choices. I still loved her on some level, even though I hated her. Does that make any sense?"

"Yes, it does to me. Although I don't think I could forgive her at all. It's remarkable that you could."

"I can't now. She crossed a line we can never rebound from."

"What line, Mason?"

"She took her pedophile boyfriend's side. When Dana testified for the prosecution against the bastard, she was a witness for the defense. Who the fuck does that to their own kid? Thankfully, the judge saw right through it. The bastard's locked up now. I'm thankful Dana's not here. She's never gotten over it."

"Who could get over something like that? You haven't either." Kiran's voice is thick. She wraps her arms around me in a tight hug. She's shaking; hot tears land on my chest.

I hold her close and kiss her head. "So yeah, you're right. She's a woman who can't understand normal thinking."

"You were so young, Mason. No one should have to go through what you did. Thank you for telling me."

"Just answering your question, Shenoy."

"What question?"

"Why you're lying in my bed instead of the couch. I don't know Gerald, but I know her. I don't trust anyone she chooses. I sure as hell won't make the same mistake twice."

She runs her fingers through my hair. "Mason, I think you have the strongest protection mechanism I've ever seen."

"Honey, you've got the same trait. Just because I'm blind doesn't mean I can't see how heated up you were."

"You told me to calm down."

"I was holding you back. Kiran, you are brave, intelligent, tenacious, courageous, and heroic. You know what that stands for?"

"Pretty sure it stands for b-i-t-c-h."

"Trust me, I mean it as a compliment."

"I know." She yawns and lays her head against my chest once more.

We're both drained. This day has been nothing but emotional highs and lows.

"Good night, Cutler. Sweet dreams."

"Sweet dreams, sunshine."

Chapter 32

Kiran

Of all the times I imagined sharing a bed with Mason, the other night was not it. But we talked, and I had a better understanding of him. In a sense, I wish I didn't. I'm still holding out hope for us. There was something needy and desperate when he kissed me that went beyond lust. But it wasn't love in that kiss. I try not to fixate on us. There *is* no us. There is me helping him out. Him being grateful but not pushing. I see flickers of the boy I knew. He still exists beneath the hard exterior of the beautiful man I crave. The man I love.

Speaking of lust, I've managed to create an entire soundtrack of raunchy parodies that play in my head while Mason runs on the treadmill. Tonight, I keep thinking of the way his powerful legs flexed and the sheen of sweat coated his body before he went upstairs to take a shower. Tonight, I think my fingers will frustrate me instead of providing any relief. This is a hot as Hades South Carolina evening when nothing stirs. Everything stands still, the heat stifling any movement.

Except for me. I am restless. Every small shift reinvigorates my craving for him.

I cannot sleep. I suck on ice chips. I pray for rain.

I eat a plum, biting the fleshy fruit and sucking the sweet juice. I wash my face and hands. I decide to take off every article of clothing. After all, my panties are drenched. It's not enough. Finally, I go to him. The oak staircase announces my arrival with each slow, longing step.

"Kiran…" he says as I stand outside his door.

I don't wait for an invitation this time. Closing my eyes, I turn the knob. It's dark and quiet except for the slow pitch rhythm of the circulating fan.

I wonder if he can hear my heart beating. It's so loud it reverberates in my skull.

"Couldn't sleep, sunshine?"

"No."

He lifts the covers and pats the empty space next to him. "Come here."

I get into the bed. He reaches for me. Grasping my arm, he pulls me on top of him. I'm suddenly in his strong arms, our bodies entwined.

"You're coming to my bed fucking naked? You think I can resist?"

"I'm hoping you can't."

He's not wearing a shirt. I feel down his side with the palms of my hands. The tattoos hide the wounds on his body, but I feel them now. He doesn't shy away from my touch. He holds me closer and rolls us over.

His kiss is still hard, but it's tender too. He didn't shave today. The gruff on his face slides along my skin.

"Are the lights off?" he asks in a raspy whisper.

"Yes, why?"

"Because I want us on even footing."

His lips travel down my neck. His tongue flicks my nipple. His teeth scrape against my skin. I beg for more.

His rough, calloused hands slide down my body. His touch is different. It's slow and lingering. His cock is a hard, heavy column against my thigh.

"God, Kiran, you're still so beautiful."

"Make love to me now."

I feel his smile against my neck. "I'm barely hanging on here. I'm planning to fuck you. You see, I want to be gentle, but I'm too hungry to do this right."

"There isn't a wrong way, Mason."

"We'll see." He's inside of me in one quick urgent thrust. He groans, his fingernails biting into my flesh. "Don't move...please."

I force myself to stay still. "Okay."

"You're so fucking tight."

"And wet."

He licks his lips. "That too." Mason leans his forehead against mine. "This will be hard for me."

"You're definitely hard."

He runs his thumb across my lips. "Pipe down on the smartassery. I'm struggling here."

I wait for him. Mason's strong body tightens. He shifts once inside of me. I moan with pleasure just from that small shift. As if that sound is a spark, he takes off. I don't even have a second to brace for this. He fucks me. His wild, primal masculine thrusts leave me quaking. I lose myself to them. To the feeling of him inside of me. He possesses every cell in my body.

He covers my face in beautiful, passionate kisses while he drives into my body like it's the Autobahn. "You feel so damn good, sunshine." I think that's what he says, but it's a garbled mess, and I can barely process a full sentence.

I hang on to him, pulling his hair and wrapping my legs around his hips like a vise. He grasps my legs to deepen his thrusts. I call his name. His breaths grow harsher, and his speed quickens. I feel myself at the edge. Then he stops. A warmth spreads inside of me.

"Fuck."

In the low moonlight, I can make out his grimace. His body clenches.

"It's okay," I say.

He buries his head against my neck. "Fail."

"You didn't fail."

"Did you come, and I missed it?"

"No."

"Then I failed."

He gets up and heads to the bathroom. I want to go to him, but he slams the door. I lay there, not sure why he is so angry. I'm not. In fact, I'm still trying to catch my breath. It wasn't a marathon, but definitely qualified as a fast sprint. He returns with a wash cloth for me. I clean myself up.

Dragging a hand through his thick hair, he sighs. "I'm so sorry, darlin'."

"Don't be. It happens."

"Maybe so, but it's still pretty pathetic and selfish."

"The last word I'd use to describe you is selfish. You're really weighing down my high."

"What high?"

"You wanted me so much you couldn't hold out. At least that's how I looked at it. To tell the truth, it made me feel a little cocky actually."

He laughs. "Don't joke."

I sigh and fall back into the bed. "You're right. It was the worst thing ever. You've officially ruined sex for me. I'll never be the same ever again. Thanks, Mason. Thank a lot."

This time he laughs harder. "I forgot how fluent you are in sarcasm." He lies down, facing me.

"Yeah, I minored in it at college. Made the dean's list and everything."

"Is that a fact?" He feels around until he finds an errant strand of hair. He promptly tucks it behind my ear. That little gesture makes me want to ride the Autobahn all over again.

"It is."

"It's been a very long time for me, Kiran."

"How long?"

"Five years."

"Are you teasing?"

He places my hand over his heart. "Swear it. I went out on a few dates over the years, but it never went beyond that."

"I see."

"Kiran, there's another problem." His mouth tightens into a grim line. "We didn't use any protection. So I failed on two counts. I didn't even think about it. I'm so sorry. We can go to the drugstore. I think there's an all-night one between here and Charleston. We'll get you the pill, sweetheart."

I lace my fingers through his. "Stop apologizing to me. I should have told you. We don't have to worry about that. I'm on birth control, and I don't have any diseases."

He releases a breath. "That's good. I suppose."

"You suppose?"

"It's really good, Kiran. I've been tested too, not that it matters."

"I wasn't tested. I haven't been with anyone since you."

He jerks his head up. "But you were with…with him for six months."

"Vik was patient with me. We talked about it a few times. I even went on birth control, but it never felt right." I don't know how to explain to him what I don't understand myself. How can you cheat on someone you're not even with? But every time I tried to be intimate with another man, it was like I was betraying Mason. He must have felt the same way. God knows, the man is Adonis incarnate, and he probably had a million offers. "We never went any further than kissing. But I stayed on the pill."

"I should not be happy about this." His grin widens. "But I am."

"Yeah, I can see that."

His fingers glide down my side, ghosting across my breasts and down my waist until his hand settles on my hip. "Hey, it's not as if anyone has pleased me. The only companion I've had is my right hand, which, although talented in its own right, is no match for you." He kisses me, sucking on my lower lip. "Do you know how many times I've imagined being inside you?"

"I'll go with one hundred and twenty-seven thousand, six hundred and two times."

He arches a brow. "That's an oddly specific number."

"Just an educated guess based on the number of times I've imagined it."

"That's your number, baby?"

"Well, I tacked on a few thousand because... Well, because you're a boy."

He laughs and pulls me against him. "Sounds accurate."

"What can I do to make it better for you?"

"You want to make it better for me? Kiran, I came. It was very good for me."

"Yeah, but is there something that I could have done?"

"Come faster maybe?"

I giggle and punch him in the arm. Ouch. Apparently, his arm is still made of steel. "Seriously?"

He presses his mouth against my forehead in a tender kiss. "First of all, I love that you're asking me that. Secondly, I need you to be a little more verbal. Tell me what you feel, what you like, how you want me to touch you and when you're close or not close. I can't see your face. I doubt it would have made a difference tonight, but I can't gauge it for myself. When I'm with you, it's way too fucking intense for me to pick up on all your physical cues alone. At least for right now."

"It makes total sense. I can do that, Mason."

"I really wish I could have taken you there, sunshine."

"Not to sound cliché, but you know what they say."

"No, sweetheart, I don't. What do they say?"

"Practice makes perfect."

He chuckles. He's left the door open, and a shaft of light comes from the hallway illuminating his naughty expression. "Right you are."

"What's up with your face, Cutler? You look like the cat who ate the canary."

"You are just chock-full of clichés tonight, darling." He traces my lips with his tongue. "Not sure what's up with my face, but you know what I am sure is up?"

"What?"

He takes my hand and slides it down his waist until it's right over his cock—his very hard, long cock. "I can guarantee I didn't eat a canary, but I sure as hell plan to have my fill of peaches."

Chapter 33

Mason

I enter the kitchen from the backdoor to fetch a bottle of water. Okay, so I really came in to see if she'll "practice" with me again. Now that my appetite is back, I'm insatiable. Luckily, she's pretty voracious herself. I'm happy to report I've learned how to please her. In some ways, the sex is more intense than ever because I get to see her beautiful body with my hands. I try to touch every inch of her.

I stop in my track when I hear the voices. Kiran's either on her phone or Skyping with her father. She has it on speaker. She thinks I'm in the shed. I head to the fridge for the bottle of water and hope by the time I gulp it down she'll be off so I can get her off. Dawdling where I have no business, I take a slow sip of the ice water. The house is sturdy, but loud voices can leak through plaster walls.

"Linda told me the truth. You're living with some boy you met when you went on vacation five years ago?" Her father's voice is ripe with disapproval and indignation. Guess Kiran kept me her dirty little secret, not that I blame her.

"It's not like that. You don't understand."

"How can I understand when you lie to me, beta?"

I should leave.

"Papa, I love him."

Nope. I'm gonna stay.

"You haven't seen him for five years. What kind of man leaves a woman?"

"You did."

Oh, shit.

He lets out a long line of words, most of which I could not understand.

"Stop it," she says. "You know Mason had to leave."

"Why didn't he come back for you?"

She could not answer that one."

"You don't even know what love is," she said, her voice wavering. "You should not lecture me on this topic, Papa."

"Someone should talk sense into you. Do you know Vik is still single by the way?"

"How do you know that? Oh Papa, please don't tell me you still talk to my ex."

"He's one of my clients so, yes, I talk to him. I'm not allowed to divulge information due to the privacy laws, but let me just say he has a very healthy portfolio. He still asks about you."

She lets out a frustrated sigh. "Well, stop telling him anything."

"He's a wonderful person."

"Then you should date him."

"He is a catch."

"I'm going to disconnect now."

"Do not hang up on me. Tell me about this boy."

"Why? You're just going to go all judgmental or maybe just mental. Either way, it'll frustrate both of us."

"Is it true he's blind?"

"Yes, but that doesn't matter to me."

"It should matter. You've always been a dreamer, Kiran. This isn't a dream. This is your life. Does he even have a job? Can he support you?"

No, he doesn't, I answer silently. He's living on a VA disability check in a house his grandma left him. His portfolio is non-existent. He can't take care of your daughter.

"He supports me like no one else ever has."

"You didn't answer the first question."

"He's still getting acclimated to his new life. Not everything is about money."

"Will you remember that the next time you want to go to Europe? Better yet, how about if you want to purchase a new car?"

"You forget, I support myself."

"You should find someone who supports you in every way. You deserve that, beta. Do you want to take care of someone for the rest of your life?"

No, that's not what she wants. It's not what I want for her either.

"Yes, I want to take care of him for the rest of my life. You know why, Papa? Because he takes care of me too. I'm not asking for your approval here. I was keeping him from you because I knew you would not understand. But I'm not ashamed to tell you I'm with Mason. Mason is the strongest, most honorable man I've ever met. He fought for this country. He protected us, Papa. He's my hero, and I won't listen to you bash the man I love."

She's saying some really nice things about me. Every sentence comes straight from her heart. But I can't invest in the sentiments. She's so self-assured about us. I want to believe in her words, to stride into the other room and make it clear Kiran Shenoy is mine. She has always been mine. She belongs to me just as I belong to her.

Maybe a hero would do that.

But there are no heroes living here.

Chapter 34

Kiran

I stand outside between the jasmine shrub and tangerine tree. The wind picks up, blowing the blossoms into the air. I close my eyes and inhale the scent as they fly past me, the petals brushing my skin. I hum along to the sad lyrics echoing from inside the shed. The song is called "Hurt." It's not the original Nine Inch Nails version, which is epically stupendous in itself. No, this is Johnny Cash's take. It's much slower and more haunting. Sometimes you can feel pain radiating from a song. Johnny Cash radiates pain like no other artist.

I knock on the shed door. "Mason, its Kiran." I say it the way I've said for the past twenty-five days. I almost add, "Let me in to your secret clubhouse."

Mason opens the door. His navy blue V-neck T-shirt is specked with gray dust. It's in his hair, and his hands are covered with it. Whatever he's working on, he's giving it his all. I'm sure it's some kind of sculpture. I'm dying to see it, but he hasn't invited me in yet. So until he gives me the super-secret password to the clubhouse, I'll do my best to keep my curiosity in check.

His muscular body takes up the entire doorframe so I can't even peek inside. "Hey, girl," he says in a way that can do battle with the best Ryan Gosling meme. His sexy, raspy voice is sugared with southern swagger.

"I'm going to the grocery store. Want to come?"

"I would, but I'm busy in here."

"Okay. I'll see you in a bit then." I turn to leave.

"Wait." He takes my arm and slides his hand down until he's touching my wrist. His fingers graze across my skin. He traces the port-wine heart-shaped birthmark. "Do you want to come in and see what I'm doing?"

What? Am I being invited into the Bat Cave? The Club House? The secret lair? "Um, yeah."

He draws a deep breath. He's nervous. "C'mon in, Shenoy."

He kicks the door open. I take a tentative step. He stands behind me. I blink to adjust to the low light. "It's too dark in here."

"Sorry," he says, switching on a light. "I forget."

I gasp when I take in the sight. The shed is much larger on the inside than I'd thought. There are several deep shelves on the far wall. On each one, there is a sculpture of a sandcastle. Some are large and regal with sweeping staircases and tall turrets like the one he made all those year ago. Others are small and more whimsical. I was wrong. This isn't a shed or a replica of a house. No, this is something else entirely. I'm standing in Mason's artist studio.

"They're spectacular. I had no idea."

"No idea of what, sunshine?"

"I knew you had skills, but this... This is beyond anything I imagined."

"A very special girl once told me I should be a sandcastle builder."

"That's one smart girl."

"She's brilliant."

I move closer, examining each piece. The details are vibrant. "You have so much talent."

His smile is full of relief. "Thank you. I'm happy you like them."

"Like them? That's an understatement."

"How did you learn all these techniques?"

"Working with clay was part of my rehabilitation. I enjoyed it so I bought a few slabs and started experimenting. It's like my hands remember what my eyes can't comprehend."

"Muscle memory, right?"

"Yeah, guess so."

"There are cases like this. Have you ever heard of Francisco Luggio?"

"Can't say I have."

"He was blinded as a teenager. But he'd always painted. He was able to resume his work, and most critics say it got better. They performed head scans on him while he was drawing. They found out the part of the brain that controls the optic nerves had activity. Science can't even explain it."

"Yeah, it is sort of like that for me. I can't see, but everything just has more dimension. Even the air is tangible. I can't explain it except it makes me happy when I'm creating something."

"I have the article. We can load it into your iPad if you want to read it."

He frowns, running a hand through his hair. "How did you know about him?"

"I've been doing research. Just reading up on different cases and stories."

"I hope you're not looking for a cure. You'll only be disappointed."

"Not a cure, Mason. Just trying to understand what it's like in your world. I'm sorry if..."

He takes my face. "No, don't be sorry. I'd be interested in reading the article."

I embrace him. "Thank you for showing all this to me."

He holds me tight. I feel his heart beat through his clothes.

"I'm getting clay on you, and you're wearing a nice dress. At least I think you are."

"I don't care about the clay, but for the record, this is a pretty dress."

"Course it is. Anything you decide to put on is pretty, sunshine. Because you're wearing it."

I turn around to take it all in again. There is a long wooden table flanked by two shorter tables. An array of coffee cans with tools sticking out of them sit on the long table. Everything from chisels to knives to string. I shudder when I spot the knives. Please God, don't let him cut himself. But I see his skills in all these creations. Mason's a true artist, talented and clever. A white sheet covers an object on one of the smaller tables.

"May I see what you're working on now?"

"Sure."

I remove the sheet. One of the smaller tables has slabs of clay on it. He's started something. It's a round figure. "This one doesn't look like a sandcastle."

"It's a different project."

"What is it?"

"You."

"Me?"

"It's my only attempt at sculpting a person, but it's probably a crappy imitation. I've been working on it for a while now. I'm having some trouble with the details. I want it to be right. Would you consider posing for me?"

I suck in a breath. He's sculpting me? It's a solid mass with a few curves. I cannot imagine it finished.

"Pose? How will that work?"

"Say yes, and you'll see."

"I'd be honored to pose for you."

"The honor is mine." His smile goes from cheerful to wicked in two seconds. "Take off your clothes, Kiran."

My skin prickles with the thought of it. "This is a nude?"

"That would be my preference. Not to mention, I will ruin your dress."

"A nude it is."

He licks his lips. "Then let's get on with it." He tugs on my dress. "Take it off."

"You do it."

"With pleasure."

He fingers the straps of my dress before sliding them down my shoulders. The fabric lands around my feet with a soft swish. He grapples with the bra. I take his wrists and move them to the hooks. My belly flips as he drags my panties down. He picks up all my discarded clothing, folds them, and places the items in a neat stack on a vacant corner of the long table.

He approaches me, only a sliver of a gap between us. "Get on the table."

He moves forward as I take a step back. My ass hits the edge. He grips my hips and lifts me onto the surface.

Mason's hands roam through my hair. It's in a tight French braid today. "May I take it down? I'd really like to capture it all wild and tumbling." He's already pulling on the rubber band.

"Yes."

I close my eyes as his fingers travel through my strands. This feels so good I'm not sure how long I can stand it. The circulating fan makes a nice breeze, but the room is heating up a degree or two every time Mason touches me.

"Did you use different shampoo today? Something with coconut?"

"Yeah, I opened a new bottle. Do you like it?"

He buries his nose in my hair and sniffs. "Mmm, I approve."

He lays me down and shifts me to my side. Mason moves one of my legs so it's slightly bent over the other. He takes my arm and places it over my breasts.

He bends down so we're eye level. "Are you all right in this position? Comfortable?"

"I'm fine."

He smiles as he plays with a strand of hair. "This is how I wanted to sculpt you. Completely naked, yet hidden too."

The way he's positioned me, all my naughty bits are covered up with my limbs. He turns off the light. It's almost pitch black except for the few streaks of filtered light coming through slats of the wood shutters. He walks over to the slab of clay on the other table. He begins cutting away the negative space, adding more definition and curves. I watch, grateful to see him in this element where his passion and talent shine. His hands are covered with clay. He walks to the small sink and washes them. When he comes back to me, they are cold and dripping wet. But I need something cool right now. Otherwise I might self-combust. He runs his hands across my body from my ankles to my ass to my hair and everything in between. His deft fingers skate across my flesh until my skin tingles. I try not to squirm as he strokes me, but I fail many times. He gives me a playful smack on the ass.

"Quit it. Behave and be still."

"Trying."

Maybe he considers this posing. I call it the moment between agony and ecstasy. Somewhere between teasing and torture.

I know he's turned on too. Hell, I just have to lower my glance to see how turned on he is. But Mason is a professional. He focuses on the task while I silently plead for release. He reaches back and pulls off his shirt. His jeans ride low on his hips, revealing the sexy indented V-lines on his lower abs. I chew on my bottom lip. A trickle of sweat travels down my back. The rotating fan offers little relief. I want to touch myself so badly.

The sculpture takes on more shape and definition as his deft hands manipulate the clay. I begin to recognize myself in the silhouette he creates. Each one of his carefully carved lines creates more drama with texture and shadow. He uses several knives, chisels, and even string to cut away the excess clay. The figure he's making isn't a life-size model, but it is very accurate. He even draws my scars. He sings softly about rainy days and Mondays while he works.

He comes back to me. His hands touch me once more. He holds my face at an angle, his thumbs traveling down each ridge and bone. This is powerful and intimate. My body isn't perfect, it's marred and flawed. It jiggles and bounces where I don't want it to. I acknowledge those areas, but I no longer dwell on them. In many ways, Mason's helped me with that. When I look at the realistic replica he's making, I see nothing but beauty. I even see beauty in the scars.

He washes his hands again. A sign he will touch me.

Don't touch me if you aren't planning to love me, to fuck me, to ravish me. The last two hours are both torture and rapture. He's working so I'm not sure what this is for him. But for me, it's been some crazy intense form of foreplay. I'm stiff and wet and full of lust.

His thumb crests across my lips. I open my mouth and suck slowly.

He swallows a harsh breath.

"Let's take a break…please."

"Yeah, you need a good, long, stretch."

I unbuckle his jeans and push them down. He lowers his boxers. I pull his hard erect form into my mouth, stroking his shaft as I draw him in. He moans and jerks as my lips wrap tighter around him. His fingers grip the edge of the table. "I need to touch you right now," he says, somewhere between a plea and demand.

"All you've been doing is touching me."

"With my hands. There are other parts of me that are fucking screaming to touch you."

He pushes me back. I watch him, not even daring to blink as he discards his clothes. He walks around the table, gripping the edges with his fingertips. After he comes around the other side, he bends and gives me a tender kiss. His mouth travels south down my body, marking his path with slow seductive kisses and swirling licks of his tongue. I lean my head back as he delves inside of me. His tongue fondles and strokes until I'm a thrashing ball of energy. I'm so warm, yet I'm shivering. He grabs my bottom and lifts me to his mouth.

"Almost, baby," I scream, adjusting his head to where I want it. Where I need it. His fingers dig into my flesh, his mouth devouring me as if I'm the sweetest dish. It all culminates into the most intense climax of my life.

He waits for me to come down from it, stroking himself as I extol his name.

He massages my legs, exactly what I need after being in the same position for hours followed by euphoria.

"Kiran, I need you," he says.

"Then take me, Mason."

He shakes his head and knocks his fist against the table top. "This is a sturdy table. I built it so I know exactly how much weight it can take. But what I have in mind is probably not safe. I know you're a bit of a daredevil, but there are some risks we don't need to take." He leans down and picks me up from the table. I feel safe in his arms as I always have. He sets me down. "On your knees, girl." This he says in his commanding voice, hard and virile. I'm under the spell of Mason Cutler. It's so powerful that time and distance cannot diminish it.

I fall to my knees. He does the same. He turns me around, his strong hands positioning my body so he's crouching behind. He pushes my hair to the side. He kisses my neck, shoulder, and then trails his mouth down my spine. "Tell me if this is not okay with you, baby."

"Mason, it's more than okay."

He lets out a manly grunt to indicate he is pleased by my answer. His body, warm and hard and strong, covers me. His fingers dip inside my sex.

"Jesus, Kiran, you're drenched."

"That's what you do to me, Mason."

He traces my seam with his erection. I struggle to keep the position and not collapse. He enters me slowly. I gasp.

"Am I hurting you?" He asks it with such guilt it tears my heart.

"No. Just getting used to it."

"I'm almost inside."

What the hell? He's not all the way inside yet?

He traces the shell of my ear with his tongue. His teeth scrape against my shoulder. I feel every inch of him. I cry out as he whispers sweet, wicked words with each movement.

"When I'm inside of you, I lose myself. Your body was made for mine. I love fucking you." Yeah, that last one almost makes me come. "Sunshine, angel, darling, Kiran." The words roll together, barely intelligible, as his speed increases.

"I'm close," I tell him, although we're breathing so hard I doubt he's heard.

"Thank God," he mutters, increasing his tempo. His finger presses into my nub in sync to his thrusts.

I close my eyes tight and let go. He follows not far behind.

I'm ready to collapse. He inches out of me and takes me into his arms. We lay there on the polished wood-planked floor, curled up in each other. I run my hands over his skin.

The wounds on his body have mended, but not healed. There is no doubt how much he suffered. It's written on his flesh as clear as any tattoo.

He takes my wrist and kisses the underside. "Don't be sad, sweetheart. They don't hurt anymore."

"I'm not sad. I'm angry at the person who did this to you. I want to destroy him."

"He's dead, Kiran."

"It's not enough."

He turns on his side to face me. "When you are consumed with hate, there isn't room for much else. I should know. For a long time, all I wanted was revenge. I'm not saying I forgive. But I was so angry. Not just at him either. At the whole world. It's funny, I hated the thought of people pitying me. All the while, I pitied myself. That's no kind of life."

"When did you realize that?"

He kisses my head. "About two minutes ago." He chuckles. "Guess I'm a slow leaner."

"You just have a hard head."

"Oh, I've got more than a hard head, girl."

I laugh and kiss his cheek. "Yeah, so I noticed. By the way, I love the sculpture."

"It's nowhere near done."

"I can see what it will be, though."

"Does that mean you'll pose for me some more?"

"Only if we can take breaks and…stretch."

He laughs. "Yeah, whenever you need it." His expression turns sober. "Seriously, Kiran, I want you to know no one will ever see this sculpture. It's just for me."

"It's turning out beautiful. I wouldn't mind if you showed it."

"I mind. There are some things I refuse to share. This piece of art and this moment with you is at the top of that list. It's just between us."

"I understand, but what about your other pieces? You have so much talent. People should see your work."

He twirls a strand of my hair. "Maybe one day."

Chapter 35

Mason

We finished the sculpture yesterday. We celebrated with a bottle of wine, which we then lapped off each other's bodies until we were good and drunk. It's the best piece I've ever done, probably because it was so personal and intimate. I didn't just want to sculpt her figure. I wanted to recreate what I had been craving in my head, my hands, and my heart. Now I will have the memory of her in tangible form. In hindsight, I'm not sure if it was the best idea. After all, I'm just layering salt on a wound that won't heal.

Dana's coming home tomorrow. I'm relieved she's safe. I can't wait to see my sister and hear all the details about her adventures in Antarctica. She e-mailed both Kiran and I quite often, but I won't relax until she's home.

It's the most bittersweet feeling. Dana's arrival marks the end of my time with Kiran. I struggle not to think about that.

Kiran, Molly, and I lie in the backyard on a bed of jasmine and orange blossoms. They fall on us like heady raindrops. Kiran suggested we go to the track at the high school today. I was reluctant until my second pass. I ran outside for the first time in almost a year with Molly right beside me. Kiran kept pace with us too. Well, at least once I slowed down, she did. The three of us ran past the point of exhaustion. The burn in my muscles feels so fucking good. The treadmill and weights have kept me in shape, but there is something about running in the open air that's both freeing and cleansing.

Kiran and I took a long, much-needed shower. We took our time, scrubbing each other clean, exploring every inch of each other's bodies.

Now, I'm here, lying beside her, the sound of a ticking clock fucking with my head. I feel differently than that first day she showed up at this very spot. But no matter how hard I try, I cannot rid myself of her father's warnings. They replay in my head causing all my insecurities to surface. What can I possibly offer her except a life of hardship?

She's been fiddling with my cell phone for a good fifteen minutes. "What are you doing?"

"Checking out your audible list. You have so many books on here."

"I've always loved to read." I gesture to my eyes. "Since this, it's my favorite form of entertainment right next to radio broadcasts of Dallas Cowboy games."

"Your tastes have changed. I did not expect to find *Pride and Prejudice* in your library."

"Yeah, well, I thought it might be decent, considering how you changed Mrs. Water's mind."

"Was it?"

"Not really my thing. I get why it appeals to you, though. You're hopelessly romantic, you know that?"

"I prefer to call myself a dreamer." A button dings, signaling I have a new message.

"New Message from ICE Dana. Would you like me to read it to you?" the automated voice asks.

"No," I reply.

"Why ICE Dana?" Kiran asks.

"Emergency contact."

"Oh, gotcha."

"What does it say?"

"She's confirming she'll be home tomorrow." Her voice has sorrow. It matches how I feel.

We're at a crossroads once more. Only this time, I have no idea what the right direction is. "Do me a favor and text her back. Tell her I can't wait to see her and wish her safe travels. Then talk about something else."

"What else is there to talk about?"

"Anything, Kiran. Just talk to me."

"Will you be my date to Sidney's wedding? It's November 5th."

"I'm not exactly comfortable getting on a plane yet."

"We can travel together. Maybe make it a road trip?" Her voice is hopeful. I want to say yes, not just to the wedding, but everything. Yet, I can't.

"I don't think so, Kirin."

"Okay."

"New e-mail from Kiran. Would you like me to read it?" the automated voice asked.

"You sent me an e-mail?"

"Yeah." Her voice is high, but I can read the disappointment in that single word. "Did I tell you I went to India?"

Well, that's a change of subject, but I'll go with it because I can't handle getting into all the fucked-up stuff I'm trying to work through. Plus, I'm curious about her trip. "No. When did you go?"

"Over the summer last year."

"With your dad?"

"By myself actually. Even though I couldn't see the North Star, I kept thinking I was close to where you were. Was I?"

"You were. I was in Kabul."

"Only one country away. I would have backpacked across Pakistan if it meant I could see you."

Everything inside of me strains at the thought. Nothing about her statement is comforting. It's ten times worse than watching her fall through the sky at thirty thousand feet. "I'm grateful you didn't know then."

"Did you think about me too?"

Only with every breath, baby. "All the time, Kiran. Tell me more about your trip."

Her body releases tension as though she held her breath on my answer. I want to tell her the truth. How I started and ended my days staring at her photo. How the other guys in my unit gave me shit when I told them I had a girl waiting back home for me. She doesn't know it, but she was with me the whole time, through every freezing cold, lonely night and every hellish hundred-degree day.

"I visited with all my relatives. The last few days, I went to Goa. It's a beach city off the Arabian Sea."

"Did you surf?"

"I did. The waves were really intense."

"Sounds like a good time."

"Not really. It was beautiful there, but I couldn't appreciate the surroundings."

"Why not?"

"It reminded me of our eight days. Anyway, I did stop at this gallery. I even met the artist."

"Oh yeah?"

"Yes. His name is Liam Montgomery."

"Sounds familiar."

"He used to be part owner of the Wilshire hotel chain before he sold his share. He's a billionaire, but he was so down to earth. His paintings are mesmerizing. He's made a real name for himself in the art community."

Is there a reason she's talking up another man to me? "Good for him."

She pries my fingers loose from my clenched hand. When did I make a fist? Must have been sometime between billionaire and mesmerizing.

"He's happily married, Mason. I also met his wife, Mary. She was lovely. Anyway, I kept in touch with them. I sent him a few pics of your sculptures."

"Why would you do that?"

"Are you angry?"

"You should have asked me."

"You're right, but I didn't want to take the risk. I was trying to help."

"Help me how?"

"He's a professional, and he collects art too. I don't know if you believe me when I tell you how talented you are, but maybe you would believe him." She squeezes my arm. "He loved them, Mason. In fact, he sent the pictures to his agent. She's in New York. Liam says she's interested. She wants to set up a meeting with you. That's the e-mail I forwarded."

"What kind of meeting?"

"To discuss representation."

"So I can make money from my art?"

"If that's what you want. I think you'd be successful."

"Who says that's what I want?"

"You don't have to go commercial. There are other options, but I just thought it might be an opportunity to get your work out there. I realize this is your passion, and it's a personal choice. But you should at least talk to her. She has connections with museums too. Will you call her?"

"Why? So you can tell your father I'm an artist now? Will that make me a little more appealing?"

"What does this have to do with my father?"

"Come off it, girl. We both know I'm not rolling in capital. And well, your family's pretty well-off. I'm not the kind of guy you bring home to dinner." Especially considering she'd have to lead me to the fucking dinner table.

Kiran sits up. It feels colder suddenly. "You're being a dick. Is there anything I've ever done or said that makes you think I'm motivated by money? Is there?" Her voice chokes, each word heavy with hurt.

I hate myself for it. "Then why did you do it?"

"For you, you asshole. I thought people should get the privilege of seeing your work."

"Yeah, maybe I can stand outside in sunglasses carrying a tin cup, and as the people flock into my exhibits, they can throw a few coins my way. Come one, come all, and see the blind man sculpt." I say this last line with the cadence of a circus director.

"I never told him you were blind, Mason."

I can be a real ass sometimes. "Kiran—"

She covers my mouth with her hand. "It's okay. Just promise me you'll give it some thought."

"Can we change the subject?"

"If you wish." She places my phone on my chest. "I updated your contacts too. You have my information now. Is that okay?"

"Why wouldn't it be okay?"

"I wasn't sure since you won't talk about the future."

"That's not true. It hasn't come up."

"Seriously?" Her laugh is so sad it makes me wince. "You won't even commit to taking me to a wedding, let alone acknowledge the fact Dana is coming home tomorrow. What am I supposed to do here, Mason? Tell me because I have no fucking idea. Should I book my ticket? Will you stay in my life? Or are you going to end us and send me away again? Answer me." She slaps my chest. "Just answer one of my fucking questions at least."

I grab her wrists. "What the hell do you want from me?"

"I want you to fight for me. For us. I love you, but you make this so hard."

"Then you should know better."

"It isn't hard because you're blind, Mason. It's hard because I love you so much and I can't stand to see you in pain. And it's hard because I'm still angry with you. I can't even express that to you without feeling like it's a dick move."

"Angry? Fucking express it, Shenoy. Don't hold back."

"Okay. I'm royally pissed. I understand you thought you were protecting me on some level, but all you did was hurt me."

"A few days of hurt is better than a lifetime of—"

"Shut up. You said something along these lines about five year ago. It wasn't true then, and it's not true now. A few days? Are you really this clueless? You think I would have gotten over you in a few days? You stupid, stupid, boy. I didn't get over you in five full years."

"I did what I thought was right."

"That's the saddest part, baby. It was so wrong."

"I wasn't going to show up there like this. You didn't sign up for this, Kiran."

"I signed up for you, Cutler. We pledged to show up as long as the feelings were still there. You reneged on our deal."

"You're still the same girl, Kiran. I know you think with your heart first and your head last."

"Shut up! You don't know a damn thing. You didn't even give me a choice, did you? You stole it from me. I swear, Mason, if you do it again, I won't forgive you this time."

"It doesn't sound like you forgave me the first time."

"I haven't. Not yet. But you don't get any more free passes from me, Mason. When you found me, I needed a friend the most. I never imagined someone like you. I always thought I was two girls. The one before the accident and the one after. I let that tragedy define and make my choices for so many years. You helped me realize that."

"You did all that on your own, Kiran."

She must not hear me because she just keeps going. The words come out with such emotion, I struggle not to hold her. "And somewhere along the way, I gave my heart to you. Years later, I tried my best to give it to someone else, but I realized it isn't mine to give. It already belonged to you."

"This is why you're angry?"

"No, you idiot. I'm angry because you put me through hell. I had no idea if you were safe. I watched every single newscast and, trust me, there are a lot of them on twenty-four-hour news cycles. The whole time I prayed I wouldn't see your face next to the word casualty. When I got to the hotel, I was full of fear and hope. You didn't show up for me, Mason. All you had to do was show up. Instead, you left me there all by myself. You broke our pact. Not only that, you lied to me. You told me there was someone else. Do you have any idea what that was like? What if I'd done that to you?"

I can't even turn those tables and conceive what I'd go through waiting for her at the hotel, only to get a letter full of lies. "I thought it would be easier."

"Easier? I hope to God your hard head can comprehend what I'm trying to explain to you. I love you. That means your hurt is my hurt. You didn't allow me to be there for you. You're not even allowing it now."

"I can barely make it through the day, and you're asking me to plan a life with you? What kind of future would we have?" Walls are closing in on me. I can't rationalize anything. There is just too much fucking chaos for me to control.

"A beautiful one, full of sunny days and happiness."

I swallow back the aching lump in my throat. Hold it together, Cutler. "I can't dream with you anymore, Kiran. It's not as easy as walking off in the sunset hand in hand."

"I never said we wouldn't have struggles. We can work through them... together. But right now, I want you to quit making decisions that don't belong to you. If you love me, fight for me, Mason. Fight for us."

This is the thing about Kiran. The thing it only took me a few days to figure out. She is a fighter. She loves with everything she has. This girl wears her heart on her sleeve in every fucking way.

I do not. "I'm sorry, Kiran."

"Why does your sorry sound so much like a good-bye?"

"Because it is."

Ever hear the sound of a single tear roll down someone's face? Someone you love with all your heart? I have. Twice now. It's gotta be the most awful sound in the whole fucking world.

Chapter 36

Mason

The road to misery is paved with good intentions. It's been forty-one days, six hours, and fifty-two minutes since Kiran left. She didn't even say good-bye. Well, she did to Molly, but not to me. She went to the hotel the night of our fight. She met Dana at the airport the next day. I only know that because Dana told me, although she refuses to offer any details of their conversation. Dana is beyond pissed at me. Even Molly, who continues to do her job with total professional efficiency, doesn't seem all that happy with her master. Not even when I offer her a cut of my steak. No sir, all the women in my life think I'm a jerk.

I keep busy so the days don't seem endless. I make it a point to go to the track and run every morning at least ten miles. In the evenings, I weed around Gram's jasmine shrub, trying to rip prickly thorns out of the ground. I've neglected it for so long I'm pretty sure it'll die soon. I take my therapy sessions more seriously now. I finally accept that I have PTSD, something I denied since the beginning. I talk about Kiran to Dr. Green, a former Marine himself. He reiterates the same stuff he's always telling me about negative coping, but I pay attention this time. Negative coping is using quick fixes that make a situation worse. Symptoms include avoidance, always being on guard, and pushing people away. The definition fits like a glove.

So I do some hard thinking and even harder work.

I put my nose to the grindstone and find myself a job. It's been a challenge adjusting to civilian life, but having a set schedule helps. I work as many hours as they give me. I'd offer to work for free if they'd let me.

The only thing I don't do is go to the shed. It's funny, the very thing that helped me cope now drives me crazy. My head can't focus, and my hands won't cooperate either.

Eventually, I start returning calls from my military brothers. They welcome me back into the fold with fist bumps, ice-cold beers, and Friday night football. And something else I can't quite name. It's more than friendship and a different kind of brotherhood bound by something even deeper than blood. I've been through hell with them.

The guys in my unit are another family. We swore allegiance to each other once, and I managed to push them out of my life. Kiran isn't the only one I abandoned. Tonight, we're all hanging around a dive bar in Charlotte. The kind of place a guy can adequately drown his sorrows. Hell, what am I thinking? I could consume an ocean of liquor and it wouldn't be enough.

"Whatever happened to the girl, Cutler?" Gunner asks.

We hit on just about every other topic. I should have been more prepared for this landmine.

"The girl?" I ask, going for nonchalance. It's a fail.

"Stop fucking around. You know who I'm talking about. The girl whose picture you taped to the top bunk so you could stare at her every night."

"Yeah, the five-year plan," Cankles adds. His real name is Richard. But he got cranky during long drills and whined about his ankles. Rule of thumb in the Marines, no one likes a whiner. You end up with a nickname like Cankles. The name stuck.

I take a long drag of my pint. "It didn't work out."

"That's too bad. I was rooting from the sidelines, Cutler," Gunner says.

"We all were," Chip adds.

"You were? Y'all had no issues telling me how stupid the whole idea was."

Joe chimes in his two cents, which is worth less than a half-penny. "Yeah, only cause it's pretty farfetched. But if you had made it, you beat some incredible odds." Joe is from Goodrich and my age. We've been friends from babyhood to boot camp. He's right. We were the craziest long-shot ever. Yet, I had no troubles betting on us. She didn't either.

"Fuck her," Chip says. He knocks his beer against mine like he's making a toast.

That is not something I can drink to.

We call him Chip on account of his two chipped front teeth. Right now, I'm debating making it a trifecta. "Fuck you, Chip. It's not her fault."

"Course it is," Captain chimes in. "She should have shown up."

"She did."

"Then she's a real bitch if she couldn't handle your injury, Cutler," Cankles hollers.

"Don't call her that," I say, my voice ripe with irritation. "You're way off base."

"Then show us where home plate is, bro. What happened?" Cap asks.

I tell them the whole sordid story, leaving out the intimate details. I'm met with complete radio silence. Either my boys are in shock or they're incredibly stealthy and have managed to leave without making a sound.

"Hello, you guys still here?"

Cap clears his throat. "Let me put a little perspective on this if I may."

"You may."

"You came up with the ridiculous five-year plan complete with a no contact clause. Then when the time comes to meet up, you're the one who ditched her. But wait, she decides to find your dumbass on her own. She steps up to help out when your sister is away. When she lays it all on the line, you end up pushing her away…again?" Cap sums it up well. Guess that's why he's a good commander.

"That is the Spark notes version, I suppose."

"Man, we were way off base. She's not a bitch."

"Exactly."

"You're the bitch."

"What? I was trying to do the honorable thing. She needs someone who can take care of her. Someone who can support her."

"Who says you can't?"

"I do." I laugh. "I work in a fishing store." I'm not on disability anymore, but it's not exactly a grand career in the making.

"Complete Fubar. What you did is not honorable. You're scared, but that's all in your own head. Don't play it off like you did it for her. It's not just your eyes that can't see." Who would have thought Cankles was a philosopher?

Whiskey. Tango. Foxtrot.

Joe breaks the uncomfortable silence. "We should have called you Confucius Junior instead of Cankles."

A few people laugh. I don't. I'm not upset. In fact, I'm appreciative in a way. It's not often someone holds a mirror up for you.

I ask Dana to point out the North Star that night.

I call Kiran.

She doesn't answer.

* * * *

Sixty-one days and counting. We're heading to the airport to pick up Dana's boyfriend. He's a fellow researcher who went to the Antarctica with her. If I hadn't fallen for Kiran as quickly as I did, I would be more skeptical. Of course, I'm still planning to size him up and give him the tenth degree.

"You're a dick." That's what I keep hearing in my head, accompanied by the lyrics of "Creep" by Radiohead. Oh wait, that's just Dana's annoying voice and the car stereo.

"Cut it out, Dana."

"Just saying."

"You've said it many times. I got the message, loud and clear."

"You really hurt her."

"I did her a favor."

She lets out an aggravated shriek, one I haven't heard since she was a teenager. "What is wrong with you, Mason?"

"Apparently, a lot of stuff."

She pulls the car over.

"What are you doing? We're on the expressway. You can't pull over here."

"We're fine. I need you to hear this." She turns off the radio. "It's going to be hard for you to comprehend cause you're a guy, but what you consider a favor to Kiran is really just saying she's a dumb girl."

"What? Where the hell are you getting that from? I would never say that."

"You don't have to speak the words. You said it with your actions. You're basically communicating she's not capable of deciding who she wants to be with. It's misogynistic, and I really can't believe my big brother, this guy I totally admire, is a complete caveman."

"You're right, but it doesn't matter."

"Say that again."

"It doesn't matter. I've called her a few times. She's not answering." A few times is a mild estimate. I've called her over twenty times and left at least five messages and eight texts. At some point, I need to accept that she's done with me. I can't fault her.

"Oh," Dana says. "I just wanted you to say the part that I was right again. Now I kind of feel like an ass for bringing it up."

"Don't. I deserve it."

The blast that took my vision wasn't the worst thing that happened to me. The worst was what occurred afterward, and it was a conscious choice on my part. I abandoned her. Then I let her go.

I left a huge chunk of my soul in that village. I let it rot away and almost die. I survived, but surviving and living are not the same thing.

Chapter 37

Kiran

The rotating restaurant at the Wilshire is spectacular. It has full views of the gulf. There are twinkle lights everywhere. The chairs and tables are draped in white silk. I only wish I matched the romantic ambience. It's hard being back here. Harder than I imagined. There are memories of us everywhere. I fight all the bitterness with my best lipstick smile.

It's not easy to do, especially in this getup. I look like I came straight out of a regency novel, but not in a good way. My peachy bridesmaid dress comes complete with lace and not one, but three petticoats. Let's not even talk about the huge bow framing my ass.

"I'm sorry. Now that I'm really looking at it, it is pretty ugly," Sidney says. She's adorable in her floor length crystal-encrusted wedding dress.

"It's all good." I may not be able to fit into a regular bathroom stall, but I can deal with it.

Sidney's a little drunk. The tiara on top of her head is crooked again. Reworking a few of the pins, I straighten it.

"Maybe it is a little over the top, but it didn't stop three different guys asking about your status."

"What did you tell them?"

"It's complicated. Is that the right answer?"

"Yes, I guess it is." It's more succinct than saying she's had her heart torn open and stomped on.

She gives me a hug. "Thanks for being here for me."

"Of course. Thank you for letting me be a part of your day. Did you think I'd bail on you or something?"

"Never. It's just I know you're sad right now."

I take her hand. "Shhh. This isn't about me. This is your day. The only sad thing we're going to talk about is how much we sucked at karaoke last night."

She smiles through her pout. "We did, but it was a blast."

"Yeah, it was."

The waiter places a drink in front of me. "I didn't order this."

"It's from the gentleman at the bar, miss."

Sidney narrows her eyes. "Eww gross. What kind of guy orders a girl a blow job?"

I know exactly what kind of guy.

I almost fall out my chair. I turn toward the bar very slowly. Not by choice. The damn corset I'm wearing is pinching everything and making it difficult to move with any speed.

There he is. The most beautiful man I've ever seen leans against the bar top. He's tall and lean with a touch of honey in his hair and a smile that can render a girl speechless.

Mason is here.

He's not playing fair either, dressed in Marine dress blues.

"He's even hotter than I remember," Sidney says. "If I wasn't a married woman, I might be tempted."

"Sidney." I elbow her.

"He's going to carry you off like Richard Gere carried Debra Winger off in *Terms of Endearment*."

"Debra Winger died of cancer in *Terms of Endearment*. You're thinking of an *Officer and a Gentleman*."

"Oh yeah, that's right."

He turns his head as if he's scanning the room. He isn't sure where I am. My body betrays me, toes curling and pulse racing at the sight of him. Behind the strong façade, he's nervous. I've ignored all the messages and texts and missed calls. If I let him into my life again, the next good-bye will destroy me. I have to protect myself.

"What's he doing here?" I say, almost to myself.

"Why not ask him?" Sid says. "Want me to come with you?"

"No. I want you to go dance with your man."

I stand and, with shaky feet, I move toward him, the triple petticoat rustling like a bag of leaves on a windy day.

If I wasn't staring at him, I might have missed the way his large hand trembled. The way he frowned and looked hopeful at the same time. Oh God, Mason, don't make me fall for you again. I shake the thought. I'm still falling. The crash might just kill me.

He straightens as I approach. "I've always loved your scent. It reminds me of home."

My knees shake as I take the last few steps toward him. "Mason."

"Hello, Kiran, you look beautiful tonight."

"What?"

"Oh, you're wondering if that's insincere. It's not, sweetheart. You're always beautiful so I can say that with certainty."

"What I'm wondering is why you're here."

"You wouldn't answer your phone."

"What else could I say to you that I haven't already said?"

"Nothing. I had things to say to you, though."

"So you came here to say them?"

"You asked me to be your date, remember? Is that invitation still open?"

"No."

He shifts his head down, not exactly defeated. More like he's gearing up for his next move. "You're here with someone then?"

"No."

He smiles.

"That does not mean you can just show up. You're crashing a wedding."

His smile tightens. "Technically maybe." He jerks his head toward the band. "But you see, I had to make good on a promise."

"What promise?"

"I went swimming with this girl once. This amazing girl who I fell in love with in just eight days. I vowed I'd dance with her at the revolving restaurant on the top floor of the Wilshire one day. I want nothing more than to make that day today."

"I don't want to dance with you."

"You have to. They're playing our song, sweetheart."

He takes my hand. I stand strong, not budging an inch. "The 'Macarena' is our song?"

"Wait for it," he says.

The band switches gears. I don't want to smile, but I can't help it. Who can resist a smile when "I Want To Hold Your Hand" is playing?

"This sounds like us, don't you think?"

"Mason…"

"You have to lead the way to the dance floor, Shenoy. I'm not exactly in tune with this place. I promise wherever you lead, I'll follow."

"I'm tired, Mason."

"Okay, then we can dance right here, sweetheart."

He takes me into his arms. I don't know if this is dancing. We're swaying. God help me, I should run away, but I can't.

"How did you get here?"

"I flew."

I look around. "Is Dana here?"

"She offered to come, but I had to do this on my own. I did bring Molly, though, but I left her at the hotel room. I figured two wedding crashers would draw attention, especially if one ate without utensils."

"You flew all by yourself?"

"Honey, I'd swim across oceans to see you."

"That's an odd statement coming from someone who asked me to leave."

"I've been working on some stuff. I've got a hard head. It takes me a while to process things. By the way, before I forget, Dana sends her best. She just moved to San Diego and extends an invitation for you to visit whenever you'd like."

"You moved to San Diego?"

"No, Kiran. Dana moved. She met someone on her trip."

"Really?"

"Yeah, they're perfect for each other. When they talk about the weather, it's in terms of climactic shift, and they both use the Latin names for animals. They're both pretty weird."

I laugh. "He does sound perfect for her."

"He was made for her. Just as I was made for you."

I ignore his statement. "You live alone now?"

"Yeah, I have been for a while. But don't worry about me. I'm doing just fine." His hand slides down my dress, his face twisting into a stern frown. "What the hell are you wearing?"

"About thirty yards of organza."

"Does this frock come with instructions or a GPS navigator?"

"It should."

"I really want to touch your skin right now," he whispers.

"I'm going to leave now."

He tightens his grip on my arm. "Wait, sunshine. I know I really fucked up. But I'm here, trying to do what I should have done three months ago. Hell, probably what I should have done five years ago. Maybe even when I was fourteen, and you ran away from me after you gave me my first kiss."

"What's that?"

"I'm fighting for you. For us. I've showed up way too late, but I'm here now, asking for your forgiveness. Please tell me I'm not too late."

"You can't just show up here, say a few romantic things, and expect me to fall into your arms."

"You falling into my arms is something worth waiting for. I'm not asking for that now. I want to make a couple of new vows to you. Will you go for a walk with me? Just one more time, Kiran. One more walk. I have so much to tell you."

I take his hand, and we head to the elevator. "I have to go to my room and get out of this dress."

"May I come with you? I promise I won't look."

I laugh despite myself.

"Where are you staying?" I ask, sliding my keycard into the door.

"Sandy Waves. I'm in the Sweetheart's Suite."

The fact he got on an airplane and came here to see me is amazing, but it's clear he's really planned everything.

I change into a sundress. I considered shorts, but he looks so handsome in his dress blues I can't even contemplate casual. At least I can breathe again. That is until Mason clasps his fingers through mine. Now I'm having a little trouble.

We end up pretty close to where we started on the beach.

"You saved my life once. And then you reminded me how to live again. I never thanked you for that. I'm so sorry for the things I said."

"You're welcome, and I forgive you." We're quiet, the sound of the lapping waves calms the cacophony of emotions inside of me. I look over at him. The man that I love. I answer the question he asked of me. "It's not too late," I say, choking on the words.

He takes my wrist and kisses the underside. "Thank you."

"When did you get here?"

"Yesterday."

"You've been here for a whole day, and you didn't tell me?"

"You have no idea how difficult it was for me not to come straight to you. I figured you were busy with wedding stuff. Plus, I had some things to do."

"What things?"

"I made Sam an offer on his store."

"What?"

"Carla was right about something for once. The house did fetch a good price. We just closed on it a few days ago. I'm staying on until next month. Then I'll move here. You said you could live anywhere. Will you live here with me? I know we'll be happy here."

"You sold it? But you love that house."

"Yeah, I do. It's going to make some great memories for a new family. Remember our dream?"

"We were just talking out loud. It was a joke."

"No, we weren't. We were planning a life together." He ruffles my hair. "It was a beautiful dream, Kiran. I want to make it come true."

"So you want us to sell books?"

He reaches in his pocket. "Books, a few sandcastles, and maybe some beach jewelry made out of shells to the tourists."

I squint to see what he's tangled around his finger. It's the twine bracelet I made all those years ago and hid in his duffle bag. "You still have it."

"You gave it to me to remind me to keep dreaming. I forgot along the way, but not anymore. What do you think about the shop?"

"It's crazy—"

"Who ever said we were normal? You and I? Give it some thought, sunshine." He swallows. His heartbroken expression cuts through me.

The bottom line is I love this man. Whatever we've been through, we belong to each other. "You didn't let me finish. Your idea is crazy...and awesome."

He expels a long breath. "You have no idea how relieved I am."

"Tell me about these vows."

He takes my hand in his and walks us to where the shoreline laps the beach. It's a full moon tonight, and the breeze is almost intoxicating.

"I vow I'll be honest with you. I'll never intentionally hurt you. I'll never stop dreaming again. If you let me, I'll love you till my last breath."

"I vow the same."

He touches my face. God, I missed his touch. He kisses me long and tender. We're both breathless when we separate. "You make my world whole, Kiran. I love you so much."

"I love you too, Mason."

"One more vow. Okay, darling?"

"Okay."

He drops to his knees and fishes in his pocket. "Kiran Shenoy, I vow to do everything in my power to make you happy and always keep you safe. Will you do me the honor of being my wife?"

I am not expecting this. I never let the dream get this far.

"Yes."

I fall to my knees beside him. He slips the ring on my finger. It's a simple white gold band with a heart-shaped diamond. There's something very romantic and vintage about the simple piece. "I love this ring."

"Linda said you would."

"What? When did you talk to my stepmother?"

"I met her in person actually. I figured she'd be the best person to go ring shopping with me. Although, I did have a few ideas of my own."

"You went to New Jersey?"

"That was my first solo trip."

"Let me understand this. You went to New Jersey to go ring shopping with my stepmother?"

He cups my face. "Sweetheart, I'm a southern gentleman. There are some things you just don't do. Asking for a woman's hand without her daddy's blessing is one of those things."

"You met Papa?" My gut wrenches, imagining that conversation. Poor Mason.

"I did."

"It's okay, Mason. I don't need his approval. I love you."

"Who says I didn't get his approval? It took three days of showing up to his office."

I shiver at the thought of everything Mason went through. When this man fights, he does it with everything. What girl wouldn't surrender?

"That's impressive, but I still can't believe you won him over."

"Well, Linda put in a good word or two on my behalf. I told him I might not be rich, but I could give you everything you need and guarantee your happiness."

"You do, baby."

"While I was there, I went to New York for a day."

"New York?" As in the city with all the whizzing cars and crowds of people.

"I met with the agent too. Well, I suppose I can call her my agent now. I showed her my portfolio."

"That's amazing. You should have told me. I would have gone with you."

"I had a lot to work out on my own. You helped me so much, but I had to take the last few steps by myself."

"I'm proud of you, Mason."

He kisses my forehead. "Thank you, darling. That means a lot. We can talk later on that subject. So now that we're finally on the same page, there's just one thing left to do."

"What?"

His grin turns wicked. "I'm gonna love, honor, and cherish you for the rest of our lives, but tonight I'm going to do all of those things…to your body."

"Well, what the hell are we waiting for?"

We fall into each other's arms.

We will never let each other go again.

Epilogue

We lived in a small rented apartment for the first two years of our marriage. It's hard starting a business. It's downright insane to start a business, get married, and move to a new city at the same time. Kiran and I worked long hours. We made some mistakes, but we sure as hell have no regrets. We celebrated our first year anniversary by jumping out of a plane together.

Dana got married. Yeah, it was to the scientist research guy. I have no doubt they'll be crazy happy and have scary genius babies with monster IQs. Last year, my sister was offered a prestigious position in Miami. I'm grateful we're not too far. Our kids will have a chance to know each other.

Kiran never excelled in making beach jewelry, but I did start sculpting again. The tourists buy up my smaller sandcastles before I can start on a new batch. The bookstore slash souvenir shop slash coffee bar isn't going to make us rich, but it does make a nice profit.

I had my first official exhibition six months ago. Liam Montgomery and his wife, Mary, even attended. Kiran was right. They are good people. Surprisingly, I sold several of my larger pieces. I exceeded my expectations. Of course, my wife never doubted my talent.

She's written two more books. I'm so proud of her. Kiran still freelances too. She has articles published in about a hundred different periodicals and is always on ten different deadlines. I've asked her to slow down. But my girl is stubborn. She promises she will though when the baby gets here. I'm going to hold her to that.

Oh yeah, we're making a baby. Isn't that awesome?

The ultrasound says it will be a girl. We're planning to name her Ellen Anita after my Grams and Kiran's mama.

Now that you're all caught up, that brings us to today. Today we moved into a little house close to the beach. I guess you could call it a cottage. The kind of place Kiran once told me she wanted to live when we were dreaming together all those years ago. Bonus, it has a nice size outbuilding I can rehab and turn into a studio. But the first project I have in mind is to plant a tangerine tree and a jasmine shrub in the backyard.

Fun fact, our neighbor's daughter is also an artist. Her name is Abigail Helms. A while back, she kicked my ass at a sandcastle building contest. Small world, huh? We commissioned her to paint the baby's nursery. She did it in beach tones, complete with a mosaic of sandcastles and sea life. I'm sure she gave me a funny look when I asked her to add a few barnacles and hermit crabs to the mix. Although, I can't see it, I can visualize how it turned out.

Kiran has been standing at the nursery door for the longest time. I wrap my arms around her and kiss her neck. My hands travel down to her protruding belly.

She tilts her head back. "I hope Ellen loves this nursery as much as I do."

"I hope your boobs get bigger soon."

She elbows me. "Mason!"

"Just kidding, baby. She'll love it. It's her daddy and mama's love story painted out in four walls."

"True."

"How are you feeling today, sunshine?"

"Wonderful."

"Yeah?"

"Another day in the sun."

I frown, wondering if I missed something. I can smell the ozone and hear the patter of rain on the roof. "I'm pretty certain it's raining."

"It is. But it's sunny too."

She's right of course.

Every day we are together is a sunny day.

Check out MK Schiller's heartwarming Where the Lotus Flowers Grow.

"This book confronts a number of economic, social, and gender issues with grace and honesty, and provides two very believable, flawed and genuinely empathetic protagonists...will linger in readers' hearts and memories after the final page."
–RT Book Reviews

Where the Lotus Flowers Grow

Even in darkness, love can bloom...

Heir to a multinational hotel empire, Liam Montgomery thinks business is everything—until he goes undercover to check out their locations throughout Asia. As cosmopolitan as Liam is, from the bright lights of Mumbai to the tranquil beaches of Goa to the bustling streets of New York, he's never met anyone like lovely Mary Costa. He can't understand why this delicate, educated woman works as a maid. Or how she is reigniting his long-buried desire to be an artist. They are apart in so many ways—especially in the things Mary won't tell him. But more and more, Liam can't imagine his life without her.

Mary knows this unexpected desire for Liam must end. It's true that his gentleness and sense of fun inspires her and makes her hopeful for the first time in her life. But she has a grim promise she feels compelled to keep—and painful experiences she fears he could never understand. And with secrets soon reaching out to separate them for good, can they dare risk a future together if it means confronting the scars of the past?

Chapter 1

Liam

I was too exhausted to sleep. Despite the twenty-two-hour plane ride, the ten-hour time difference, and the three bloody bourbons consumed on the flight, sleep refused to come. That's how I found myself wide awake at the ungodly hour of three a.m., studying the pale glow of a Rajasthani moon. At precisely 5:36 in the morning, I finally decided to make my insomnia useful and call my secretary, Monica Penny.

"Hello Miss Moneypenny," I said, imitating the Sean Connery brogue. It made her giggle every time.

"And who would this be?"

I could imagine the blush that crept around her face whenever we played this game. At sixty years young, she'd always been formal and efficient, but when I burst into Bond, she acted like a giddy schoolgirl.

"Montgomery. Liam Montgomery."

"It's gotta be five in the morning there."

"Five thirty-six, actually." Can we go over the schedule and your notes from the meeting yesterday?"

"I love the way you say 'schedule.' But seriously, Liam, you have to be exhausted."

"I am, but I can't sleep. May as well be useful."

"Fine. Well, I booked the rest of your flights. You'll leave for Mumbai on Saturday and Goa the following Saturday. Then back to New York on Sunday." She went about the specific details, meetings, and agendas that would take place over the coming weeks. I had most of it memorized, but I needed her to remind me of all the upper management at each hotel.

By the time we'd finished, the sun had crept slowly over the horizon. I opened the window to let in some air.

"Make sure you wear plenty of sunscreen, drink lots of bottled water, and buy a Pashmina scarf."

"What kind of protection will a Pashmina scarf offer me?"

"Nothing, but it's a really nice gift for your secretary."

"Noted."

"Liam, what's that sound?"

I blinked, taking in the huge hulking creatures that flew across the sky, their shrieking calls growing exponentially with the rise of the golden sun. Their cackles drowned out all other noise.

"Birds."

"You're kidding?"

"Afraid not, Moneypenny. The wingspan on these birds would give Hitchcock a heart attack." I ducked outside the window to get a closer look. Another flew by, nearly grazing me. Holy shit...was that a falcon? I banged my head against the sill as I backed away.

"Fuck."

"What happened?"

"Just banged my brain a bit."

"Are you all right?"

"I'll live."

"I'm sure you will, seeing as you have a very hard head. Which reminds me, Natalie called." Moneypenny's typically soft voice hardened over Natalie's name. "She asked about your schedule, too. She's trying for an Indian visa since she's filming a shoot in Hong Kong." Her heavy sigh gave the birds a run for their money. "I thought you broke up."

As if my bloody head wasn't already aching.

"We didn't break up. We were never going out. She rings when she's in or around the same general vicinity as me. We get together. That's all."

"Liam Montgomery, I maybe older than you, but I know what a booty call is."

"Booty call?" I almost dropped the phone. "I believe the kids are calling it a hook-up these days. Yes, that's the correct terminology."

"I don't like her. She's very rude."

"Well, it's good you're not sleeping with her then. But in any case, please send two dozen roses to her hotel in Hong Kong with a note relaying my sincere apologies. I'll be far too busy these next three weeks to entertain her."

"I'll send it right away," she said, sounding incredibly happy at being assigned the task.

"And Moneypenny?"

"Yes."

"Make the note sincere, yeah?"

She huffed over the phone. "What do you want me to do? Quote Shakespeare?"

"That's a nice touch."

"Fine. I'm sure I can find a line from *The Taming of the Shrew*."

"You're a funny girl. I have to go."

"Be careful, Liam. I'll tell Stephen you arrived safely."

I wanted to tell her not to bother. My half-brother could care less. In fact, he'd probably be happy if I hadn't arrived safely, but I simply thanked her instead. Keeping up appearances had become second nature. If anyone looked below the surface, they could easily identify the large fissures in my family, but we'd done an outstanding job at plugging the leaks.

What looked like a hawk came to the window next. He perched on the ledge, fanning his large wings. It appeared more curious than anything, staring me down as if to say I was on his territory, not the other way around. I could almost hear his taunting thoughts: *You wish you had my freedom.*

I did.

He flapped his wings before swooping down toward the grounds. I followed his descent across the infinity pool, the manicured gardens, and finally the water fountain. Prabhat, the manager here, had given me a brief tour yesterday. I told him to get rid of the eyesore. It wasn't in a spot guests would go to, but the crumpling stones blemished the otherwise spotless façade. Not to mention it was a haven for mosquitoes and the water looked dirty. He went on about how he agreed with me, insisting it would be no problem. So why it hadn't been done in all the years he'd been general manager?

I focused on the shining figure standing next to the fountain. It looked like every ray in the sun was pointing at her and reflecting off her at the same time. That was until I realized that her long white skirt and scarf had tiny mirrors patched into the embroidery. She moved with grace despite the large pot balanced on her hip. She placed the pot on the ground. From within, she took many small silver bowls. Ten, to be exact. I counted as she placed them around the fountain, occasionally swiping the tiny broken stones gathered on its ridge. The strike of a match against the box cut through the air as if even the birds had decided to be silent out of respect for her. She lit each bowl. Who lit candles in the daylight? Was it some type of religious ceremony?

When she was done, she fell to her knees in front of the fountain and removed her scarf. Her hair cascaded in dark waves. A soft echoing music filled the air, the melody haunting. She looked toward the sky.

Whatever she prayed for, I wanted her to have it.

My fingers twitched. I wished for a piece of charcoal, a paint brush, or even a fucking pencil. The once-familiar longing had been absent from my life for many years.

Her gaze drew back to the fountain.

"What's so interesting?" I asked, as if she could answer me. I didn't know what was so interesting for me either. I blamed it on a combination of sleep deprivation, curiosity, and bad bourbon. Whatever it was, I couldn't look away.

A single flower in the middle of the pool opened up. The bud stood out in ethereal white above the still, dark waters. What the hell kind of flower grew in water? A lily? No…no, this wasn't a lily. I knew this. I racked my brain until the memory finally came.

Mum sitting at the rickety kitchen table, her elbows bent in concentration as she tried to fashion some kind of pin. She based her design on the tropical flower book she'd checked from the library. She swore under her breath as she tried to shake off the arthritis before it settled into her fingers.

I tapped the book with my pencil. "What is it?"

"A lotus flower. I want the pin to look like this. Isn't it lovely?" She prattled on about some stone she'd found at the thrift store.

"No, Mum, it's very ugly" was my flippant reply. I hated her doing this kind of work. It only made her hands hurt. It was the reason all my weekends were spent at street fairs instead of hanging with my mates. Hell, it wouldn't have been so bad if we made money from it. In the end, I felt so guilty for my outburst, I finished the pin for her, bending the stiff silver wires with small pliers, following the lines in the book, until they resembled petals. I pasted the cheap stone in the center.

Mum said the lotus flower was special. I didn't see anything special about it then, and I certainly didn't now.

I couldn't see Lotus Girl's face…not from this angle, ten stories up, but I imagined it anyway. She was as enamored with the flower as I was with her.

I wasn't the only one watching. He came from the shadows and stood in front of her. My hand clutched the sill. She straightened, but there was no fear in her posture. I recognized his uniform and shape as the driver who'd fetched me from the airport.

Their voices didn't carry, but even if they did, I doubt I'd understand what they said. It didn't matter, though. Their body language slashed through any language barriers. He was taller than she was, but she looked him in the eyes when she spoke. She patted his arm, a docile gesture meant to comfort. She kept an ample amount of space between them, each of her movements careful, perhaps even guarded. His words were accompanied with shakes of his head, his hands barreling though his hair, and finally a defeated slump in his shoulders.

I chuckled to myself. *Sorry, mate, but at least she's letting you down easy.*

He took her hand and pulled it toward his mouth. She yanked it back so fast, his lips met nothing but air.

Don't go embarrassing yourself, bro. No bird is worth that. As if to contradict me, a fucking Pterodactyl soared past, squawking loudly. I stumbled back.

Bloody birds.

Once I regained my balance and confirmed my heart was still tucked inside my chest, I shifted my attention back to them. He kept talking, closing the gap between them, his fingers curling around her arm. In reaction, I tightened mine into a fist.

You're starting to piss me off. Keep your fucking hands to yourself before I come down there and break them.

Her stance stiffened. She slapped his hand away. Whatever she said, she spoke it with force, pushing his chest so hard he staggered back.

"Good for you," I said. "Let the wanker have it."

She uttered some final words that must have been harsher than any slap. He shrunk against her voice, shoving his hands in his pockets. She grabbed the large pot and walked away...well, more like sashayed. The girl glanced back once more, but not at him. At the flower in the fountain. I swear, even from this distance, I could see her regret at being disturbed, her solitude ruined.

I felt it, too.